Also by Janelle Scott

The Red Kettle

Entitled

Janelle Scott

Order this book online at www.trafford.com
or email orders@trafford.com

Most Trafford titles are also available at major online book retailers.

© Copyright 2018 Janelle Scott.
All rights reserved. No part of this publication may be reproduced, stored in a retrieval system, or transmitted, in any form or by any means, electronic, mechanical, photocopying, recording, or otherwise, without the written prior permission of the author.

Print information available on the last page.

ISBN: 978-1-4907-9195-1 (sc)
ISBN: 978-1-4907-9194-4 (hc)
ISBN: 978-1-4907-9193-7 (e)

Library of Congress Control Number: 2018913280

Because of the dynamic nature of the Internet, any web addresses or links contained in this book may have changed since publication and may no longer be valid. The views expressed in this work are solely those of the author and do not necessarily reflect the views of the publisher, and the publisher hereby disclaims any responsibility for them.

Any people depicted in stock imagery provided by Getty Images are models, and such images are being used for illustrative purposes only.
Certain stock imagery © Getty Images.

Trafford rev. 02/23/2019

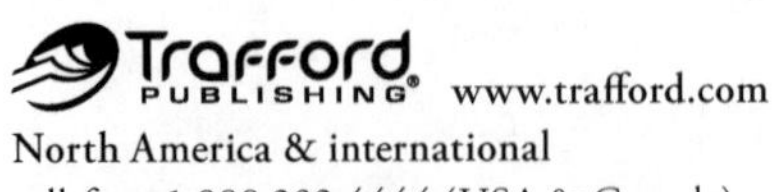

www.trafford.com

North America & international
toll-free: 1 888 232 4444 (USA & Canada)
fax: 812 355 4082

Entitled

Believing oneself to be inherently deserving of privileges or special treatment

Author's Bio

Janelle Scott was born in Sydney, Australia, where she still lives. Her first published piece was in the Bexley North Public School magazine, *First Bell*, when she was 8 years old.

Janelle has a lifelong interest in reading and can usually be found with a book in her hands. Over the years, she has attended many workshops on the craft of writing and has produced short stories and poetry. Janelle works part time as a medical typist but still manages to find time in her busy schedule to write. Her first book, *The Red Kettle*, was published in 2015.

Website: www.janellescott.com
Email: janelle.scott2511@gmail.com

Acknowledgements

My love and heartfelt thanks to my daughter, Julie. Without your encouragement and hours of proofreading, this book would never have happened.

Thank you also to Wayne, Corey, and Kirrily for your valuable input.

One

She hardly reached the height of the doorbell, but she was a determined little thing. Her curly golden hair was uncombed and needed a wash, but so did her face, with two tear streaks from her blue eyes to her trembling chin. The door opened, and a kindly face looked down at her. "Oh, my darling girl, what're you doing here? Where's Mum?"

The little girl turned and pointed towards a car parked in the driveway with one door open, from which protruded a pair of tightly leather-clad buttocks, slim legs, and gold sandals. The rest of her was trying to retrieve something from the back seat.

"Mum's just getting my things. Can I stay with you, Auntie Marg? Mum said she has to go away for a while, and I would be a nuisance."

"Of course, you can, darling. Go inside now and see if Uncle Ken can find you some ice cream. Would you like that?"

Her little face lit up with a smile, and dragging her worn and torn teddy bear by one paw, she disappeared into the cool house in search of Uncle Ken and the promised ice cream. Margaret closed the front door and went across to where her sister was now wholly visible standing beside the car. "Okay, Tiffany, what's the story this time?"

"Well, Scottie and I have heard of some work down the coast, and we can't take Meredith with us. She would just be in the way. Can you look after her for a couple of weeks? Will let you know how long we'll be away once we line up the work."

Margaret shook her head in disgust. "Why can't you get any work in Sydney? It's not as though you're fussy about what you do, is it?"

"Don't be such a bitch," her sister replied. "It's all right for you with Mr Suburbia inside supporting you. I have to work for a living, and I don't have many choices. Are you going to look after Meredith or not?"

Margaret reached down for the small suitcase that Tiffany had thrown on the driveway in temper. "Of course, we'll look after her, for her sake, Tiffany, not for yours. Go and say goodbye to your daughter and be on your way. Just let me know when we might expect you back to play at being mother again." Margaret followed her sister back into the house, and within a few minutes, Tiffany was disappearing down the road in a cloud of exhaust smoke.

Meredith was looking a bit cleaner after Ken had washed her face and hands, but the ice cream smeared around her smiling mouth was a delight to see. "Where's she off to this time?" Ken asked his wife.

"Tell you later. Not important now."

Ken took Meredith into the family room and propped her and Teddy up on the lounge with a few of her favourite books. She loved to look through them, slowly turning the pages while telling Teddy what the story was about. She had an amazing memory for a 3-year-old, and there were always a few new books waiting for her each time she came to visit.

Margaret had never seen any of the places Tiffany had lived in as her sister was constantly moving houses and changing her lovers. Meredith's father was long gone, and his present whereabouts were unknown. She had seen the latest "love" on Tiffany's Facebook page and was not impressed. He looked rough and tough, and she was concerned about his appearance and his apparent influence on her sister.

In the twelve months that Scottie had been around, Ken and Margaret had been asked nearly every month if they could mind Meredith for a few days. It was not unusual for her to stay with them for weeks, but they didn't mind the extended time they had to spend with her. They loved the little girl as though she was the child they had never been able to have.

They feared for her safety as Scottie had a bad temper according to Tiffany, who had arrived late one Saturday afternoon with Meredith, a suitcase, and a black eye. When Margaret challenged her about leaving Scottie, her sister defended him, saying that it was just an accident and that she had tripped when he pushed her. It was all Margaret could do to say, "Why do you let him abuse you, Tiffany?"

"He didn't abuse me. I just told you. I tripped when he pushed me, and I fell on the floor. Anyway, mind your own business. I just want you to get Meredith out of his way until he calms down. He doesn't like it when she whinges."

"Tiffany, I swear to God that if he ever hurts that child, he will have more to deal with than he even knows is possible," said Margaret.

"Oh, get off my back. Just take Meredith for a few days." And with that, she turned and went back to her car without even saying goodbye. Her daughter was peeping from behind her teddy bear and clutching Auntie Marg's hand.

"Bye, Mummy," she said tearfully as the car roared up the road.

"Come inside, darling, and you can have a lovely bubble bath. Would you like that?"

"Oh yes, please, Auntie Marg. Can I have some books on the lounge with Teddy when I am all dry?"

"You certainly can, but I think something to eat after your bath would be better before the books, don't you? I'll get Uncle Ken to get one of your favourite meals ready. Would you like an egg and toast fingers or chicken nuggets?"

"Chicken nuggets, please. Do you have something Teddy can have too?"

"I'm sure Uncle Ken can find something not too messy for Teddy but a bath first for you, Miss Meredith."

When Meredith had been bathed, fed, and read to, she was put to bed in the room kept for her use with lots of cuddles and kisses. Teddy was also dressed in a pair of pyjamas that Margaret had made for him out of an old shirt of Ken's.

Within minutes, there was silence from the small bedroom where Meredith slept, but she didn't like sleeping in a darkened room. On one of her shopping trips, Margaret had found a ceramic fairy light that plugged into the wall power point and gave a soft glow. Meredith was thrilled with it and settled into sleep quickly once her fairy light was turned on.

Back in the kitchen, Ken was cleaning up after dinner and was immersing the dishes in the sink. He turned when Margaret walked into the kitchen. "Do you want a cuppa, love?"

"I think I need more than a cuppa, but in the absence of any alcohol in the house, that will have to do tonight. Isn't my sister the absolute limit?"

"She certainly is," replied Ken. "She's a walking disaster. I don't think she has ever grown up, but then again, she was the golden-haired daughter, wasn't she?"

"Yes, I was known as the smart one, and she was known as the pretty one. She could bat her baby blue eyes at Mum or Dad and would be forgiven for almost anything. No wonder she has grown up irresponsible and living the crazy life she does. I don't see any chance of her improving anytime soon."

"Me either," said Ken. "I just hope that nothing happens to that darling little girl asleep in the other bedroom. I love her as though she was our own, but unfortunately, she isn't."

Two

Three weeks had gone by, and there was no word from Tiffany about when she would return. Mobile messages had gone to voicemail, and although the lack of returned calls was not unusual, Margaret had a bad feeling about this trip south with Scottie. She didn't trust him and knew that he had a drug habit as told to her in one of Tiffany's drunken rants.

Each time Margaret heard of a motor vehicle accident, she ran to the television to see if Tiffany's car was involved. One item of interest was a huge drug bust in the Riverina where itinerant workers were harvesting cannabis in a purpose-built hydroponic warehouse. There were scenes on the television of the police arrests, and Margaret thought she saw a car like Tiffany's parked beside a shed, but it had different-coloured number plates.

Meredith was having a wonderful time with her Auntie Marg and Uncle Ken. They took her to the park most afternoons when Ken got home from work. She was allowed to paint on big squares of paper at the kitchen table and delighted in creating a string of paper dolls. She was such a happy little girl and helped clean up her mess before bath time each night. The kitchen soon became decorated in her artwork, and the paper doll strings were hung on the curtain rail in her room.

Best of all, she got to play with Scruffy. He was a rescue dog of mixed breed, brown and white, with one funny ear and a tail that wasn't quite straight. His name suited him perfectly. Meredith spent many happy hours throwing his ball or rescuing his squeaker toys from wherever they had been hidden. Scruffy didn't mind at all being included in the trips to the park, even though he wasn't allowed off the leash, but he had such fun with Meredith.

Ken and Margaret even let Scruffy stay in Meredith's room each night. She went to sleep with one arm around Teddy and the other hand hanging off the side of the bed, ready for Scruffy to lick or sniff if he felt the urge. He curled up in his bed, and his soft snores could be heard from the doorway. He had the use of the doggy door, so he didn't need to disturb anyone if he needed to go outside at night.

It was always sad to see Meredith's crestfallen face when she knew she had to leave Scruffy behind, but she was assured he would be glad to see her anytime she stayed over when "Mummy needed to go away for a while." Ken and Margaret didn't say a bad word about Tiffany in front of Meredith as they wanted her time with them to be happy and as close to a family situation as possible, given the life they could only imagine she had with the two irresponsible adults she lived with.

It was almost a month before Margaret received a call from Tiffany. "Hi. We'll be back tomorrow, so have Meredith ready by two o'clock. And don't be loading her up with more books to bring home. She has enough toys to sink a ship, and every time we move, I have more crap to pack. Okay?"

"Fine. Thanks for letting me know you're still alive. Did you not get all my other messages, or did you not think to check your daughter was okay?"

"Coverage was scrappy in the Riverina, and we were so tired every night I couldn't be bothered, so don't get crabby. See you tomorrow."

"I assume that was your lovely sister" came a voice from the family room.

"You guessed right, charming as always. Will be here tomorrow afternoon at about two, and in her words, 'don't be loading her up with more books to bring home,' which is fine with me. They would probably only be thrown in the bin. She doesn't exactly appreciate literature, and I doubt she has ever read a book to Meredith in her life. For that matter, I don't think she has read one herself that wasn't R rated."

Tiffany and Scottie arrived the next afternoon four hours late and in a different car to the one her sister had left in. "New wheels?" enquired Ken.

"What business is it of yours?" barked Scottie while he leaned against the front of it.

"Well, Scottie, I don't suppose it's any of my business. It was just a question, so you needn't get your back up. Meredith is ready to go home, but you are welcome to come in for a while, if you'd like to."

"Nah. Had a long drive. Just want to get home and chill," replied Tiffany and then raised her voice and shouted, "Meredith, get in the car! We're going home!"

The little girl appeared behind Margaret, again dragging Teddy by the paw, and slowly walked across to her mother. Tiffany grabbed her quickly and almost threw her in the back seat. "Took you long enough. You'd better smarten up, young lady, when I get you home. No more living the high life and being treated like a princess. Now sit still while I put your seat belt on and stop looking like you just lost your best friend!" she barked at the little tearful girl.

It brought tears to Margaret's and Ken's eyes when the little girl pressed her face to the window and waved goodbye to the only two people in the world who were kind and gentle to her.

"No thanks from the lovely Tiffany as usual," commented Margaret. "What on earth does she see in that creature who is her latest lover?"

"Well, they say love is blind," commented Ken. "But it doesn't have to be stupid as well."

They went back inside and sat at the kitchen table, both deep in thought. "Where do you think they got that car from?" said Ken.

"It wouldn't surprise me what they'd been up to. Did I tell you I saw a car like hers at a drug bust in the Riverina the other day but it had different plates?"

"No, you didn't. They've arrived back, and hopefully, there is no reason why we should be worried. Come in the lounge room. I want to talk to you about Meredith."

Ken patted the seat beside him on the lounge. "Come and sit down, love. I think we need to do something to ensure that Meredith doesn't continue the life her mother is living. She's only Three years old, but it won't be long before she becomes aware of what her mother gets up to – the men she brings home, the drugs, the alcohol, and who knows what else goes on. This latest 'love,' the charming Scottie, leaves a lot to be desired in a role model for our niece. Do you think we should try and talk some sense into her when Scottie isn't around?"

"I agree with you, but Tiffany is getting government benefits for Meredith, and I worry that is the main reason for her keeping her. Poor little kid is just a means of cash, I suspect. Maybe just keep quiet for now and offer to have Meredith stay over more often? That would work for Tiffany. She keeps the cash, and she keeps Scottie happy with Meredith out of the way. As the old saying goes, 'There is more than one way to skin a cat.' Do you want to give it a go?"

"Okay, but there is one thing I want to do to try and safeguard Meredith, if ever she is in trouble."

"What's that?" enquired Ken.

"You know how much she loves her bear, so I thought I would make Teddy a new outfit."

"How's that going to safeguard Meredith?"

"Well, Teddy's outfit will have a vest with a lining that has our names, address, and phone numbers written on it. I will tell Meredith what I have put there, and if ever she is in trouble or worried, she can show it to an adult, and they will be able to contact us. Tiffany doesn't need to know about it and wouldn't be interested enough to investigate the bear's new outfit, but it will be a contact if ever necessary. What do you think?"

"You crafty woman, no wonder you were known as the smart one."

"Glad you agree. Now I had better get my sewing machine up and going. Teddy needs a new outfit."

Three

It was only a few weeks later that Margaret received a phone call from Tiffany demanding that they look after Meredith for an uncertain amount of time. When Margaret enquired why, she was greeted with "It is none of your business. Is the answer yes or no?" Of course, her answer was yes.

The next day, Meredith was delivered to the front door of Auntie Marg's house, again trailing Teddy by his paw. As soon as Tiffany was out of sight, Margaret took Meredith inside for her treat of ice cream with chocolate sprinkles. It was early afternoon, so it wasn't going to spoil her dinner, and she would have time to take a bath but this time with Teddy being given a wash as well. He was starting to look dirty and bedraggled and needed sprucing up before his new outfit was put on and the details on the inside of the vest explained to his little owner. Margaret didn't like asking her niece to keep a secret from her mother, but it was in the child's best interest.

It was Meredith's fourth birthday during the time she stayed with her aunt and uncle. Margaret tried in vain to contact Tiffany and ask if she wanted to celebrate with her daughter, but the calls always went to voicemail with no response forthcoming. A birthday party was arranged for the Saturday afternoon, and a few of the neighbour's children were invited as Meredith had played with some of them in the past. Even Scruffy received a reluctant bath and blow-dry so he wouldn't be a smelly guest.

A shopping trip was undertaken a few days before the party so Meredith could choose some new clothes. There was certainly nothing suitable in the clothes she had brought with her as most of them didn't fit or were not in a wearable condition. The Party Clothes Shop was in the next suburb, so Ken, Margaret, and Meredith decided to start there. One look at a pink tulle dress with sequins sewn on the bodice caught the little girl's eye, and she shyly tugged on her aunt's hand. "Can I have that one, please?" she ventured as she pointed out the pretty dress.

"How about we see if they have one to fit you and a pair of shiny shoes to match? Would you like that?"

There was no need for Meredith to answer verbally. Her shining eyes and wide smile said it all. When she was dressed in the pink dress and had been fitted with shiny, soft ballet shoes, she looked beautiful. It brought tears to Margaret's and Ken's eyes as they watched her twirl around in front of the mirror. It took some persuading to have the outfit taken off and packed in a bag to take home. Meredith insisted on carrying her treasures and kept on peeping inside to make sure they were still there.

Next was a stop at the specialty cake shop to choose something appropriate for a 4-year-old. The sample one the party girl chose was pink and decorated with fairies, the number 4 in the centre, and chocolate sprinkles around the sides. Perfect. It was to be collected on the morning of the party, complete with candles. Another stop for plastic bowls, plates, table decorations, balloons, and shopping was complete. They decided to have lunch in the centre and then take the tired but happy little girl home.

Margaret tried several times over the next few days to let Tiffany know about the forthcoming party but was unsuccessful. She had no idea where her sister currently lived, so she could do no more than leave messages and hope Tiffany didn't go ballistic about her organising a party for Meredith. It was hard to tell which way her sister's mood would go, and much of this depended on her unstable relationship with Scottie. She knew her sister drank to excess at times but had not seen any evidence of drug use when she brought Meredith to them or collected her. The times between visits to Margaret and Ken were getting shorter, and Meredith's stays were becoming longer. This didn't bother them at all as they really enjoyed looking after her but were always conscious that she was not their child.

The birthday party was a spectacular success, and Meredith had a wonderful day, twirling around in her pink dress and silver shoes. Scruffy had a new pink collar, chosen by Meredith, who couldn't be talked into any other colour. She explained to Margaret in a very serious tone, "Scruffy's feelings will be hurt if he and I don't match." Teddy wore his silver vest, and both the dog and the bear smelled a lot better than they had done the day before.

Another week passed, and finally, Tiffany phoned her sister. "Can you keep Meredith for another few days until Scottie goes down south again for work? He doesn't like her being around him."

"That's fine. She can stay for as long as you like. She's no trouble at all, and we enjoy having her with us. Are you going south too?"

"No, not this time. I'll pick her up after he leaves. Will let you know when, okay?" And the call was disconnected.

"Charming sister again?" queried Ken. "How much longer is Meredith staying? Not that I mind, and you know that too, don't you? It's just that I worry about her when she goes back home. We don't even know where she lives, but at least someone can contact us now that Teddy is wearing a new vest."

"I'm not happy about the situation either. I would rather see Meredith more frequently so I can keep an eye on her and make sure she is being looked after as much as Tiffany is capable of looking after anything. It worries me, though, that Scottie doesn't like her being around when he is home. Given a choice, I think my sister would choose Scottie over Meredith any day as long as she doesn't lose any money on the deal."

Meredith was becoming more reluctant to leave each time Tiffany came to collect her but couldn't or wouldn't explain why. It seemed to be more than leaving her loving aunt and uncle behind. Before Tiffany was due to arrive, Margaret again explained the details on the inside of Teddy's vest and how she could show them to any adult if she needed her auntie's or uncle's help. It was difficult explaining to the little girl why it was best she didn't show the inside of the vest to her mother. Margaret got around it by saying that "Mummy knows how to contact us. You know she phones when she is coming to get you, so it is more for people who don't know us. Do you understand, my darling?" Meredith just nodded and slowly packed her bag to go home with her mother.

The phone at Ken and Margaret's rang two weeks later, and a stranger asked, "Is this Ken and Margaret's place?" Margaret answered that it was. "Hi, I'm Holly, Tiffany's next-door neighbour, and Meredith asked me to ring you. She said she couldn't wake Mummy up. I've rung for an ambulance. She's still alive, but I think it might be a drug overdose from the look of the bedroom. Can you come and get Meredith? I have to go to work soon, and it's not a good idea for her to be here in case DoCS [Department of Community Services] becomes involved."

"I don't even know where my sister lives," Margaret stammered. "If you give me the address, we'll leave right now. Thanks, Holly, for letting us know. Is Scottie around? I don't want to run into him if I can avoid it."

"No sign of the creep." After Holly offered the address, she said, "Okay, see you when you get here. Your niece is one smart little girl, knowing how to get help when she needed it."

Ken was standing in the doorway, waiting for Margaret to explain the conversation that had upset her so much. "Tiffany again?" he enquired.

"Not Tiffany but about Tiffany. That was her next-door neighbour, Holly, whom Meredith went to for help when she couldn't wake her mother up. The ambulance is on its way, and we need to go and collect our niece. Oh, Ken, this can't continue. Something will have to be done."

"Okay, don't worry about it now. We'll go and get Meredith and bring her home and then worry about your sister later. By the way, where're we headed?"

Margaret gave him the address, and his only comment was "Charming part of town. Mightn't have any wheels on the car if we leave it parked for too long."

Four

After her discharge from the hospital, Tiffany again asked if Meredith could stay with them as Scottie had returned from his work down south and wanted some "kid-free time." Margaret didn't agree as quickly as she usually did, and Tiffany sensed the hesitation. "What's wrong? Are you tired of the kid?"

"No, we never tire of having Meredith stay with us. Ken and I have been talking, and there's something we'd like you to do before taking some 'kid-free time.' When you bring Meredith over, allow an extra hour or so. It's important, Tiffany, so don't just fly in and fly out like you usually do, okay?"

"Whatever" was the disinterested reply. "See you tomorrow morning, about ten."

Around eleven the next morning, Tiffany called out at their front door. "I'm here. Now what's so important? Could you make it quick as Scottie gets impatient if I'm gone too long?"

"Come in, Tiffany." Margaret opened the door wide. Meredith had already taken her suitcase down to what she called her bedroom. Scruffy was barking excitedly at the back door as soon as he saw his little friend. "Meredith, I think Scruffy wants you to play with him. How about you go and find his ball and ask Uncle Ken if he will give you some dog treats?"

"Tiffany," Margaret started off, "you know we love having Meredith with us, but after the scare you gave us when you had to go to the hospital, we would like to make a suggestion."

"Yeah, okay, whatever. But make it snappy, okay? My man gets aggro, and that is not a pretty sight."

"Firstly, we'd like you to take out an insurance policy on your life, with Meredith as your beneficiary, and we will pay the premiums each year so that it remains valid."

Tiffany interrupted with a laugh and said, "You're the eldest, so you'll probably be gone long before me."

"With your lifestyle and apparent drug and alcohol abuse, I think you already have a head start. Now please let me finish. In the event of your untimely demise, the money from your policy would be invested in a trust fund for Meredith to be used for her education, including university, if she wants to do that. You would also need to make out a will with those instructions and making Ken and me Meredith's guardians until she reaches the age of eighteen. Do you agree?"

"Well, I don't like the idea of an insurance policy on my life. What if I don't agree?"

"If you don't agree, we may be forced to try and take a legal action to have Meredith removed from your custody and placed in our care. It's entirely up to you. You have one week to set all this up. Be responsible for once in your life, Tiffany. This is important for your daughter's future."

"Is that all? Have you finished?"

"Yes, Tiffany, that's all for the moment. I'll expect to see you back here in a week with what we have discussed put in place. You know me well enough that I mean what I say, and I say what I mean."

Tiffany picked up her bag and left, slamming the front door of her sister's house in temper. Tiffany was smart enough to know that her sister would go for the jugular if Meredith was hurt in any way while living with her and Scottie. They had planned to go south for a few months, and Tiffany needed her sister to look after her daughter so they could be together and have the lifestyle Scottie had introduced her to – sex, drugs, and rock 'n' roll. Unfortunately, it was more of the former and less of the latter. She had been backed into a corner, but it was no skin off her nose if her sister was going to pay the premiums on the policy, the cost of the will, and guardianship papers. She would do what her sister had demanded, and to hell with her. She had a life to lead, and she was going to damn well do it.

The next day, Tiffany organised the life insurance policy for accidental death for half a million dollars with Meredith as the beneficiary. The money was to be held in trust and used for Meredith's education until the age of eighteen. After that age, release of funds was at the discretion of Ken and Margaret. They were hoping that Meredith would go to university and make something good of her life. The annual premiums were to be paid by Margaret and Ken, and a direct debit was set up. A visit to a solicitor, and the will and guardianship papers were organised, and Tiffany had to go back in two days to sign them. At least she didn't have to pay the bills.

When the papers were ready, Tiffany turned up on Margaret's doorstep one afternoon and thrust them at her sister. "There you are, just as you demanded. Hope you're happy now." And she went back out to her car, which she drove at speed up the road.

"If she keeps driving like that, the ink won't be dry on the insurance policy," Margaret remarked to Ken.

Only a week later, Tiffany rang and asked if they could look after Meredith for an extended amount of time. Margaret readily agreed, as Tiffany knew she would, and Meredith was brought over the next day, with two suitcases this time. "How long do you want us to have Meredith here this time, Tiffany? Looks like she has quite a few clothes with her."

"Well, probably a few months. We've moved out of the rental place, and Scottie and I are both going south to the Riverina again. Will let you know when we get there and check the place out." Tiffany got back in the car and didn't even bother saying goodbye to her daughter, who was standing at the front door with a suitcase on either side of her and Teddy dragging on the ground.

Tiffany's phone calls were few and far between, and she was very vague about where they were working or what the work was. The only indication of location from Tiffany was that they were in the Riverina. Margaret and Ken didn't think they would be fruit picking as that was too physical for them, but of concern was the amount of drug dealing that went on in that area. Although, as Margaret correctly pointed out, you couldn't believe a word Tiffany said and since she had been with Scottie, she had gotten even less truthful, if that was possible.

Some weeks later, they were surprised to see a police car pull up in their driveway. Margaret opened their front door and admitted the two policemen. She called for Ken to come into the lounge area. Fortunately, Meredith was out in the yard chasing after Scruffy and his latest squeaker toy.

"Hello. Are you Ken and Margaret Cunningham?" They confirmed with a nod. One of the police looked at Margaret and asked, "Is your sister Tiffany Bannister?" Again, Margaret nodded.

"What's happened to my sister, Officer? Has she had an accident?"

"No, not an accident, but I'm sorry to tell you that she's in Wagga Wagga Hospital with a gunshot wound and is critically ill. The man with her, Scottie, was a well-known drug dealer and was fatally shot."

"Shot? Why, how?" stammered Margaret.

"I'm sorry, I can't release details until there's been an enquiry. Once your sister is stabilised in Wagga Wagga, they are going to fly her to Sydney for specialist treatment. I'll get someone to let you know when and where she's been transferred so you can go and see her. It should be sometime tomorrow if they can get an air ambulance to bring her. She's too ill to come to Sydney by road. Is there someone we can get to come and stay with you? I realise it has been a terrible shock."

"Thanks, Officer, but we'll be all right. I'll write down both our mobile numbers so we can be contacted when Tiffany arrives, and thanks for taking the trouble to find us."

The two officers left, and Ken and Margaret could hear Meredith laughing while she played with Scruffy out in the backyard, fortunately unaware that her mother was critically ill.

The next day, they had news of Tiffany's condition and her transfer to a major Sydney hospital. She was in ICU, and they could visit for only a few minutes as her condition was still critical. Margaret asked one of her neighbours if Meredith could stay with them and explained the circumstances of her sister's hospitalisation. It was daunting for Margaret and Ken when they saw Tiffany lying so still in the bed, wires hooked up to beeping monitors with the sound of her oxygen-assisted breathing. Their stay with her was very brief, but the doctor looking after her took Ken and Margaret aside when they emerged from her room.

"Your sister is very ill," he directed at Margaret "and the next forty-eight hours are critical. She has suffered damaging upper chest injuries from the bullet, and we haven't been able to remove it yet. She's not fit to undergo an operation at this stage. You can come for a brief visit tomorrow." He patted Margaret's arm and went on his way down the corridor. Margaret took a seat in the nearest chair with a shocked look on her white face.

"Oh, Ken, she looks so ill. I hope she makes it, but the doctor didn't sound too confident."

"We'll come back tomorrow. Maybe she'll have improved by then. We can only hope she comes through this and will be okay. What are we going to tell Meredith? Do we need to say anything yet or see how Tiffany goes?"

"Well, as Meredith hasn't seen Tiffany for some time and doesn't ask about her very much, maybe we just keep quiet for now. If her mother's condition improves and they move her to a ward without all that equipment beeping, it will be less traumatic for Meredith."

"I agree with you, Margaret. It would be all too much for the little girl at this stage."

For the next two weeks, Ken and Margaret made regular visits to the hospital for very brief stays to see how Tiffany was going. She didn't seem to be improving and looked worse every day. They asked to see the doctor looking after her so they could get some updated information.

"I think you'd better sit down" were his opening words to Ken and Margaret. "Tiffany has taken a turn for the worse and now has an infection. We're keeping her heavily sedated for the pain, but her chances of survival have dropped to about 10%." There was nothing either of them could say to the doctor. Again, he patted Margaret's arm and walked away from them.

"What do we do now?" Margaret tearfully asked her husband. "Should we bring Meredith into the hospital? It might be the last time she sees her mother alive."

"I don't think we should. Tiffany looks absolutely dreadful, and the noise of the monitors beeping would be enough to scare any 4-year-old. Let's just wait and see what happens in the next twenty-four hours. Maybe she'll recover and surprise us all." He didn't believe that, and he knew his wife didn't either.

It was a sleepless night for both of them. In the early hours of the morning, Margaret's mobile, which was on her bedside table, rang. It was the hospital letting them know that there had been a change in Tiffany's condition, and unfortunately, she was rapidly deteriorating. They were advised that they should come to the hospital as soon as possible. Once again, Margaret asked her neighbour if she would look after Tiffany, and she readily agreed to come to their house as the little girl was sound asleep.

Ken drove to the hospital as fast as the speed limit would allow. The last thing they needed was to have an accident before they even got to see Tiffany. They approached the ICU with great trepidation, and Margaret was shown to her sister's bedside. Margaret sat as close as she could to Tiffany, given the restriction of the equipment keeping her alive, and reached for her hand. She put her mouth as close as she could to Tiffany's cheek and tried to whisper in her ear, "You're not to worry, little sister, about your daughter. Just try and get well and come home to us. We'll look after Meredith for as long as it takes for you to recover." Margaret held Tiffany's hand until the nurse tapped her on the shoulder and said that it was time to go, and Ken gathered his sobbing wife into his arms.

"She looks awful, Ken. I don't think she's going to make it," Meredith said through her tears.

They were shown to a waiting room and were told that a nurse would come and get them if Tiffany deteriorated any more. It was only a few hours when a nurse came out of the ICU and beckoned them to come into Tiffany's room. "I'm so sorry," said the nurse. "Your sister is not expected to live for much longer. Come with me, and you can sit with her, if you would like to."

Margaret nodded, and she and Ken followed the nurse back into the ICU. Tiffany was still hooked up to the monitors, but they could see from the tracings on the screen that her heartbeat was slowing. It was only minutes later that she breathed her last breath, and Margaret started crying. Ken sat with her, holding her hand and trying to give her comfort, but Margaret was distraught. The nursing staff let them know that they could stay with Tiffany for a while longer, but then she had to be moved from the ICU so her bed could be prepared for another patient. Neither of them could speak and just nodded, holding hands until their knuckles were white. All Margaret could repeat was "What a waste of a young life."

Margaret got through the next week with a lot of support from Ken and her neighbours. The funeral was organised, and Margaret just went through the motions. It was all just a blur. Meredith was told that her mother had an accident and couldn't be saved, so she had gone to heaven and was with the angels. The little girl seemed to accept this explanation and why she wouldn't be seeing her mother anymore. Margaret and Ken assured her that she would be living with them and Scruffy now. They had decided Meredith shouldn't go to the funeral because she was too young to understand and would be better staying with neighbours and some children on that day.

Margaret contacted Holly, Tiffany's previous next-door neighbour, to tell her the news. Tiffany apparently had few friends; as she had moved to a new place so many times, it was difficult to maintain friendships. It was a short service at the funeral parlour, followed by a cremation. A sad ending for such a short life.

Five

There were a lot of decisions to be made in the weeks after Tiffany's death. Ken contacted the insurance company and a solicitor to draw up a trust fund for Meredith. Tiffany's will was read and the guardianship papers were put into effect. They were also investigating the adoption of their niece as they agreed that it would be the best thing for the little girl. Within three months, most things were put in place. The terms of the trust fund allowed them to draw money for Meredith's education for as long as the money lasted. They hoped that it would be enough to get her through school and possibly a university degree, if that was the way she chose to go.

Neither of them had ever been to university, and they were denied jobs that returned a good salary. They were happy to supply the day-to-day expenses for Meredith, but a good education was a must. A private school a few suburbs away enrolled Meredith for the next year on compassionate grounds. Most of the pupils had their name on the enrolment list from the time they were born, but when Meredith's situation was explained, she was given a place. Ken remarked, rather cynically for him, that at least the school knew that the dollars would keep coming in because of the trust fund. For this remark, he got a poke in the ribs from his wife.

Meredith seemed to settle into her new life with her aunt and uncle. For the most part, she was a happy little girl; but occasionally, there was a glimpse of her mother's behaviour from childhood that Margaret remembered. There was the odd temper tantrum when things didn't quite go to plan for Meredith, but neither Margaret nor Ken let her get away with bad behaviour. Mealtimes could be a challenge if she decided she didn't like something her aunt had cooked, even if she had eaten it many times before.

She seemed to settle into school and made a few friends in her class. She loved learning and was proud to bring home whatever finger painting or project she had completed that day. Her teacher reported that she was in the middle of the class with her reading ability and loved story time. At the parent-teacher interview, Ken and Margaret were told that Meredith could be very strong-willed when it suited her and, at times, was disruptive in class. They weren't happy about these comments, and both hoped she wasn't going to exhibit too many of her mother's less likable traits.

By the time Meredith was eight years old and starting primary school, she was not getting the marks on her school reports that her intelligence would suggest were within her abilities. Again, Ken and Margaret were advised that Meredith could sometimes be a problem with her disruptive behaviour as she liked to be the centre of attention. The only thing that worked with her was sending her to the principal for detention. This kind of notoriety was not to Meredith's liking.

As she advanced towards high school, Ken and Margaret did their best to keep her in check with her behaviour. It really hurt when she would come out with "Anyway, you're not my parents, and I don't have to do what you say. You only look after me for the money my mother left you." This kind of comment earned her a lack of TV time and whatever other punishment fitted the crime.

Meredith was unpopular with a lot of her peers. She was developing into a bully, and the principal of the high school soon brought this to her aunt and uncle's attention. They despaired of where this young woman was going to end up. She was intelligent and well mannered when she needed to be, and she attained good marks but had few friends. Those who did share lunchtime or travelled home with Meredith were unfortunately very much like her – burgeoning bullies. They were at their wits' end. How had that sweet little 4-year-old turned into this unlikeable 14-year-old teenager?

Margaret and Ken were often greeted with grunts whenever they asked her to do something as simple as putting her dishes in the dishwasher. "Whatever" was another favourite word of hers, accompanied with a dismissive wave of her hand as she left the room. They were coming to the unhappy conclusion that they had Tiffany No. 2 on their hands. They hoped she would take a different path from her mother, which was of drugs and alcohol, but were not confident that their wishes would be granted.

She managed to get through to year 12 and the higher school certificate without being expelled, although she had come very close on several occasions. Ken suspected it was the constant dollars that kept her there for the most part. It certainly wasn't her sweet personality.

Meredith was accepted into university for a business management degree but informed Margaret and Ken that she wouldn't be staying with them in their suburban wilderness. She was going to live with some other students in a house close to the uni but expected "the trust," as she referred to it, to pay for her accommodation. She was less than pleased when the executors of the trust informed her, at a meeting Ken had arranged, that the money had been invested for her education, not her living expenses. It was their advice that, with a very expensive private school education under her belt, she might want to work part time in a coffee shop or a bar. This did not go down well with Meredith, and she hurried out of their office, slamming the door on her way.

Ken just shook his head at her behaviour but heard the executor ask him, "Didn't they teach manners at that school?" Ken remarked that Meredith didn't learn anything that Meredith didn't want to know about.

Margaret and Ken were quite relieved that their niece would be moving out of the house. They were tired of her tantrums, her sense of entitlement, and her bad attitude towards them. They had done their best for her when her mother had been killed, but it never seemed enough. They were happy she would be doing a business degree as she had expressed on several occasions that she was not going to be poor like them but wanted more for herself than a box in some suburban wilderness. Meredith totally ignored the fact that Ken and Margaret had kept a roof over her head when there was nobody else in the world she could have gone to.

Six

Ten years later

Meredith Cunningham's parents, Ken and Margaret, had come to a life-changing decision. They had their property on the market, and the price should be sufficient to buy a longed-for luxury motorhome to travel around Australia. They had paid a deposit on one that they particularly liked and were thrilled with their choice. They felt it was time they did what they wanted to do, not what Meredith thought they should.

They had topped up her bank account and paid down her credit card with their own savings when the trust was not earning enough interest for Meredith's endless demands. Ken's recent retirement payout meant that they now had time to travel, and the sale of their property would provide them with the means to do so. With the pension they would receive and some careful investments of his superannuation, they should be able to have a few years of travelling where they wanted and doing what made them happy. The golden goose (or, in their case, geese) was flying the coop.

A phone call to Meredith the next day went to message bank. That evening, she returned the call in an irritable voice with the opening question "What's wrong with one of you now?" And she was stunned when her parents told her their plans. "Don't do anything until I come over there! Are you both mad?" she screamed down the phone. Thirty minutes later, her silver Mercedes sports car hurtled up the driveway and screeched to a halt, swiftly followed by the slamming of a door. Ken and Margaret just looked at each other and raised their eyebrows.

"Incoming missile," Ken commented wryly.

They had prepared what they were going to say as Meredith was predictable when things didn't go her way. First, she yelled her displeasure, and then she slammed a few handy items around and burst into tears. Her parents were now immune to this childish behaviour and had vowed to stand firm and united throughout the expected tantrum.

All Meredith was concerned about was how this life-changing decision of her parents had affected her. During the drive from her place to theirs, she had come to the conclusion that there would be no more financial support, and she couldn't believe how selfish her parents were being. This crazy scheme of theirs was going to totally disrupt her life, and she was furious about it. Her parents had never denied her anything at all throughout her life, and now she was faced with a cash drought. She was not sure how she would manage and was angry that they hadn't consulted her first before selling the family home and disposing of what she saw as her future entitlement. Her parents were wise enough to know that, had they consulted Meredith, she would have tried to talk them out of this "madness" as she called it. She was now faced with a situation that she couldn't change or be pleased about, and she was not happy – at all.

After an hour of shouting, crying, and hurling the closest objects at the wall, Meredith came to the unhappy conclusion that not only had she lost the battle but she hadn't won the war either. This was the first time in her life that her parents had held firm and denied her whatever it was she wanted, and she didn't like the feeling of defeat. She returned to her car, once again slamming the door, and reversed at speed out of the driveway. She had gotten nowhere with squashing her parents' plans, and it seemed that she would be faced with a very dire situation. Her parents had told her that all financial support was going to cease today.

MC Events Management Company had been Meredith's creation, with a lot of financial assistance from her parents. They did not expect any kind of monetary gain from the venture and were happy that their beloved daughter had been such a success in creating a company. They were just hoping that the company made enough to support Meredith in her new financial state. Their plans had been made for their trip around Australia, and for once in their lives, they were going to put themselves first.

Her apartment was paid for, but her weekly expenses for beauty treatments, entertainment, clothes, and general "Meredith maintenance" were way outside her monthly salary. In addition to her considerable personal expenses were the costs of running her car and having it washed and polished regularly, strata costs on her apartment, electricity, and so on. A plan was needed. Poverty was not on Meredith's wish list, but as her parents had decided to withdraw their support, she was now financially on her own – and it terrified her.

However, her current lover, Foster, may be her saviour in this economic dilemma. He had told her he owned his apartment; she knew he drove a very nice top-of-the-range BMW and was always well dressed. He had a secure position as a consultant with one of the larger finance companies and was up for promotion in the near future. *This may turn out better than I thought*, mused Meredith.

Meredith had met Foster at one of the conferences she had organised almost twelve months ago. She had liked his well-groomed looks and his way of speaking. They had exchanged mobile numbers and had met up again a week later for dinner. They talked about their younger lives, school, friends, and so on.

Foster told Meredith that he had spent some time in London when he was in his early twenties after leaving Western Australia for the "big wide world" as he put it. When she asked him about his family, he told her that he was an only child; and when he left Australia, his father had told him not to bother to come back. He had been to university, where he attained a degree in commerce, and was supposed to go into the family business, but it didn't interest him, so he saved enough money and went to England. After a few years, he returned from the other side of the world and had lived in nearly every state and territory, with the exception of Western Australia for obvious reasons.

"I assure you, Meredith, I love Sydney, and this is where I am going to stay." That was music to Meredith's ears, especially the part that he was going to stay in Sydney. If she played her cards right, he could keep her in the manner to which she had become accustomed.

After Foster told Meredith he was staying in Sydney, she decided to start her campaign of linking his surname to hers when they met midweek for dinner at La Gondola. Meredith planned on spending the night at his apartment and stepping up her campaign to be Meredith Cunningham-Browne soon – or at least before her bank account emptied and her credit card maxed out. It was now more crucial than ever before that she marry Foster. They had been going out together for almost twelve months; they looked good together and enjoyed each other's company. They liked a similar lifestyle of dining out, late Sunday breakfasts usually on the terrace of his apartment, the theatre, and anything else that put Meredith in the social spotlight.

Her beauty routine needed an upgrade if she was going to have a hyphenated name. She was not going to walk around with dark roots showing in her glossy blond hair, spray tan becoming blotchy, or chipped nails because she couldn't afford to maintain her appearance. Meredith felt that she needed to be exceptionally well groomed to keep her clients coming back to her company. She was wrong.

The clients of MC Events Management Company felt that if she wasn't so expensive to maintain, then perhaps she could have organised events at a lesser price; however, no one was in any doubt that they certainly got value for money. The events booked by clients were well organised and held at amazing venues, and the food was always top class. It was testament to Meredith's success that many of her clients booked a year ahead to make sure that they could secure the date they required.

Saturday night was to be a fundraiser for a children's charity and had been booked for several months. The venue had been secured, two-thirds of the tickets sold, menu confirmed, and drinks ordered for delivery on the day. All was going well, and Meredith felt confident that her staff could manage any details that had to be changed. She often attended the functions to make sure that everything went according to plan, and it was also a chance for her to secure new business. At least half a day was required for Meredith to get herself presentable for this occasion, so Wednesday afternoon, she took time away from her business. The staff from her office attending the event were going to see Foster for the first time. She liked to keep her private life out of the office, and nobody had seen her with him as far as she knew.

"Good morning," she said cheerfully as she approached the partitioned office section of the company. There was a mumbling of greetings, none too enthusiastic, Meredith noted.

"Are we not happy today?" she enquired of the office in general. There were more mumblings, and a few slightly raised voices of "not really."

"And why would that be?" she persisted with a sarcastic tone in her voice.

Tasha, one of the more forthright girls, stood up and eyeballed Meredith with the statement "We are not happy today because we have a lot of work to do before Saturday. Our boss has not been here to help with it, nor were we able to contact her."

Meredith was rather taken aback as she was the boss, but she had been absent for half a day yesterday and an hour or two the day before. What they didn't understand – and she had long given up on trying to explain to them – was that she had a certain level of grooming to keep up. Her hair needed constant attention with colour, streaks, treatments, or a cut to keep it in the perfect condition Meredith had to have. Her nails were manicured weekly to ensure they were always perfect. The other girls were not so attentive to their grooming, but it completely escaped Meredith that they didn't have the disposable dollars that she had – or used to have.

Meredith turned on the heel of her Jimmy Choo shoes and disappeared into her office. She was a bit stunned by Tasha's comment but realised that there was a big event on Saturday, and she probably should have been in the office. Oh well, she was the boss, and the buck stopped with her, so if the job didn't get done, it was her head on the block. She shelved the idea of telling them about Foster this morning as it was obvious there was an air of discontent in the outer office.

She buzzed for her PA, Suzy, to come in for the morning instructions. Suzy appeared in the doorway, and the first thing Meredith noticed was that she had a run in her pantyhose. "Please provide an explanation for the run in your pantyhose," Meredith barked at Suzy as she pointed her manicured nail at the offending run. "You know I insist on immaculate grooming here." Suzy stammered and managed to get out that when she was dropping her little girl, Larissa, off at preschool, she had caught her leg on one of the stroller bags and had torn her pantyhose.

When Meredith enquired, "And why didn't you have a spare pair with you to change into?" Suzy replied that it was not her pay week, and she didn't have any money to buy another pair or the time to do so before she got to work. She also told Meredith that her little girl had to go without medicine as she couldn't afford it, so pantyhose was last on her list. Meredith was not the least bit interested in the budget problems of her staff and said with a point of her pen that Suzy should sit down and start taking notes.

Personal budgeting was a completely foreign idea to Meredith. All she knew about money was that when she needed more, she had two options. The first one was to ring her parents and quote the amount required and where it should be deposited, and the second was using her credit card. This system had always worked beautifully – for Meredith.

After giving Suzy two days' worth of work to be done in one day, Meredith picked up her Michael Kors bag; and swinging it over her shoulder, she went out through the office without a backward glance, telling anyone who happened to be listening that she was going to lunch. Meredith was one of the city's A-listers and was always off to lunch or dinner to build up her client base for the company. That was her story anyway. She had told the staff to never ring her mobile as a text message would do, and she would get back to them when convenient.

Janelle Scott

Most of the staff were glad to see the back of her and her demanding ways for a few hours. They could enjoy a coffee break in the middle of the afternoon without The Old Bitch (TOB) poking her head out of her office and calling for someone to do something urgently. It was almost like being given a short holiday. The majority of them worked hard but didn't feel at all appreciated, even if Meredith did pass out some tickets for shows or sports events that she wouldn't be using anyway. The pay was above average, and that was about all that kept most of them working for MC Events Management Company.

Seven

Promptly at seven on Wednesday night, Meredith arrived at La Gondola. She was dressed casually in a long one-shouldered alabaster crepe dress, silver leather sandals, a stunning blue enamelled necklet, and a light cashmere wrap. This outfit was combined to do the best for her blond hair, recent spray tan, and blue eyes. Under her arm, she held a small Dolce & Gabbana leather clutch bag that only contained her essentials – lipstick, credit card, and valet parking ticket. It would not have done to bring a large though stylish bag containing everything she would need for her planned overnight stay. That bag was safely stored in the boot of her car, parked by the valet service just down the road.

She was very aware of the effect she had on the heartbeat of most of the males she passed as she sauntered one block to meet her potential husband – in her mind anyway. She was greeted by Marco, the owner, and was ushered to the bar, where Foster was waiting for her. She knew how to make an entrance and did so with style everywhere she went. Foster stood up from his bar stool as Meredith approached.

He smiled at her, took her elbow to guide her to the other bar stool, and asked, "How have you been? I've missed you, even if it's only been a few days." And he leaned forwards to place a light kiss on her upturned cheek.

Meredith beamed at him. "And I've missed you too, my darling," the last bit being added for good measure. Endearments fell easily from Meredith's lips, and her whole day was peppered with them when speaking to clients in person or on the phone. The exception to this largesse of endearments was her hapless staff, who more often than not were summoned from their desk by the command "My office – now." It saved Meredith time and trouble to remember their names. It was pointless, in her opinion, committing their names to memory as they were not her friends, and she never gave their personal life a thought.

"You look lovely tonight, Meredith," Foster said softly, "good enough to eat, in fact. But dinner first?"

Meredith smiled suggestively and said, "We don't have to have dessert here." Foster correctly interpreted that to mean that Meredith Cunningham would be quite happy to be the dessert course, and that thought was very appealing. They were shown to their table, and after cocktails had been ordered, Foster reached across the table to take Meredith's silky smooth, recently manicured hand in his. The campaign to link her name and debts to Foster had begun.

"You are a most remarkable young woman. You've obviously worked extremely hard to develop your successful events management company, yet you always look so relaxed and sparkling. How do you do it?" he enquired.

Meredith tilted her head to an appealing angle and replied, "Well, I am organised and a dedicated hard worker, and I enjoy bringing a plan to fruition. I meet lots of interesting people along the way as I met you. Of course, some of my staff work harder than others."

Foster just nodded. "I thought as much. I wish I had more colleagues with drive and determination, but all they seem to want to do is take long boozy lunches."

After a few more exchanges about work and office issues, Foster told Meredith that it was his dearest wish to run his own company but realised that it took a lot of capital to really get going and manage for a year or so until business built up. Not being one afraid to ask questions, she subtly managed to find out most of the details of Foster Browne's financial status, wishes, and dreams. While this conversation (some would say interrogation) was going on, Meredith was working out, on a separate level, where she could fit in and whether it was worth pursuing this man. Although Meredith didn't handle her own finances all that well mainly because she hadn't had to, she had a good working knowledge of what it cost to run a successful company. From the time Meredith started her company, she made it a rule that she and the accounts team had regular updates on the financial health of MC Events Management Company.

During the main meal, she made a few pertinent suggestions of how Foster might be able to start his own enterprise while still being a consultant with the company now paying him. She also knew that a conflict of interests could be a minefield, but she thought Foster was savvy enough to be able to work out a way to manage this. If this was not the case, she was more than willing to assist wherever she could to achieve her desired result.

When the waiter left the dessert menu on the table, Meredith said softly to Foster, "I think we could have dessert somewhere quieter than this, don't you? We're not far from your place, and my car is in the valet parking just down the road. What do you think?"

Foster was not thinking with his head at that particular moment, but somewhere farther down his anatomy was taking charge. "I think that's a brilliant idea. I'll meet you in the foyer shortly." Meredith had already expressed the wish that she would like to go to the ladies' room and freshen up; this news was delivered with a flirty wink.

They met up in the foyer and, hand in hand, left La Gondola Restaurant. Meredith was very pleased with herself that this man had the makings of her next golden goose. He was very easy on the eye, available, and a man who would go places – with her exceptional guidance, of course. They would be a power couple – she could see it now in the gossip columns of the Sunday newspapers: GOLDEN GIRL OF THE A-LISTERS TEAMS UP WITH THE NEWEST

FINANCIER or something along those lines. They certainly made a physically striking couple with her light-coloured hair (albeit chemically assisted to blond from mousy brown) and his dark good looks.

She gave an audible sigh, and Foster asked, "Are you tired?"

She turned her head and replied, "No, my darling, looking forward to dessert. Aren't you?" The double entendre was not lost on Foster or his nether regions.

Foster saw Meredith to her car in the valet parking and kept a close watch on her car in his rear-view mirror. It was only a short trip, and she followed his car into the underground garage of his apartment block. Within minutes, Meredith had retrieved her bag from the boot of her car and slipped her arm through Foster's as they went across to the lift. She had stayed overnight at Foster's a few times, but now there was a clear purpose in her mind.

"This is a lovely way to end the evening," she purred in her best silky-toned voice.

They ascended to the twentieth floor, and when he opened the door to the apartment, there was a stunning view across the city. Meredith had a beautiful apartment, but this one was magnificent, and it had her style written all over it. "How beautiful. You must love coming home to this every evening," she cooed.

"Yes, it's a nice apartment, but I do get lonely here by myself." That was music to Meredith's ears. Foster slid open the glass doors to the balcony and settled Meredith at a table while he prepared their drinks.

"Champagne for you, darling?" he enquired. "I have some Moët chilling or Veuve Clicquot. Which would you like?" *Oh, this is getting better all the time.*

"Moët would be perfect, thank you." *Just like you, Mr Foster Browne.*

Foster appeared on the balcony, handed Meredith her glass of champagne, and touched the rim of his to hers in a toast. "May we always be as happy as we are tonight."

"I'll drink to that," she replied in her sexiest voice.

Adjourning to the bedroom seemed to be the next logical step, and after a particularly satisfying sexual encounter, Meredith mentioned, "I should probably go home before morning." But it was not delivered with any sort of determination to do so. All it took was a soft touch on his arm and a slow smile from him, and she turned into his arms, putting her hands behind his head and pulling him towards her willing mouth. After another sensual kiss, they gave up the idea of her going home and went back into the bedroom to continue where they had left off not five minutes before.

Wednesday night became Thursday morning far too soon for both of them. Meredith, for her part, had never had a lover who made her feel so feminine, so adored, and admired. It certainly ticked all the boxes for her – so far. They were in no hurry to leave their love nest, but hunger rumblings were becoming too audible to ignore. Laughingly, they decided that maybe "dessert" had worn off, and it was time to eat some real food. Foster made the comment "Man cannot live on love alone" as he swung Meredith around in a circle and finished the move with a kiss. Meredith had not missed the words "love alone" but was wise enough to not make any comment – at this stage. She would, however, tuck that thought away for another time.

"Come, my darling, breakfast awaits." Meredith tucked the "my darling" away with the "love alone" comment. She was very happy with the way this was going.

"I just need to let my PA know what I expect her to do until I get to the office, and then I'll be ready to leave."

Over breakfast, Foster and Meredith arranged to go sailing on Saturday and perhaps pulling into a harbour bay somewhere that they could swim. Foster would be borrowing the yacht from one of his colleagues, and fortunately, it came complete with crew, including a top-class chef. Meredith was rather pleased about the chef as she would struggle to put a sandwich together, if anyone even considered that was something she would attempt. Foster was not a confident sailor and didn't want to make a fool of himself by running a million-dollar yacht aground. It sounded like the perfect day out to both.

The prospect of spending a whole day with Foster was very tantalising, but Meredith had no intention of looking like a drowned rat. A bikini over her spray-tanned and waxed body, Gucci sunglasses, shady hat by the latest fashion find, and a deckchair were more what Meredith had in mind. There was work to do on her appearance before Saturday, and as soon as Meredith arrived back in the office, she rang for appointments with her usual beautician. The campaign to have a hyphenated surname was well and truly underway.

Saturday was perfect for sailing, and they spent a few hours anchored in a sheltered cove while the crew served a delicious lunch and poured champagne into chilled glasses. *Ah, this is the life. I could get really used to this.*

Foster had a swim and playfully shook cold water over Meredith's sun-warmed body. Initially, she was annoyed but quickly covered her anger, and he didn't seem to notice the downturn in her mood. The crew furled the sails and motored back into the harbour as the sun was setting, and it was a natural progression to go back to Foster's apartment to "freshen up" as she called it.

"Let's go to our favourite restaurant for dinner," he suggested. "I'll ring and see if we can get a table for 8 p.m. Is that all right with you, darling?"

"Sounds wonderful" came her voice from the en suite as Meredith dealt with the ravages of being in the open air all day, albeit under an awning. Meredith had no intention of going home tonight and planned to spend the latter part of the evening enjoying Foster and his luxury city apartment.

Eight

Meredith had left a string of broken hearts behind her, according to her. In reality, though, most of the men felt they had made a lucky escape from her clutches, constantly twittering on about herself, what she had just bought for her beautifully appointed apartment, her wonderful job, and all the fabulous people she got to meet. After a few months, they got tired of being the listener and not being able to get a word in edgeways about what was happening in their world. It was unlikely that Meredith even noticed when they were no longer around as she was so wrapped up in herself.

She only had three female friends, and they had been at the same private school many years ago. Throughout school and in their later teen years, Jacinta Coutts, Rochelle, Courtney Tynan, and Meredith Cunningham made up a tight little clique. They went everywhere together, spoke the same kind of language, had the same likes and dislikes, and were almost clones of one another except for their looks. Meredith was tall and willowy and had light brown hair. Jacinta was slightly shorter but had waist-length glossy brown hair that she was always playing with, much to the annoyance of her friends at times. Rochelle Woodham was a fair-skinned girl with a slight frosting of freckles across her nose and the wildest, untamed red hair. Courtney was the quietest one of the group and a real head-turner with her jet-black pageboy bob and her curvy figure, but she was completely unaware of it.

Through their teens and into their late twenties, they met up for the occasional lunch or dinner and kept up to date with what one another was doing by Facebook and emails. Jacinta's job as a flight attendant had her travelling all over the world, and Rochelle's marketing company also kept her busy, but the girls tried to get together for birthdays or other important events. As their thirtieth birthdays loomed just over the horizon, there had been no engagements, weddings, or births, although they were all hoping these occasions would eventuate. Courtney's conversation was usually about her horse and the ribbons she had won at the last show. This didn't interest the other three too much as they were definitely not of the "horsey set."

Meredith usually wanted to know if Courtney had met anyone who might want to use her events management company. If the answer was in the negative, then she immediately lost interest and turned the conversation back to herself and all the marvellous events she was organising, and this information was unashamedly peppered with name-dropping. The other three girls were used to Meredith's self-centredness and were not bothered by it. It was just part of who Meredith was.

Over the years, they all had their share of lovers, but none of them had yet made it down the aisle or even into a long-term live-in relationship. They were just too bound up in their burgeoning careers to really pay much attention to the current man in their life. They all felt that they really didn't need a full-time male and were almost proud of the fact that they could get along quite well without one. Things were about to change.

Meredith had met Foster and was very keen to link his name and bank account to hers. For the time being, she was going to keep his presence in her life to herself. Foster was jealously guarded territory as far as Meredith was concerned, and even though she enjoyed the company of her friends, she was not yet prepared to show off her latest find. She wanted to make absolutely sure this time that this particular man was going to stay in her life.

Entitled

Meredith had never been so determined to link her name with another man, but as her thirtieth birthday had passed, she was becoming aware that her financial future needed a partner to help support her lifestyle. She didn't feel as though she loved Foster, but she certainly liked him and his prospects. An added bonus was that their sex life was improving every time they were together. All in all, they had a relationship that suited Meredith, and that was all that really mattered to her. She also expected him to be well groomed with good manners and always put her first. She thought that it was her responsibility to look her best whenever she had a date with Foster so that he was proud to have her with him. Her hair was immaculate, nails perfect, and make-up professionally applied. She was punctual, and the first time she was shown to Mr Browne's regular table in Shangri-La Hotel, it caught her by surprise and caused a stab of jealousy she wasn't expecting. *How many times had he been here, with whom, and when?* flitted through her brain. She realised that, for the first time in her life, she was jealous of a man she hadn't known existed a little over a year ago.

She saw him crossing the room towards her, and her heart skipped a beat. He was so handsome and self-assured as he greeted people on his way through the restaurant. A nod here, a smile there, but he was still moving towards her. He sat down opposite her and took her hand in his. "I'm so glad you could find time in your busy schedule to have lunch with me."

Meredith almost purred as she replied, "I would find time for you no matter how busy I am. I love our midweek lunch or dinner dates."

"Now what would you like to drink? Your usual Moët?" enquired Foster as he signalled for the sommelier to approach their table.

"Oh, that would be lovely, but I do have to go back to work this afternoon, and I don't want the staff to see me giggly. I have to set a good example," she replied.

"Okay, we'll share a bottle so that we can both go back to work in a reasonably sober condition. I have a client coming at 4 p.m., as I told you, and he wouldn't like his financial adviser to be under the weather while shuffling his millions around," Foster joked.

"Meredith, you look beautiful. There are heads in this room that are constantly turning this way. I feel like the luckiest man on earth."

Meredith just smiled demurely and touched Foster gently on the back of the hand. His dark brown eyes twinkled at her, and he signalled for the waiter to take their order. *You are the luckiest man in the room, Foster, because I can open doors for us that you don't even know exist. We will be the darlings of the social set.*

The food was delicious, the champagne was perfectly chilled, and the company was everything Meredith had ever wished for. *Is this what falling in love feels like*?

Lunch was over all too soon, and it was time for them to go back to the real world. They reluctantly returned to their respective offices but not before making arrangements to see each other on Saturday. To Meredith, that seemed like a lifetime away, but she would use the time to have a beauty treatment and the highlights in her hair touched up. After all, she was investing in her future.

Upon arrival back at the office, she was greeted by telephones ringing and girls and guys looking harassed; and in her relaxed state, she didn't quite take in that there was obviously a crisis occurring. She went into her office and shut the door, mainly so that she could use some breath spray to cover the smell of alcohol, and then rang for Suzy. "What's happening?" she asked in a sharp voice.

Suzy always seemed to be the bearer of bad news, and this was no exception. "The chair covers and tablecloths for the charity ball on Saturday night have been damaged in transit and can't be replaced in time. I have rung all over Australia, but it's a busy time of year, and I can't find an exact replacement."

"Why didn't you ring me?" Meredith barked at Suzy.

"What would be the point? You don't answer your phone, and you didn't answer the text either. You have been gone for almost four hours, and we had to try and do something, so don't get angry with me," Suzy retaliated. She had had enough of Meredith's absences and the blame being put on anyone and everyone else.

Meredith had forgotten about the charity ball on Saturday night and now realised that it clashed with her date with Foster. Damn, some fast thinking was required here. She was good in a crisis and calmly asked Suzy to get her a coffee so they could try to avert a disaster. This charity ball was worth a lot of money to her company, and she didn't want to be known as unreliable. Suzy's words had stung, but they had an element of truth about them, and she couldn't deny that. When she was with Foster, all thoughts of the outside world and her place in it vanished.

Swinging into action, Meredith sent Suzy out into the main office to bring in the staff directly involved with the seating and decorations for the ball. As they trooped into Meredith's office, each looking as though they were going to the gallows, she announced that she needed them tonight to get this crisis sorted, but she would provide a meal and pay them overtime if they agreed to do so. They looked at one another in astonishment. This was a first – dinner and overtime. Maybe TOB had a heart after all, but she had hidden it well to date.

She asked Suzy to take coffee orders for the staff and get them delivered to the conference room. She set up the whiteboard and asked around the table for ideas of what they could do to dress up the chairs and tables at such short notice. The brainstorming began, and ideas were written on the whiteboard. It was the first time the staff felt that they had an input into MC Events Management Company. They were usually told, not asked, so they were a bit hesitant to put their hand up with an idea in case they were ridiculed.

Meredith was euphoric after her lunch date with Foster, so her usual style of cut and thrust was missing. The staff were a bit bewildered by this change in attitude and gradually started contributing ideas to the crisis meeting. Bit by bit, they came up with a whole different look for the ballroom to be used on Saturday night. They could access the materials required from their warehouse, and as long as they kept to the colours the charity had requested, it would be okay – hopefully.

At 6 p.m., Meredith realised Suzy was not in the room, and she needed her to organise food to be delivered while they finished the final details. She sent Hayley to track Suzy down and, upon returning to the room, reported that she had found her crying in the corridor. When Meredith asked what was wrong, Hayley replied that after Suzy had ordered the food, she had had to arrange for a friend whose child went to the same preschool to pick Larissa up, and she would be charged an extra fifty dollars, which she couldn't afford. These sorts of arrangements were a foreign land to Meredith, but she informed Hayley to tell Suzy she would pay the fee as it was her fault her PA had to work late. Hayley nearly fell over with shock but thanked her on Suzy's behalf.

Meredith called it a day at 9 p.m. and thanked the staff for staying back and pulling this event out of the fire. They were all a bit taken aback by this show of courtesy as they were used to just doing what they were told with no thanks whatsoever. As they left the building, Andrew suggested that maybe TOB had found herself a bloke at last. "Poor bugger," he added. They all laughed but didn't realise how close to the truth they were.

Nine

Saturday's date with Foster would need to be changed as she had to attend the charity ball. She realised for the first time that if her staff had refused to work back, which they were quite entitled to do, she would have been in dire straits. It had cost her some overtime, coffee, and dinner, but that was small change compared with losing the account of this particular charity and possibly her good reputation too. It was a slow climb to the top in this business, but one mistake, and you could find yourself right off the A-list. It was hard to get to the top and even harder to stay there.

Tomorrow she would have to phone Foster – an email would just not do – and reorganise their date. She would be devastated if he didn't find time for her over the weekend or didn't understand why she had to cancel. Then she had a thought that perhaps he might like to be her partner to the ball. She knew he owned a dinner suit, so she would give it a try.

Mid-morning, she rang his office, but he was at a meeting, so she left a message that Meredith Cunningham from MC Events Management Company had phoned. She wasn't sure if he spoke about his personal life at the office, so she erred on the side of caution. An hour later, he phoned and apologised for not being in the office when she had called. She explained about Saturday night, and he said that he didn't mind where they went as long as they were together. Problem solved. She organised for the company car to collect him from his home, and she would meet him at the venue as she had to be there much earlier. Meredith's master plan for the end of the evening was that they would go back to Foster's in the company car.

She had not managed to create a very successful business by being a wilting vine, but over the years, she had become somewhat ruthless. From her earliest childhood, what she wanted, she got, but she felt that Foster Browne was no pushover. They were both in their thirties, and neither had yet been married mainly because of their careers, which he had confirmed came first with him; but of course, that was before he had met Meredith. She understood this perfectly because that had been the rock many of her romances had perished on. However, this time, she felt quite differently. She wanted this man in her life – forever. She would do whatever it took to bring about that result.

What to wear? She went through her wardrobe like a woman possessed, throwing thousands of dollars' worth of clothes onto the bed, some still with the price tag attached. It was easy to be an impulse buyer when you had a bottomless bank account or a constantly replenished credit card. Meredith had never bothered looking for bargains, and charity shops were an unknown world to her. In her mind, if you worked hard, you were a success. If not, then you were a failure. Simple.

She finally found, in her cavernous wardrobe, an electric blue Grecian-style dress that she had bought for a special date with one of her previous lovers. However, the lover was gone before the transaction had appeared on her credit card. She had pushed the dress to the back of the rack, still in its plastic clothes bag; but when she brought it out, she realised that this was the one to stun. She searched through the stack of see-through shoeboxes – arranged in her wardrobe in colours and styles – and found a pair of silver Italian high-heeled sandals that just gave her extra height to be able to look straight into Foster's deep brown eyes.

Now all she needed was some serious bling. She knew her mother had a stunning sapphire and diamond necklet and earrings that had been handed down through the family and would one day be hers. No harm in giving it an airing instead of it sitting in the silk-lined velvet box on her mother's dressing table. Without any hesitation, she called her mother, even though it was 10 p.m. and her parents were probably in bed.

She was still angry about their proposed defection from her life, but she had a plan. When the phone was answered by her mother's sleepy voice, Meredith cut in with "Mum, you know that diamond and sapphire necklet and earrings that Granny gave you?"

Her mother replied, "Yes, I know the one, but I don't have it anymore."

"Why? Where is it? You know I wanted to have that when you die. What have you done with it?"

Her mother spoke softly and said, "I sold it last year. We needed the money, and I never wore it anyway."

Meredith didn't even wait for a reason about why this particular set, which she felt entitled to, had gone from the family. She was more upset that she would now have to find something else to provide the bling for her stunning dress, and she didn't have much time. Meredith's parting comment was delivered with a certain icy edge to her voice. "Well, thanks for nothing." And she hung up the phone with more force than was strictly necessary to disconnect the call.

At Meredith's beautifully appointed apartment, she threw the phone onto the bed in temper. Damn, where was she going to get something fabulous by Saturday night? She rang Jacinta in the hope that she might have something suitable, but her call went to message bank. Then she tried Rochelle, even though it was doubtful that she would have anything as stunning. Meredith thought Rochelle was just a little bit suburban and lacking in style, but it was worth a try. She had to have a necklet and earrings and quickly.

Rochelle sleepily answered the phone on about the fifth ring, and Meredith launched into her request for a stunning set of jewellery to wear on Saturday night. Rochelle woke up enough to say, "You must be joking, Meredith. All mine are fake, not like your genuine diamond ones. You wouldn't be seen dead in what I could offer. Good luck with your search, and I'm going back to sleep now."

She knew it was no use asking Courtney. She was definitely not a style queen. She was more country girl, even though she had never actually lived in the country, but was quite at home in jodhpurs and shirts. Her job as the manager of an equestrian centre did not lend itself to high heels and short tight skirts. It was a constant source of annoyance to Meredith that Courtney just did not bother to glam up a bit, but as Courtney pointed out when she had had enough of Meredith's criticism one day, "We can't all be the queen of style when we don't have incomes to match yours." Of course, Meredith had never bothered to divulge the fact that her parents gave more financial support than the wages her friends earned monthly.

Meredith then had an idea that perhaps she could "borrow" a piece from one of the many A-listers that she rubbed shoulders with at functions. Who could she ask? She sat down on the bed at midnight and started to make a list of possible women from whom to borrow a piece. Meredith was so focused on what she wanted to happen for her that it didn't cross her mind they probably borrowed their jewellery from designers who were eager to show off their latest work and had to return it after the event at which it was showcased.

The blue dress hung in its plastic shroud on the outside of her wardrobe, beautiful in its simplicity, but Meredith didn't see it like that. All she saw was a dress that would maximise her good looks but just needed some jewellery, and she was determined that was how she was going to go to the charity ball. Many futile phone calls early the next morning didn't bring any luck.

In a last desperate bid and during the time she should have been getting ready to go to work, Meredith remembered that one of her previous lovers had worked in a jewellery design studio. It didn't matter to her that they had not seen each other for about three years – she needed jewellery, and he could get it for her.

"Darling," she purred into the phone when her ex answered.

"Who's this?" he queried.

"Why, it's me darling, Meredith. You must remember me. We had such wonderful times together not that long ago, didn't we?"

"Did we? Anyway, what do you want? You must want something, Meredith, as it's the first time I've heard from you in three years."

"Well, darling," she persisted, "I was wondering if you might just happen to have a stunning piece of jewellery that needs to be seen by about 1,500 people at a charity ball on Saturday night. The only problem, if it is a problem, is that it must be diamonds or diamonds and sapphires as I am wearing a stunning blue dress. I just thought it might be a chance for you to showcase a piece of your work. What do you think?"

"Thanks for the opportunity, Meredith, but the only thing I would like to see around your neck is a noose for the way you treated me. Have a good day." And he hung up the phone.

Meredith was a bit taken aback; after all, he had finished the romance. *Some people are just so hard to get along with. You give them an opportunity, and they throw it back in your face. Well, that's his bad luck.*

Meredith had never been taught to take any responsibility for her actions and just went through life with a sense of entitlement. So far, it had worked just fine – for her.

Ten

When Meredith arrived at work, almost two hours late, Suzy rushed up to her with a concerned look on her face and started to tell Meredith about the latest fiasco. Meredith just spun around and said to Suzy, "Oh for goodness' sake, can I just get my coat off first? And a coffee would be nice too." The hapless Suzy almost ran out of the office to do her boss' bidding. She promised herself that, one day, she would get a better job; but for now, with a small child to rear on her own, she was stuck with TOB.

Suzy returned with Meredith's coffee and quietly placed it on her desk. Meredith pointed at the table and tub chair seating to the side of her desk and told Suzy, "Over there," without so much as a thank-you.

After a few sips of her coffee, Meredith realised that Suzy was still standing in the room. She looked up from the papers in her hand and asked, "What's the matter now?"

Not wanting to be the bearer of bad news but forced into the situation by her position as Meredith's personal assistant, Suzy took a deep breath and informed her boss that there had been a lot of people who had cancelled for the charity ball, and the seating would have to be reorganised.

Meredith's reply was typical. "Well, get on with it then. Find someone to help you. Suzy, don't bother me with trivial details. I have to find a necklet and earrings to wear before the event."

Suzy spun around and, with raised eyebrows, left the office to find someone to help her reorganise the tables so it didn't look as though a lot of people had cancelled. She hoped Meredith's necklet choked her. Well, not really, or she would be out of a job. Better be careful what she wished for.

While sipping her coffee and examining her recent manicure, Meredith remembered she had a silver leather belt encrusted with Swarovski crystals that might just do the trick. One of her heavy white gold chains with the letter *M* encrusted in diamonds should pull the whole outfit together and dazzle Foster when he saw her.

Meredith had emailed a long list of duties to the staff who were setting up the venue for the ball. She checked her list just once more to see that everything was to be looked after by someone on her team and then set off for the first of her beauty appointments for the day. She had tried on her dress and shoes the night before and was more than happy with her image in the mirror, but she felt she could do with a light spray tan to give her skin that special, polished, sun-kissed look. She would make sure it was an all-over tan. *Just in case,* she thought as she imagined her evening with Foster.

She had booked the company car to take her to the ballroom in plenty of time for the start of the event. Even though she had not physically done any of the work, it had been her organising (giving no credit to any of her staff) that had pulled this off. Now all she had to do was be the public face of MC Events Management Company and do what she did best, circulate and charm. She would have been mortified had she known that most of the women thought her to be shallow, condescending, and fake in her praise when she told them, "Darling, you look just marvellous. That colour suits you perfectly, and you seem to have lost a little weight too," which they translated into *I have to say something positive to you as you're paying $200 each for the privilege of being at my event. I'm glad you're not wearing the same colour as me, and even though you are still overweight, you might feel better if I tell you the last little lie.*

Jacinta and Rochelle had been roped into coming to this event but not as paying guests. Their brief, delivered by email from Meredith, was that they should work the room and tell as many people as possible how wonderful MC Events Management Company organised this type of occasion. They were to give out business cards – subtly, of course – and for their work, they would get to eat a meal in the kitchen or somewhere else out of sight. The other reason they had been invited was to see her latest find and hopefully future husband, Foster Browne. At their last luncheon a month ago, she had dropped hints about her latest lover, and tonight they were to see him.

Courtney had not been invited to help at the event as she was off on some cross-country ride with a new man she had met at the equestrian stables she rode from every weekend in Centennial Park. Meredith wasn't disappointed but rather relieved that Courtney could not attend as she would probably wear something unsuitable. She could not be relied on to dress up to the level that Meredith expected and had given Jacinta and Rochelle strict instructions on the type of dress they were to wear and the minimum amount of grooming that would be acceptable. As usual, Meredith did not take into account the difference between her earnings and that of her other three friends. It never crossed her mind that her friends also lacked the desire to be anything like her.

Right on time, Foster appeared in the doorway of the ballroom. Meredith had been watching out for him as she told the company driver to text-message her when Foster arrived at the front of the venue. She didn't want to make her excitement too obvious, but she was quivering inside. This was a feeling she hadn't known for a long time, and it felt delicious.

She glided across the floor to him and gave him a light hug and an air kiss in the direction of his cheek. It wouldn't do to ruin her make-up this early in the evening.

"Foster, darling, I'm so pleased you could come tonight. There are some people I would like you to meet." And she expertly guided him across the room to introduce him to the people on the board of the charity they were fundraising for.

As they were crossing the dance floor, Foster leaned closer to her and whispered in her ear, "You look absolutely ravishing tonight."

Meredith just looked up at him with the sexiest smile she could muster and replied, "Thank you, darling. That's so sweet of you to say."

It gave her immense pleasure to see the looks on Jacinta's and Rochelle's faces as she slowly walked past them with a handsome man by her side. When she was out of hearing, Jacinta whispered to Rochelle, "Is that the next victim?" And they both burst out laughing. They had known Meredith for a long time and were well aware of her patronising attitude towards them and how she used them if she could. They had agreed to come tonight not to help Meredith but to see if they could find themselves a man. After all, they were getting on, and their biological clocks were ticking louder each year. They had met men through their jobs of flight attendant and marketing executive, but as they travelled a lot, they never seemed to be in the same place as the man they had recently met. Many a romance had foundered on the difficulties of conflicting timetables.

It was finally time for dinner to be served, and the guests made their way to their allotted tables. The master of ceremonies introduced himself and informed everyone that there would be a silent auction and many opportunities as the night progressed for great prizes and entertainment throughout the evening. Meredith, of course, was seated with Foster, and she had made sure that she sat where the best lighting was to be had – shining on her, of course. She was no amateur at being the centre of attention as that had been her position for most of her life. However, things had a way of changing, and Meredith was unaware that her privileged existence was about to undergo a downturn, and there would be nothing she could do about it.

Eleven

Monday saw Meredith arrive at the office on time and in a good mood. Both situations were unusual, but the staff would be happy with anything that saved them from her wrath and unreasonable demands. "Good morning," she cheerily greeted her staff, already assembled in the boardroom as instructed by emails over the weekend. "Well, it was a very successful event on Saturday night, and a lot of money was raised for the chosen charity, so thank you, one and all, for your efforts."

This was greeted by a stunned silence. Nobody had ever heard Meredith say "thank you for your efforts" in the whole history of the company.

"There will be a luncheon held here at 1 p.m. today, so don't hit the vending machines in the foyer too heavily." And with that, she turned on her very high and expensive heels and disappeared into her office.

"She must be getting laid," one of the more outspoken guys whispered. There was a lot of laughter at that comment, even though it had been delivered sotto voce.

"It won't last," said another.

"What? The good mood or the sex?" queried one of the guys who had worked almost sixteen hours straight on Saturday.

Lunch was duly delivered and devoured by the staff while TOB was at one of her beauty appointments. Her absence elevated the mood in the room, and it was a welcome respite from the usual atmosphere of the place.

"Back to work, everyone," advised Suzy. "She will be back by 3 p.m. so we had better look as though lunch was just a blip on the radar of our day."

Just ten minutes later, Meredith swept back into the office and announced to the staff, "I am exhausted. It's been such a busy day." Then she disappeared into her office with a throwaway comment to Suzy: "Coffee, Suzy, and be quick about it." It looked like TOB was back.

Meredith and Foster had not really discussed their possible future. They very much lived in the moment, and the next high-profile event was all that interested them both. It was time for Meredith to take their relationship to the next level. Foster was climbing the corporate ladder in his company, although to Meredith's mind not quickly enough. They had never discussed their income in depth, but it was mutually assumed that there was plenty of money in the pot for the lifestyle they both aspired to.

It was not even on Meredith's agenda to reveal to Foster that her parents were a couple of grey nomads travelling around Australia on some whim that had seen the family home disposed of to fund this ridiculous idea. She was careful to give the false impression that she had a wealthy background and would, at some time in the future, inherit money.

Foster had never declared to Meredith that "his apartment" was actually company owned. The previous tenant was on a twelve-month secondment to a big bank in London and would no doubt want to move back in on his return, the date of which had not been confirmed but would be sooner rather than later. Rent in the same area was expensive, but Foster felt he could manage it with a bit of financial juggling. After all, he had a rich heiress in his arms most nights of the week who did not need to know why he had decided to move from one apartment to another.

In his mind, there was no harm in allowing her to think that he was actually accumulating property when, in fact, he was not an owner of any real estate. He guessed that Meredith would only hitch her wagon to a successful man, not one whom she saw as below her financial status. Through his business dealings, Foster had learned that it was not necessarily what you said but more what was left unsaid.

He had planned a special dinner for them, and he was going to propose marriage. He had to make sure that this bright and shiny star did not move from his orbit. He needed her on his arm at corporate functions and in his bed as much as possible and was as sure as he could be that she would accept his proposal.

Foster was paid a commission on the amount of clients and financial portfolios he brought into the company, and during the time he had been with Meredith, his mind was more on her than his job. He was getting a little low on funds but not seriously enough to worry just yet. He enjoyed her company, the sex was good, she was a social asset, and they liked the same kind of lifestyle.

They had discussed the possibility of children, but neither of them saw themselves as parents. A dog, however, was another matter altogether. Meredith had one time expressed an idea that she wouldn't mind having a miniature apricot poodle. She didn't mention that the dog would serve as a fashion accessory tucked into a specially designed bag. She made the point that dog hair made her sneeze and that poodles didn't have that effect on her. The real reason was that she couldn't stand dog hair on her clothes or furniture.

In his ignorance of the real reason Meredith would tolerate a poodle, he managed to locate a breeder on the NSW North Coast who had a miniature female apricot poodle available in four weeks. She asked him all sorts of questions about where the dog would be housed, who the owner would be, and so on. It was like trying to adopt a child, except a lot less expensive. He must have answered all the questions correctly because then money was transferred, and the pup was to be flown to Sydney on a regional airline. Foster organised to take an afternoon off work and collected the poodle, which he named Pamela, from the airport. He had arranged for a friend in the office to keep the pup with him for the night until he could give her to Meredith.

This was a risky move because Meredith had not expressed a strong desire to have a dog, but to Foster, it was a cute way to deliver the engagement ring he was planning to put on Meredith's finger the next evening. A caterer had been organised to deliver food and perfectly chilled champagne to his apartment for this celebration. Timing was everything because the previous tenant was due back in Australia in six weeks, and he would have to move out. He surmised that Meredith wouldn't ask too many questions about his relocation if she had a shiny ring on her finger and a puppy to take care of.

Saturday night was looming, and Foster had taken delivery of the engagement ring he was planning on giving Meredith. He had bought it at a jeweller who assured him that his about-to-be fiancée would not know it was cubic zirconia instead of diamonds unless she was a trained gemmologist. Foster knew Meredith was only interested in bling and not its origins, so he was fairly sure he would get away with the very much cheaper ring. After all, this was the carrot before the donkey, and he couldn't afford a solid gold carrot.

He picked Pamela up from his friend and placed the diamanté collar around the puppy's neck with the ring pinned on with a pink ribbon. He had bought a fancy dog basket for her but hadn't figured out yet how to stop her from barking and giving the game away when Meredith arrived. Perhaps he would just put the puppy in the farthest room and turn the music up a bit. Surely a little dog couldn't bark that much? Could she?

Foster went to Meredith's apartment and brought her across the city to "his" place. The dinner was due to be delivered by the specialist catering company in thirty minutes. Drinks were poured, and he took Meredith by the hand and led her out to the terrace.

"Darling, I have so enjoyed our time together. I think we have something special, so I have organised a lovely dinner for us to share and toast our future." Just then, the doorbell chimed, Foster let the caterers in and paid them, and they disappeared like the morning mist.

"Sit down, darling. I'll open the champagne, but first, I need to do something else." Meredith was consumed with curiosity but loved the attention and the aroma from the covered dishes spread out on the white tablecloth. Foster appeared from the hallway with a small bundle in his arms. At first, she couldn't identify what it was he was holding, but then she saw a pair of brown button eyes and a sparkly circle glinting in the light.

"What on earth have you there?" She laughed. "It looks like a bundle of curly rags." And then the bundle lifted its head and stared straight at her. Foster brought the bundle across and gently placed it on Meredith's lap, which caused her to jump up, and Pamela fell to the floor, giving a yip as she did so.

This wasn't going to plan for Foster, but always ready to rise to a challenge, he picked Pamela up and said, "She is part of my surprise. Just pick her up gently and see what is attached to her collar."

Meredith did as he asked and gasped when she saw the sparkling ring at the end of the pink ribbon. Foster was still on one knee on the floor of the living room and reached out for Meredith's hand. "Meredith, will you do me the honour of being my wife?" For once in her life, Meredith was speechless; but after inspecting the ring, she decided this was probably a good deal. She thought she loved this man; the ring was spectacular, the proposal was cute, and the puppy wasn't bad either.

"Oh, Foster, you have made me a very happy girl. I accept." And so Foster, Meredith, and Pamela became a twenty-first-century family.

Twelve

The next day at his apartment, Foster began hesitantly to speak to Meredith. "Darling, I think we should seriously think about combining our assets now that we are going to be married. Where would you like to live?"

Meredith, reclining on a sun lounge out on Foster's balcony, lifted her head from the social pages of the newspaper and replied, "Well, somewhere with a water view and, of course, with the right postcode. We can't just live in the 'burbs. We wouldn't know anybody or at least anybody I would want to know."

Foster pursued the sale idea and presented Meredith with a list of real estate possibilities that he had downloaded from the Internet. She ran her eye down the list and identified the three most expensive properties available. "I think these three have potential," she stated and handed the list back to Foster. "Why don't I tell you what I cannot possibly live without and then you look at them until you find the perfect home for us?" He was quite happy with this idea mainly because he didn't really want Meredith to have too much to do with their financial future and the reshuffling of money that would have to be done.

"How about we find an apartment to rent for a year at least, somewhere we both would like to live? We could then sell both our properties and invest the money until we find just the right place for our forever home. This will be less stressful for you as you won't have to deal with the inconvenience of open house showings, and we could be settled before the wedding. I'll look after the real estate, and you look after the wedding plans. That way, we will each be doing what we're best at, don't you think?" he said as he raised his eyebrows enquiringly.

"Wonderful idea, darling" came the answer from a distracted Meredith, who had just seen her arch-rival in the events management arena featured in the social pages.

Foster went to the wine fridge and brought Meredith a glass of champagne. "Let's toast our wonderful future together," he said as he clinked his glass against hers. "To us." And the deal was done. Foster now had carte blanche to organise the sale of Meredith's apartment, which would give a sizeable cash injection into his plan for financial stability. It was very timely as he was running short of funds and needed to move out of the company-owned apartment within a few weeks.

He left Meredith still reclining on the sun lounge and offered to take Pamela for a walk. Meredith thought Pamela was quite cute, and she was happy to tuck her into a specially made bag and install her in the office, but it was Suzy who had to see to regular toileting sessions for the poodle. There was no way Meredith was going to be seen taking the dog on a lead across to the park for this purpose and then scooping up the results for depositing in a bin. That was definitely not on the agenda. After a month or so, Meredith got bored taking Pamela with her and most times left her with Foster to cope with. She had a wedding to plan and an apartment to be packed up by professionals, who would then transport her belongings to her new home with Foster.

Meredith and Foster's engagement appeared in the social pages of a major Australian newspaper, where they were described as a "new power couple." Meredith wasn't sure if her parents would see the full-page coverage in whatever godforsaken place they were at the moment, but not wanting to take the risk they may decide to come to the wedding, an email was duly sent. This informed her parents that she was only having a small wedding and wouldn't dream of interrupting their long-awaited holiday. Also, she didn't expect them to foot the bill as Foster was quite wealthy in his own right.

When her parents received this email, they were delighted for several reasons, namely, that their daughter had found someone who would put up with her and that they wouldn't have to foot the bill for what they knew would be so over the top. They were also relieved they wouldn't have to go to an event where they would feel right out of their social comfort zone.

The wedding and its creation took centre stage during Meredith's working day. She employed another secretary to take Suzy's place, and it was then Suzy's job to totally look after Meredith's wedding day. Suzy's life was full enough working long hours, looking after her daughter, and paying the bills as a single parent. She did not need any more pressure, but of course, Meredith was totally unaware of the impact her demands were having on Suzy and, what was more, wouldn't care.

A special screened-off area was created in the boardroom of MC Events Management Company totally devoted to her wedding. This was where invitation designers were summoned to appear with the best designs they had for Suzy to look through and create a short list for Meredith's perusal. Caterers were given "the greatest chance of their career," according to Meredith, to showcase their culinary skills. Venues were examined and discarded until Meredith found one that suited her particular style. Special appointments had to be set up with bridal gown designers – out of hours, of course, as Meredith couldn't be expected to risk crossing paths with someone who may leak to the press what she could be wearing.

By the end of the first month, Suzy was exhausted from the wedding preparations and having to train her secretarial replacement. The staff were advised by email that it was only going to be a small wedding of select guests. (Take that to read no staff would be invited.) Nobody was disappointed by this email. This was one circus they were happy to not be commanded to attend.

Since she and Foster had been together, the few friends that Meredith had previously socialised with had gradually drifted away from her social circle. She realised that she didn't have anyone close whom she could ask to be her bridesmaid/attendant/matron of honour, so in desperation, she came up with the idea that she would have Suzy's little girl, Larissa, scatter rose petals down the carpet in the chapel aisle in front of Meredith's entrance. That way, she would not upstage Meredith or cost much.

"Suzy, could you come in here?" came Meredith's voice from the inner sanctum. Suzy sighed and rose to her very tired feet one more time to see what was required now. "I have an idea I want to run past you. I would like your daughter to precede me into the chapel and scatter rose petals on the carpet as I walk down. What do you think?"

There was silence from the other side of the desk. All Suzy could think was *Oh lord, how much is this going to cost me, and how can I get out of it?*

"Well?" Meredith raised her eyebrows enquiringly.

All Suzy could mutter was "Um, I need to think about it."

"What is there to think about? You don't have to do anything. I'll organise for a dress to be made for her, my choice of style, of course, and I'll pay for it. She is well behaved, isn't she?"

This last sentence put Suzy's hackles up. "Of course, she is well behaved. What sort of child do you think I am raising?"

"No offence meant. It's just that I think she would be a rather cute addition to my wedding, and she would get a nice dress and shoes out of it. You could take her home after the ceremony as there is no need for her to go to the reception. It will be a late night." The last sentence was delivered at Suzy's angry face. "Oh, and by the way, I will give you $500 in cash to buy yourself something suitable to wear when you bring her to the chapel."

Suzy nearly fell over with shock. She had never had a spare $500 to spend on anything, let alone a new outfit. She already knew how and where she would spend that windfall, but Meredith would never know. "Thank you, Meredith. Just one thing – my daughter's name is Larissa in case you might want to include her on your wedding invitations." Suzy made her exit with a broad smile on her face that she had no intention of letting Meredith catch sight of.

On Saturday morning after being given $500 cash to buy "something suitable," Suzy and Larissa headed for the Eastern Suburbs of Sydney to a pre-loved designer boutique that she had seen from the bus window on her way to work each day. There was always something wonderful showcased in the window, and Suzy was sure she could get a dress there that would suit and cost her nowhere near the money she had been given. They had a system whereby you could purchase an outfit at a greatly reduced price, wear it, and return it dry-cleaned and ready for sale with a 50 per cent rebate on what you had paid as long as it was within the same season.

As they got off the bus, Suzy gently reminded Larissa that she was not to touch any of the dresses no matter how pretty she might think they were. She was to sit quietly where Mummy put her and play with her doll, and if she did as she was told, there would be an ice cream in it for her. Suzy didn't usually bribe her daughter, but these were exceptional circumstances. It was considerably more upmarket than her usual choice of shopping venues – Vinnies or the Salvos.

The racks inside the boutique were filled with clothes in all colours of the rainbow and divided up into sections of daywear, casual, resort wear, and so on. Suzy headed for the daywear section and, with help from the salesgirl, chose three outfits that she thought would suit. Her final choice was emerald green silk that flowed like water over her slim body, and she felt wonderful in it. The salesgirl made the usual comments, and Suzy had already seen the price tag, which was $120, leaving her $380 to save.

When she took it over to the register, she was told, "Oh sorry, but you can't return that after you wear it because the season is almost over." Tears filled Suzy's eyes, and the salesgirl reached out and touched her shoulder. "I haven't finished my spiel yet." And she smiled. "Because there is no return, you can have it for half price. Sixty dollars, and it's all yours."

Suzy was absolutely thrilled. She was going home with a dress that made her feel fabulous, and she didn't have to return it. It was a dress that she hadn't had to scrimp and save to buy, and she still had $440 of the money Meredith had given her. One of the girls at work would loan her a bag, and she had a pair of pale gold sandals that would suit quite well. A trip to her local charity shop should take care of a stunning pair of earrings, which was all the dress needed. *Oh, this was a lovely way to spend a Saturday morning.*

There was a little tug on her hand, and a pair of blue eyes looked straight into hers. "Are we getting ice cream now?" a soft voice asked.

"We certainly are, sweetheart. You were so well behaved in the shop, and I'm very proud of you. What flavour do you want?"

While all the wedding planning was going on, Foster was just as busy organising their future accommodation. Within a month, Meredith's apartment had been cleared and packed and her belongings transported to the apartment Foster had found that suited her list of requirements. Her apartment was listed for sale and, in market speak, was described as "a very desirable residence" with a price to match. There was a lot of interest, and the apartment was sold privately well above the reserve price. Meredith had left the sale organisation in Foster's capable hands – and he was rubbing them together with glee. The sale went through without a hitch and the cheque deposited into the investment account Foster had set up through his business.

Meredith was savvy where events management was concerned but had never had to worry about property prices, interest rate fluctuations, and the myriad of financial details that went along with buying and selling. Foster also needed Meredith to think that "his" property was being sold and the profits invested. His story was that his company had been thinking of purchasing a city apartment for the use of executives for the short or long term, and they had asked him if he would be interested in this proposition. He explained to Meredith that it too would be a private sale, so no inspections or open house viewings were required. Everything was going according to plan – or Foster's plan anyway.

Meanwhile, the wedding arrangements were all coming together. The editors of the social pages in the major newspapers had all been notified of the time and venue of the wedding. Suzy was run off her feet with all the last-minute changes to seating arrangements, but finally, the day arrived bright and sunny. Meredith's designer gown by Vera Wang had been delivered to her suite at the harbourside hotel where the reception was being held and several rooms had been booked. Flowers were to be delivered in chilled containers as she didn't want droopy flowers pictured in the social pages. She offhandedly informed Suzy that she could use one of the cheaper hotel rooms for her and Larissa to make sure that they arrived on time and in reasonable condition. They could also stay there for the night, but breakfast was not included in their tariff. Suzy held her composure but did some high fives with Larissa when Meredith was out of sight.

The limousine was booked for Meredith to alight from alone, Larissa was to be waiting at the chapel with her basket of rose petals, and Foster was to make his own way there. She had "graciously" suggested that he book a hire car, but her company would pay for it. At the appointed time, the circus left town for the chapel.

A few of Meredith's employees were waiting outside the chapel. They had been warned in a staff memo that there was to be no photography and definitely no throwing rice or confetti. It was made quite clear that if any of these conditions were breached, there would be consequences. Most of the employees wouldn't want a photograph of TOB anyway, and if they were going to throw anything, it would not be as lightweight as rice or confetti. They were only there to see Suzy and Larissa looking gorgeous – and they did not disappoint.

Larissa wore a beautiful pale pink dress and had flowers tucked in her dark curls. She had a firm grip on her basket of rose petals and was shyly smiling at anyone who looked her way. Suzy was stunning in her flowing silk dress, and her earrings added a touch of glamour. She looked a million dollars, and nobody would guess that her whole outfit had cost her $75, and she still had $425 in change tucked away in her emergency account.

Foster was in the chapel, as instructed, waiting for his bride to walk down the aisle towards him. As the organ thundered into the traditional wedding march and at a touch on her shoulder from Meredith, Larissa stepped forwards and started scattering rose petals as Suzy had practised with her in their hallway at home. In the absence of any adult attendants for the bridal couple, Suzy had been commanded to be a witness with Travis, a colleague of Foster's from his company.

The bride and groom were photographed from almost every angle possible, and Larissa was dismissed from her duties. Suzy took her daughter by the hand and went over to mix with her work colleagues. Larissa was certainly the centre of attention with them as they all knew how much she had looked forward to this day and being able to wear a beautiful dress making her feel like a princess. They also knew how many hours Suzy had put in to pull off this event for her demanding employer.

Meredith Cunningham and Foster Browne were linked in matrimony until parted by death – a chilling thought on this happy occasion.

Thirteen

Meredith and Foster returned from their month-long honeymoon in New York and Paris, and it was time to resume work at their respective companies. The new bride was delighted with the view from their leased apartment and was able to tolerate Pamela being in a corner of the terrace that was the size of most three-bedroom homes. Foster was disappointed that Meredith had not bonded more with Pamela, but then again, Meredith was the centre of her own universe. Her self-absorption suited Foster's plans because, as long as all was right in Meredith's world, his world was a happy place. It was time for Meredith to re-establish her company as a considerable amount of time had been spent on the wedding, to the detriment of other projects.

Meredith's idea of dinner preparation was instructing Suzy to book a restaurant table. She was not a working wife who struggled with shopping on the way home and had the week's meals planned in advance. She had never been, nor ever wanted to be, a domestic goddess. The refrigerator in the apartment could have hidden two grown men within its walls, but it was far from well stocked. Yoghurt, milk for coffee, strawberries, chocolate, champagne, and a selection of white wine did not take up much room in its cavernous interior. Bad luck for Foster if he felt like sneaking into the kitchen for a midnight snack of real food. His only hope was when the chosen caterers placed leftovers in the fridge.

Each weekend when the papers were delivered, Meredith would drape herself on the largest lounge, instruct Foster to "make a coffee, darling," and proceed to try to find articles or photographs of herself and Foster at some event where they had appeared, even if only for a short time. Meredith continued to spend money on new outfits for each occasion as she was often heard to say, "I wouldn't be seen in the same thing twice."

The credit card Meredith insisted on having, although attached to Foster's bank account, got quite a workout each week. The beauty treatments alone would keep a suburban family of four fed for a month. Foster was becoming gradually more concerned about the mounting bills as the money he had invested was no longer keeping pace with the credit card spending. He tried several ways to bring it to Meredith's attention that they could just not continue living in this expensive way. His wife's usual response was "We earn it. Why not spend it?" What Meredith didn't know, and had never bothered to find out, was that Foster's income was dependent on the amount of business he brought into the company. Although he was on a healthy retainer, this was insufficient for the rapidly increasing debt Meredith was running up. It wasn't worth his skin alerting Meredith to their real financial situation as he knew he would be seen as a failure for not providing enough money to support their lifestyle.

The apartment suited Meredith to perfection. The rent was not her problem, and the garage was more than adequate for her car. Foster had to find street parking as Meredith had made it quite clear that getting into a car with the possibility of bird droppings decorating the roof or windows was not going to be her dilemma. Foster was learning what battles he might win, and this was not one of them. Also, the location of the apartment meant that it was only a ten-minute drive to MC Events Management Company, which again pleased her.

Foster had supposedly been looking at properties that they might purchase but was deliberately sabotaging the success of this process by lying to Meredith regarding negative aspects of each apartment. Fortunately for him, Meredith was quite happy with the apartment they were renting and was in no hurry to relocate. It was becoming more evident to him that his wife's aspirations about a suitable property no longer matched the steadily diminishing account where their money was being held.

Every so often, he read the paper's finance section and would make pointed comments to Meredith about the interest rates on investments being low and that it would be better to just be careful and see how the market moved. He generally chose a time when his wife was relaxing either on the terrace or on the lounge, and her reply would usually be "Foster, please don't bother me with the minutiae of life. I have enough to do running my company."

They had been married for two years, and Meredith had started scanning the travel pages in the weekend papers. She felt that, with all their hard work organising the wedding (Suzy's efforts being totally overlooked) and moving into their apartment (again ignoring the fact that Meredith had done nothing more than retrieve her handbag from the car as everything else had been outsourced), they deserved a European holiday. Foster was in the kitchen trying to find something to eat in their almost empty refrigerator, so she didn't see how his face paled when she asked, "Darling, do you think $25,000 would be enough for our holiday?" Momentarily stunned by the dollars required, he stalled his answer by having a sudden coughing fit.

"Are you all right?" Meredith enquired from the living room, where she had not bothered to put a foot to the floor and see if her husband was actually okay.

"Yes, I'm fine, thanks. Be with you in a minute. Would you like a champagne while we talk about our holiday?" Meredith answered in the affirmative, and Foster duly opened a bottle and carried two glasses in to where his wife was relaxing, with Pamela curled up on another area of the living room in her basket. Pamela was definitely not allowed to sit on Meredith's lap or even next to her. Any trace of a pet on her latest clothing acquisition was not the plan.

It was Foster's problem to try to find a holiday that would satisfy Meredith's high-living idea but one that would fit in with the money they could afford. He was finding it more and more difficult to hide the fact that their living expenses were outstripping his ability to keep up with them. Meredith was unaware of the fact that the "sale" of his property was fictional and that their combined assets, in fact, were approximately half of what Meredith thought they were. Foster's lie had resulted in Meredith believing they had more funds available to them than they actually had. He was feeling more and more anxious and pressured as time went by. His lie was now coming back to haunt him.

Several destinations were discussed and discarded for reasons that bewildered Foster. Meredith did not want to go on a scenic cruise down a European river. "Really, Foster, how could I take enough clothing for several changes a day and fit it all in one of those ridiculously small wardrobes?" The fact that Meredith had not, to Foster's knowledge, ever been on a cruise ship and seen the size of the wardrobes was totally beside the point. Coach travel was featured heavily in the travel supplement, and Meredith's comment, predictably, was "Oh really, Foster? Do you expect me to queue for breakfast with a bunch of old-age pensioners? It just won't be happening."

And then Meredith spied an advertisement that just might be worth her time to consider. "Foster, here's something that would appeal." With the level of enthusiasm in Meredith's voice for something she had found in the travel section, Foster felt this would not be good news – at least for him. With a big smile on her face, she passed the travel section over to him, and then he really felt ill. A full-page advertisement for a thirty-day European holiday complete with a personal guide, a chauffeur-driven car, five-star hotels, and meals provided with wine for $80,000 (airfares included). He nearly choked when he saw the cost.

"That sounds lovely, darling, but thirty days is a long time for us to be away from our businesses, don't you think?" he added hopefully.

Her immediate reply was "Well, Suzy, can manage for a month by herself, even if she has to work overtime. You will just have to take leave, won't you? I want to go on this holiday, so make it happen, Foster." And she turned away, picked up her almost empty glass of champagne, and made a waving motion with it for Foster to refill it. He was becoming somewhat disenchanted by his beautiful wife, and he often felt as though he was the hired help.

He knew that if he didn't come up with some money for the holiday Meredith had chosen, she may well start asking very difficult questions about why this wasn't going to happen. After all, she was an astute businesswoman when it came to cajoling clients into spending money on events; and most of the time, she got her own way. He thought that if he started dropping hints about how their lifestyle was affecting their bank account, she may trim back this ridiculously expensive holiday idea; but in his heart, he knew that it was a vain hope. Meredith had made up her mind that this was the holiday she deserved, wanted, and was going to have. She had pictured herself telling their business acquaintances (because they had no friends) about this wonderful second honeymoon they were going on.

Foster tried to stall for time in booking this "once-in-a-lifetime trip" as Meredith liked to call it. According to the advertisement's fine print, which he read but Meredith had no patience with, a deposit of 25 per cent was to be paid on booking and would not be refundable if the holiday was cancelled within three months of the date to leave Australia. Foster was in a panic. He had to come up with $20,000 within the next week or so, and he had no idea how he was going to do that, let alone follow up with another $60,000 to complete the cost of the trip.

No spending money had been mentioned, but he knew – with bitter experience from their honeymoon – just how much money Meredith was capable of spending within 100 metres. He imagined, with horror, how much she could spend with a chauffeur to carry her purchases and a large limousine to store them in. He envisaged purchases appearing on the credit card for some time after returning from their "trip of a lifetime" as it was now referred to. He felt ill, but no visit to a doctor could make him feel better. He felt the net closing in, and a silken noose around the neck would still be a noose.

Fourteen

Monday morning arrived, and Foster left for work with a heart that felt like it had been filled with lead. He was distracted when driving and almost had a collision with a very expensive-looking car. He couldn't stop thinking about the $20,000 deposit he had been instructed to find and pay today to the travel agent. He felt quite ill about the whole holiday idea and would have to do some creative accounting to come up with the deposit and then another $60,000 final payment within a few weeks. What he was going to do about spending money, he had no idea. He didn't even want to think about what expenses would be going on the credit card.

He was angry with himself that he had lied to Meredith right at the start when his ego had won out over common sense. His wife was a very attractive woman, and he was proud to have her at his side, but her attitude towards money had not altered. What she wanted, she expected to have, and he had allowed that attitude to continue right up until the present day. He knew he should have told Meredith that it was a ridiculous price to pay for a holiday, but from experience, he knew there would be a backlash, and he just didn't have the stomach for an argument. She gave no thought to how their expensive lifestyle was being funded, and as long as she got what she wanted, there were no waves created in the seas of the Cunningham-Browne partnership.

Upon arrival at his office, Foster immediately opened up his computer and checked the balance of the several bank accounts he had money secreted in. He had originally kept Meredith's house sale money in a separate account to his, but over the past two years, he had depleted it by almost half. It would now be a financial impossibility for them to buy an apartment of the quality that Meredith expected, and she was under the impression that the two million dollars her property sold for was still intact and had been combined with the "sale" of Foster's apartment but slowly growing, although the interest rates on investments were low. Foster regularly made comments about how much better it was to rent than buy because their "nest egg" could remain whole. Meredith didn't know that this particular egg was leaking yolk fast.

He did some calculations regarding the holiday and felt even more panicked than when he had left home only an hour ago. It was worse than he had anticipated. If he told Meredith their true financial situation, he would have to reveal that he had lied about having a property to sell, and not telling her they were using her money to live on. He could not make the excuse that she had never asked. Foster had lied by deceit, and now that injudiciousness was coming back to haunt him in a big way. He was trapped in all these lies and didn't know how to get out of it. He picked up his coat, walked past reception, mumbled that he had a client to see, and continued out of the building.

He couldn't refuse Meredith this holiday because of the questions she would ask and the answers he didn't want to give. What a mess. He walked down the street near the office, bought a coffee at his usual cafe, and crossed the road to the park, where he sat on a bench and put his head in his hands. The truth would probably mean the end of his marriage, and the fury of Meredith was not something he wished to encounter. He had been subjected to it on one or two occasions when she didn't get her own way, and it was terrifying. She lost all control and threw things, smashed glasses, and screamed like a banshee. Added to this was the very real possibility that she would want her money back, and he didn't have it to give to her. It would not matter to her that the vast majority of what she thought they had, had been spent to keep her in the lifestyle to which she had become accustomed and saw as her right.

Foster knew either he had to confess to Meredith, which he considered a very unattractive and dangerous option, or he would have to find the money some other way. He ran through the options in his head. He was not a gambler, so trying to win money in a casino on a card game or roulette wheel was out of the question. He could use the money that was left and invest it in a short-term high-risk enterprise, but again, this was fraught with the danger of losing it all if the investment went pear shaped. Then he would have even less than he had now. Cutting down on their living expenses would be a very unappealing option because it meant he would have to fight that battle with Meredith, who had no interest in reducing her spending. Again, questions would be asked, and he really wanted to dodge that scene and its predictable conclusion.

Upon returning to the office an hour later, he sat down at his computer and, in desperation, made the biggest decision of his working life. He would do some creative accounting. He oversaw a considerable number of different types of accounts that he managed for large and small companies. There were also people who had traded with his company for many years, and in the good times, they had built up quite substantial portfolios. Shares were invested at various levels of risks, and some of the accounts had been ticking over for years without any client involvement. Twice yearly updates were sent to the clients to keep them informed, and these half-year statements had been sent only last week. If he was careful, he could move some money around; and as long as he had it back in their accounts in five months, he would be okay. However, for one of those months, he would not be earning much commission while he was on this ridiculously expensive holiday.

The first thing he had to do was pay the $20,000 deposit and get Meredith off his back in the short term. He had no idea how he was going to try and rein in her spending in the meantime because he knew, from experience, that she would want a whole new wardrobe for her European adventure. This was in addition to what she would buy while she was away. Her constant spending sprees were terrifying, but so was her wrath if he refused her.

The credit card was always edging close to the top of its limit, but somehow he managed to keep paying some of it each month. There was no way he could pay the deposit to the travel agent without getting a new credit card or a huge credit limit increase. It had to be a second card, and he would use it only for the travel expenses. Foster chose to ignore the obvious fact that if he was having trouble paying down one card, then two was not a step in the right direction, but it was the only thing he could think of now. And so he took that step on the road to almost certain financial ruination that had started with a lie three years ago when he was trying to impress a very forceful and sexy woman who was now his wife.

In the afternoon of that fateful day, Foster developed his plan of how to shuffle money around so that it wouldn't be noticed for some time. He was confident of having it back in the accounts before the next half-yearly statements were due to be sent out. He had very good IT knowledge, gained while working in other companies both here and overseas, and knew how to set up accounts that were multilayered and very difficult to trace through the financial network. He put this knowledge to work, and over the next few weeks, the deed was done. He had transferred a total of $1.5 million from a variety of unsuspecting clients, most of whom would be able to take a downturn in their financial situation, but he still had enough conscience to feel badly about the smaller investors who had trusted him with their life's savings.

Foster was disgusted with himself, firstly, for being dishonest all those years ago when he let his ego dictate his actions; secondly, for stooping to temporary theft, which he would despise in any of his colleagues; and, thirdly, for being too weak to come clean with his wife and make her aware of their real financial situation. He wasn't sleeping well as he was fully aware that if any of the investments failed or there was a downturn in the economy, he would be financially screwed. If he couldn't return the money to its rightful owners before the five months were up, he would more than likely be found out and charged with embezzlement – right on the heels of being dismissed in disgrace. Even if he didn't get a jail sentence, being able to then obtain another position in the finance sector would be lost to him forever, and he would be unemployable. All he could imagine in front of him, if his creative accounting failed, was financial oblivion.

A few of his colleagues made some comments about how he was losing weight and looked a bit rough around the edges. He just smiled and joked back about how his wife kept him on his toes. Some of the girls had met Meredith and felt quite sorry for Foster because they thought he was a genuinely nice guy married to an absolute nightmare. On the few occasions that she had socialised with his work colleagues, she was all sweetness and charm; but as females did, the girls could sense that she was as tough as steel underneath all that grooming and expensive clothing. The guys just thought that they wouldn't mind twenty-four hours alone with her.

It became a habit of Foster's to sit up half the night with his computer on, watching how the markets were performing. He was constantly doing calculations regarding the movement of money to get a bigger return as he desperately needed these investments to work. He still had to pay $60,000 for the remainder of the European adventure and almost had enough money earned to siphon it off. It was a delicate balancing act, and so far, it was all working out. Their trip was to take place in three months, and they would be back before the money had to be returned to the various accounts.

With a rare show of courage, Foster broached the subject to Meredith of her reducing her spending because of the cost of the holiday, and the result was predictable. "I am not going to Europe looking like I don't have a bean to my name, Foster. It's bad enough that we live in a country at the bottom of the world that is at least a year behind the continent's fashion houses. You can go over there in any old thing if that is how you want to look, but let me tell you this – I won't be wearing anything that I already own. I'll be shopping over the next two weeks for my holiday wardrobe, and you will just have to suck it up." This was followed up with the instruction "I'd like a glass of champagne while I look through the latest *Vogue* issue." Foster dutifully headed for the kitchen.

He had known it was a vain hope to suggest Meredith reduce her spending, but he was angry with himself that he had once again backed down. He asked himself, "What are you, a man or a mouse?" And he made a squeaking noise that said it all.

Fifteen

Meredith had to organise someone to come and stay in the apartment while she was away to look after Pamela as she didn't want her mixing with other dogs who weren't purebred. On some levels, Meredith was taken with her, but it was primarily as a fashion accessory than a beloved pet. Once again, Suzy was commanded to help.

"Suzy, come in here, please," Meredith called out from her office. The "please" on the end of the command usually meant that it was something for Meredith's benefit.

With a sigh, Suzy thought, *What does she want now?* She left her desk and duly presented herself in the doorway of Meredith's office.

"I have a proposal for you," she started off. "As you know, Foster and I are going away on a European adventure, and we want someone trustworthy to come and stay in our apartment for that time and look after Pamela."

"I'd have to take Larissa out of school, Meredith, as we live quite a way from here. I'm not keen to do that but will think about it and let you know."

"Ah, but you haven't heard the advantages yet. You might change your mind. I will give you $500 per week on top of your wages for the inconvenience. With my credit card, you can stock the fridge and cupboards before I leave and use a hire car to get Larissa to her school and you to work. It would cost me nearly the same to send Pamela to a top-of-the-range kennel for a month, and I would rather her stay in her own surroundings. I am quite fond of her, you know. Also, there have been break-ins around the area in the last few months, and I would rather have the place look like someone lived here. What do you say? Yes or no?"

While Meredith had been speaking, Suzy had done some quick calculations and could see an enormous benefit to her savings account. It was an attractive option to be able to get Larissa to school in a car rather than taking the bus. "Okay, I'll do it for you, Meredith. Thanks for the offer, especially about the car. I couldn't manage it without that as it is too far, with no direct public transport from here."

"You don't have a car?" Meredith asked in an amazed voice. "Why not?"

"It's really quite simple. I can't afford the running costs, and I would have to park it on the street where it wouldn't be safe from the rather dodgy neighbours." Suzy thought, *She really has no idea how the other half live.*

"Oh, and while I'm away, I will expect you to run the show. You're quite competent, and you can always contact me by email, but I'm sure you'll manage. I'll pay you overtime as I don't trust anybody else to do a job as good as you do."

"Thanks, Meredith. That's very kind of you. I'll look after the company while you're gone and hope you have a lovely holiday." Suzy almost floated out of the office. She would be able to afford a short holiday on the coast where her daughter could run in and out of the waves instead of dodging litter on the streets where they lived. Life was looking pretty good to Suzy. They would have a beautiful city apartment to live in, a car to get Larissa to school and her to work, and cupboards full of food, plus about $2,000 for her savings account. Bliss.

Suzy had been instructed to go and buy an extensive and expensive set of luggage in the city and bring it back to Meredith's apartment in a hire car. Meredith had phoned the store and given them her credit card details with an authorisation for Suzy to collect the luggage on her behalf. "I'm going on a European adventure," she said on the phone to the salesperson. "So I need a set of high-quality luggage, and my assistant will come and collect it this afternoon." After discussing what was required, Meredith informed the salesperson of her credit card details; however, the cost was somewhat more than what she had expected. Meredith's pride wouldn't let her ask for a cheaper option, so she just took a deep breath and put the phone down at the end of the transaction.

Ten minutes later, her mobile rang, and it was the salesperson she had just spoken to. "I am sorry to phone you back, Mrs Cunningham-Browne, but there seems to be a problem with your credit card. I am sure it is just a little hitch, but would you mind checking with your bank that the transaction can go through? I wouldn't like your assistant to have to wait when she arrives." All this information was delivered in an apologetic tone with just the right amount of firmness that suggested a problem needed to be sorted sooner rather than later.

Meredith rang Foster at the office, and before he had time to finish his name in greeting, he heard his wife shouting at him, "You had better get my credit card sorted, Foster! I have just been extremely embarrassed by a salesperson telling me they couldn't charge $18,700 for the luggage I had selected! Ring me back when you have fixed it!"

Foster had not said a word. He could not believe that his wife had just spent almost $20,000 on luggage. He felt nauseous and headed for the gents, where he promptly lost his lunch into the toilet bowl. "How on earth am I going to get another $20,000 together?" He could feel a third credit card looming. *I am just digging a deeper hole*, he thought.

Foster left his office and went into a different bank from the one he had his other credit cards with. They were somewhat reluctant to offer him a card with a $25,000 limit as he was not already a customer, but he assured them it was only a backup card for when he and his wife were away in Europe on holiday, and the debt would be cleared on their return. The bank representative offered to take him into an office to discuss this further, and Foster felt a little more confident that they would grant his request.

An hour later, after regaling the bank officer with embellished details of his earning capacity and downplaying the cost of their upcoming European holiday, he returned to his office with the bank's assurance that he could have the card and credit limit he had requested. After he phoned Suzy with the details as Meredith was in a meeting, which usually meant she was at the beautician's, Suzy left to collect the luggage. *My employer has just spent a year of my rent on luggage. Unbelievable.*

For the rest of that afternoon, Foster spent some time siphoning money out of a few old accounts and into a false account so he could top up Meredith's credit card. On one hand, he was relieved that he had dodged another spectacular scene with Meredith, but he could feel the financial hole he was digging getting steadily deeper. He had started digging with a small shovel, but it now looked like he would need a mechanical digger. Their spectacularly expensive holiday was looming, and Foster was anything but thrilled. He could hardly dredge up a smile these days as he was so worried about what he had done at work but felt reasonably confident that his creative accounting deception (he didn't like to think of it as theft) would stay hidden while he was away.

Meredith was flinging unwanted clothing onto the bed, uttering, "So last season. Just get rid of it all while I'm gone, would you, Suzy? I am not likely to wear it again. Take anything that fits you, but don't wear it in the office. I don't want the hired help to think that I am a soft touch." Suzy already knew that from her years of working for Meredith, not with Meredith as she was reminded on occasion.

Suzy had a plan for the unwanted clothes, but she was not about to tell her boss. They would be going to the recycle shop where she had bought her wedding guest outfit, and with the money, she would buy something that she could wear to the office. Although Suzy was paid well and made her income stretch as far as possible, she was always mindful that she had to dress well at work. She carefully chose classic designs in plain colours and had her own style by adding jewellery she had found at markets, garage sales, or charity shops. This month of house-sitting and pet minding was turning into a very welcome bonanza for Suzy, and she was grateful for every bit of it.

Times were a bit tough bringing up a young daughter while renting and relying on public transport. Spending money on treats was a distant dream, but maybe with the extra money from this unexpected windfall, they could spoil themselves – just a little. Her parents were deceased, and Larissa's father had departed soon after a few weeks of broken sleep and a sexually unresponsive partner. No financial support was forthcoming from him as his whereabouts were unknown.

The packing had been completed, mostly by Suzy acting on Meredith's instructions. Foster made a few breathless trips taking the luggage down to the stretch limousine that had been ordered. Meredith was taking no chances that an ordinary sedan would fit all her luggage in, and Foster was already feeling quite apprehensive about the excess weight fee that would be charged by the airline.

They would be back in just under five weeks, and Foster would pull out all stops to get the "borrowed" money back into the accounts where it belonged. He just hoped he had buried the money trail deep enough in the computer system that it wouldn't be discovered while he was away. Nobody else had passwords to his accounts, so he was confident it would be safely hidden, though no one can ever be 100 per cent sure of anything except death and taxes.

Suzy and Larissa, who was cuddling Pamela, stood on the apartment balcony and waved the travellers goodbye. Foster returned their wave, but Meredith was busy giving the driver instructions about how he would be helping her husband unload and assist with their baggage into the terminal. After all, she couldn't be expected to help, could she? The driver nodded in all the right places but really had no intention of getting out of the vehicle when they arrived at the airport. He was blissfully unaware of Meredith's spectacular temper when thwarted, but he was about to see it in real, living technicolour. She hadn't built a thriving company from the ground up without intimidating or coercing many people along the way, and a driver of a limousine (whom she considered her private chauffeur and therefore in her employ to do what she ordered) was small potatoes. He would be helping, and that was that.

Upon arrival at the overseas terminal, Foster helped Meredith from the car, and she stood tapping her foot and waiting for the driver to assist. His version of assistance was to flick the boot of the limousine open. Foster headed towards the open boot and proceeded to pull one piece of luggage after another onto the trolley that the driver had at least managed to bring to the back of the vehicle. When it was obvious to Meredith that the driver was going to get back in the car, she almost ran onto the road to head him off before he could open the door. "Go and help my husband," she commanded as she drew level with the driver.

"Not on my jobsheet, lady. I drove you here, and that's all I have to do."

Meredith was furious. This was not going to plan at all. She reached down, took off her high-heeled shoe, and proceeded to hit the driver on the shoulder with it while shouting, "Do you know whom you are dealing with, you cretin?" The driver had had enough of her by now and took the shoe off her and threw it across the road, fortunately being empty of cars in that moment. Meredith was making quite a scene but looked ridiculous hopping around on one foot while still trying to get the driver to help Foster.

Once Foster realised what was going on across the other side of the vehicle, he hurried around and took Meredith's arm to steer her back onto the footpath and out of the way of the approaching traffic. He made the mistake of asking, "Where is your other shoe?" He had been unaware of the attack she had made on the driver.

Meredith pointed to the roadway, spluttering, "This cretin threw it over there. You had better go and get it, and don't get run over. I have enough problems without you being killed at the airport."

As soon as the driver could see that the boot lid had been closed by Foster, he got in the vehicle and took off as fast as the speed limit would allow but confident that he was going at a speed that Meredith, in her one shoe, could not catch him. What a tale to tell when he got back to the depot. He pitied the poor sucker who was going on holiday with her, if that temper was any example of her usual behaviour.

Back at her employer's apartment, Suzy was making a spectacular dessert for herself and Larissa with Ben & Jerry's ice cream, luscious big strawberries, and chocolate topping. Suzy could only ever afford generic ice cream, and strawberries were off the menu unless they were on special. She carefully carried the treats on a tray out onto the terrace, where Pamela was having a marvellous game of chasing with Larissa. Suzy was so glad to see her daughter playing with the dog as they couldn't have one in their tiny rented unit, and vet bills were beyond their household budget. This was going to be a lovely four weeks, almost like a holiday, even though she had to work, but there were the evenings and weekends to enjoy living in this luxury.

Pamela was exhausted after playing but not so tired that she passed up the last bit of ice cream left in the bottom of Larissa's dessert bowl. "Don't let her have chocolate, Larissa," Suzy warned her daughter. "It will make her very sick, and we don't want that to happen to her. She is such a lovely little dog."

There were two beds in the guest room, and after they had hung their clothes in the huge wardrobe, they settled on one of the beds, and Suzy read a bedtime story to Larissa. "Can Pamela hear it too, please, Mum?" And so Pamela was settled on her new best friend's lap while the story was read to the child and the very tired dog – child tucked up in bed, dog relegated to her beanbag on the floor beside Larissa. Suzy was so happy and relaxed that she was asleep in the twin bed in five minutes.

Sometime in the night, she heard her daughter stir, but then she drifted back to sleep. In the morning, there was a child's head on the pillow and another head that looked distinctly like it might be Pamela. Suzy stifled a laugh as she looked at the two "girls." She could just imagine the scene if Meredith had walked in. Better that she was on her way halfway across the world.

Sixteen

The Cunningham-Brownes were having a marvellous holiday on their European adventure as Meredith was happy to tell anyone who stood still long enough to listen. She had to drop into almost every sentence that their chauffeur (whose name she hadn't bothered to learn) had been wonderful, carrying their bags, driving them to all the wonderful cities, settling them into their hotels, and generally making sure they were looked after as they deserved. Foster felt ill every time Meredith started on about their holiday and hoped that nothing had been discovered in the accounts while they had been away. His appetite was poor because he was so worried, but unsurprisingly, Meredith hadn't noticed his downbeat mood.

The end of their holiday was approaching, and Foster started to receive emails from work commencing with "We know you are on holiday, but . . ." and then continued to ask for information that was starting to unsettle him. There was nothing specific, more a general undercurrent of enquiry about some old accounts that didn't seem quite right and if he would be able to clear up the matter for them. There was no hurry, but sooner rather than later was the general theme.

Foster was rattled and couldn't decide whether to ignore the emails and pretend he hadn't received them or give a vague response along the lines of "I will sort it out when I get back in a week or so. I would be happy to go through it with you then as I don't have the details with me." He needed to buy time, and time was something he didn't have much of to sort it out before anyone found out what he had done. *What had gone wrong to make them ask all these questions?*

Foster was restless every night during the last few days of their holiday, and Meredith was becoming irritated with him. "Oh, for goodness' sake, if you can't lie still, go in the other room, Foster. I need to be rested when I get up in the morning. We have a big day ahead of us, and we're going home in a few days. I don't want to arrive back in Australia looking haggard." Foster was quite fed up with Meredith and her constant picking, made worse by his heightened state of anxiety. He couldn't even think about how much money had been spent on the contents of those boxes and carrier bags that occupied half the hotel suite.

Going into the other room of the suite didn't afford him any sleep either. He couldn't turn off the thoughts spinning around in his head about what had been found out at work, if anything, and how he could bluff his way through it and recoup the money he had "borrowed." He was restless and turned the TV on to try to distract himself from his thoughts. The news was on, and to his dismay, the headline was the current financial global crisis and the repercussions it was having on the world economy. He had been so busy travelling from city to city the last few days, and with the time difference, he was out of touch with the world money markets. The headlines did not bode well for the dollars he had to recoup. He just hoped that it was not too late to recover the money when he returned to work.

Meredith was unaware of Foster's anxiety and was only interested in what destinations lay ahead for their last days of travelling. Foster was finding it difficult to even respond with a smile when his wife asked his opinion or pointed out a place of interest. All he could process was *What am I going to do if it has all gone pear shaped?* And to that, he had no answer.

Finally, the day of leaving for home had arrived. Meredith, as usual, was giving orders to all and sundry; and finally, the limousine was packed, ready to leave for the airport. The multitude of boxes and bags had been despatched by courier the previous day and would be home before they were. Foster dreaded the excess baggage cost going home, but he felt too overwhelmed and anxious about the financial crisis awaiting him at the office. He couldn't sleep on the return journey and had drunk too much alcohol on the plane, leaving him feeling nauseous and dehydrated. He was in bad shape by the time they landed in Sydney, and it was all he could do to get the bags into a hire car for their trip back to the apartment.

Meredith was angry with him because he looked a wreck. "How do you think it makes me feel when we have just come back from a marvellous holiday, which many people will envy, and you look like you have been dragged through a hedge backwards?" she railed at him.

"Meredith, at this moment, I don't care what anyone thinks, and that includes you." His wife was so shocked at his attitude that, for once, she had no reply.

Suzy and Larissa were waiting in the apartment for the travellers to arrive back, and a welcome-home dinner had been prepared for them. Suzy didn't plan on staying around once they arrived, and she had their bags in the foyer ready for a quick departure on the last day of their hire car usage. Larissa had really bonded with Pamela, and Suzy knew she was going to miss the little dog, but that was the way it was for them. Their month of house-sitting and pet minding was up.

Suzy had been watching for Meredith and Foster from the balcony while Larissa had her last play with Pamela. When the car pulled into the kerb, Foster alighted from one side, and Meredith waited until he came around and opened her door. The luggage was pulled from the boot by Foster and loaded onto the footpath while Meredith headed for the front door, carrying nothing heavier than her handbag. Suzy smiled to herself and thought, *Some things never change.*

The lift doors opened, and Meredith appeared in the doorway of the apartment. "Hi, Meredith," greeted Suzy. "We hope you both had a wonderful holiday. There is dinner prepared for you and will only take a few minutes to heat in the microwave." Suzy was not sure if her boss even knew how to use the microwave, but Foster probably did, given Meredith's lack of culinary skills. "Good to see you back safely. We'll head off now."

Meredith surprised her with "Oh, don't go yet. I have some gifts for you both." Suzy nearly fainted with surprise. "Foster will bring the luggage in, and I'll get them for you as a thank-you for looking after my home. Where's Pamela?" Meredith realised that the dog was not in the room.

Suzy had the horrible thought that Pamela had probably headed back up onto Larissa's bed and didn't want Meredith to find her there. She knew the dog would be in trouble, and it wasn't really her fault. "I'll go and find her. She is probably asleep in her bed. Won't be a minute." And Suzy hurriedly left the room.

Foster finally appeared in the apartment with a load of luggage. Meredith swooped on one of the smaller bags and brought out some packages that were sitting at the top. "Here's yours, Suzy. Hope you like it. I got it in Italy. Here's yours, Larissa. It's just something little I thought you might like."

Suzy's eyes welled up with tears when she unwrapped the beautiful Murano glass necklet. "Thank you so much, Meredith. It's truly beautiful, and I'll really enjoy wearing it." Then Larissa unwrapped a music box decorated with nymphs that Meredith explained she had bought in Greece. Larissa's eyes widened in delight as she had never had anything as beautiful given to her. The shopkeeper had assured Meredith that *Larissa* meant "nymphs" in Greek mythology, and she hoped she hadn't been conned.

Suzy could not believe that Meredith had gone to the trouble of buying something for her daughter that was so beautiful and appropriate for her name. She was stunned at the thoughtfulness that had been shown with her gifts. It gave her food for thought that, even though her boss was hard shelled, maybe she had a soft centre that she kept well hidden.

While the gift giving had been going on, Foster had deposited the luggage in their bedroom, greeted Suzy and Larissa with a kiss on the cheek, and thanked them for looking after everything. He went to the fridge, and his wife's voice rang across the room. "Don't you think you had enough on the plane given the state you're in?" Foster didn't even respond and reached into the fridge for a bottle of champagne and a chilled glass, which he took out onto the terrace. Suzy was embarrassed and thought it was time they went home.

"Come on, Larissa, say 'thank you' to Meredith and Foster for your gift, and we'll go home. We have some unpacking to do before I have to go to work tomorrow and you are back at school." Suzy turned to Meredith. "I had a wonderful stay in your apartment and can't thank you enough for the extra money. It was like a holiday for us. I hope we haven't spoiled Pamela too much, but she's a beautiful little dog, and Larissa enjoyed having a pet for a month. See you at work in a few days, and thanks again for the gifts."

"I am unimpressed, Foster," she said angrily as she slid the door open and stormed out to the terrace.

"I don't care, Meredith. You might have had a wonderful European adventure," he replied with a sneer while he waved his glass of champagne in her direction. "But I didn't. You treated me like the hired help, spent too much money, and I will have to pay for all your shopping, most of which I consider unnecessary." By this time, Foster was getting a little drunk and was throwing caution to the wind. He hadn't slept properly for the last week, was in a state of high anxiety about what he would find when he got back to work, and was not in any mood for Meredith's complaints.

"Well, darling, you will just have to work a little harder, won't you?" And with that last comment, Meredith turned on her expensive very high heels and stalked back inside.

Foster stayed on the terrace and finished the bottle while he stared unseeingly at the harbour ferries moving back and forth, the Opera House lighting up for the evening, and couples strolling arm in arm around the waterfront. He was miserable and frightened. Another bottle was consumed, and by that time, Meredith had retired to bed after her usual one-hour beauty routine.

The apartment felt claustrophobic to him, and the physical evidence of Meredith's excessive shopping was impossible to ignore. He had received several more emails at the end of their time in Europe, each one more pressing than the previous with probing questions and a commanding tone. It was obvious to Foster, even in his inebriated state, that this can of worms was not going to go away anytime soon. He didn't think there was much chance he could bluff his way out of this mess he had created. Obviously, someone had lifted a rock and found something distasteful underneath. He thought he had hidden his tracks well, but computers were only as good as the last hacker who didn't manage to breach passwords.

I need to get out of this apartment and get some air. Meredith won't even know I've gone. Foster decided to go for a drive to get away from Meredith and the visual evidence of their financially disastrous holiday. He knew he was over the legal alcohol limit, having consumed two bottles of champagne, but he was beyond logical thought. He staggered a little when the night air hit him as he emerged from the apartment and went to the underground car park, where he started up Meredith's car. His car was 100 metres or so away down a side street, and he didn't think he could walk that far. He slowly drove her Mercedes out of the garage and made a left turn to head to the northern side of Sydney Harbour. He knew he was too drunk to drive, but he was also too drunk to care.

Fortunately, at 3 a.m. there was very little traffic on the roads. Foster managed, more with good luck than judgement, to make it to the Pacific Highway, running north from the city. He had always liked the peace of Lane Cove National Park with its winding roads and a bridge across the river. It would be just the place where he could sit for a while and think about what he would do when he went back to work.

He turned left off the Pacific Highway and, within five minutes, was weaving his way down the winding road – not always on his side of the centre line – towards the river. He misjudged the last bend in the road, and before he could gather his wits about him, he had broken through the wooden rail along the riverbank and hit air with no road beneath him. The roof of the car was visible from the bridge, but there were no cars around to see it. Foster was in no state to extricate himself from the car, and two minutes later, there were only bubbles coming to the surface.

Seventeen

Meredith woke the next morning to a silent apartment and assumed Foster had gone to work but then realised that his wallet and watch were still on the bedside table. Initially, she wasn't too concerned as she had told Foster to sleep in the other room if he couldn't lie still. After her usual beauty routine, Meredith wandered out into the lounge area and then into the second bedroom, but there was no sign of Foster, just Pamela sleeping on the second bed, which she immediately vacated when she saw her.

Meredith was about to phone his mobile when the intercom buzzed. The security camera vision was of two police officers. She enquired of them, "Yes, what do you want?"

One of them replied, "We would like to speak to Mrs Cunningham-Browne, please."

"Come on up in the lift, top floor, and I will let you in." Within moments, there was a knock on the apartment door, and Meredith opened it for them to enter. "Yes? What can I do for you at this early hour of the morning?" she asked as she stepped aside to let them in.

"Mrs Cunningham-Browne, I'm sorry, but we have some rather bad news." Meredith thought something had happened to her parents and asked if it was an accident in the Northern Territory.

"No. I'm sorry to tell you that your husband was involved in a motor vehicle accident last night in Lane Cove National Park and did not survive."

It took a moment or two for her to realise what they were saying. She dropped down onto the nearest chair with a shocked look on her face. "Do you know what happened?" she asked.

"What we do know is that he was unable to get himself out of the Mercedes before it became submerged. Is there someone we could call for you?"

Somehow it registered with Meredith that they had said "Mercedes," which Foster's car was not. "What car was my husband driving?"

"It was a black Mercedes registered to his company."

"But that's my car. You mean he took my car and drove it into the river? How dare he do that?" It was obvious to both police officers that she was more upset about her car than her husband's death, but they put her reaction down to shock.

The officers offered to take Meredith to the hospital to identify her husband and again asked her if there was someone they could call for her.

"No, I'll be all right. Thanks, but as I don't have a car, I will accept your offer of transport."

"We'll wait downstairs for you if you are sure you're okay."

"Yes, just go. I'll be down in a few minutes when I get changed."

Meredith dealt with the identification of her husband at the hospital and then turned to the officers. "What am I supposed to do now?"

They suggested that she contact her husband's family and then make arrangements for him to be taken to the funeral home. Meredith's reply surprised the officers when she said, "This is very inconvenient. We have just come back from a European adventure, and I have a huge backlog of work to get through in the next week or so, and now I don't have a car. Can't this wait?"

"Well, Mrs Cunningham-Browne, these things usually take a few days to organise. But given the circumstances of your husband's death, there will be a report to be prepared for the coroner to make sure there are no suspicious circumstances."

"There is nothing suspicious about his death, Officer. He consumed two bottles of champagne last night, the empties of which are still sitting on the kitchen bench. He was drunk, and now he's dead. It's really quite simple. Oh, and by the way, where's my car at the moment?"

"We'll leave you the phone numbers you'll need to recover it, although after several hours in the water, it's likely to be a write-off."

When they were out of earshot, the older officer commented, "Well, I've come across all sorts during my career, but this is a first for me that the new widow was more upset about her car than her husband."

Meredith walked out the front of the hospital and hailed a taxi to take her to work. When she arrived, much later than she had intended, she walked past everyone and closed the door to her office without so much as greeting anyone. One of the workers commented, "Well, doesn't look like we're getting any souvenirs."

She was in shock that her husband had been so stupid to drink, take her car, and then get himself killed into the bargain. *What am I supposed to do now?*

She buzzed for Suzy to come into her office. Suzy was all smiles. "Welcome back, Meredith. I didn't expect you until tomorrow. We have lots to discuss about what's been happening with the company while you've been gone. Would you like a coffee now or later?" Meredith looked at Suzy with tears in her eyes, something that her PA had never seen before. "What's the matter, Meredith? Are you ill?"

"No. Foster took my car when he was drunk last night and drove into the Lane Cove River. I now don't have a car or a husband, and I don't know what to do."

Suzy dropped into the closest chair with shock. "Oh, Meredith, that's dreadful. What can I do to help?"

"Have you ever organised a funeral, Suzy? I have no idea where to start, and I am at an absolute loss about this whole procedure."

Suzy got herself together. "Back in a minute, Meredith." And she headed for the door to get Tom to bring in two strong coffees.

He couldn't help but ask, "What's going on? Has Foster run off with someone? Wouldn't blame him if he did."

Suzy rounded on him and said, "Just get the coffees, Tom. It's much worse than that."

Suzy assured Meredith that she would help in any way she could. She suggested that, firstly, she would ring Foster's family, but Meredith then told her he was an only child, and his parents were deceased. Then she came up with a list of other things that would need to be done. Meredith just sat with a stunned look on her face while Suzy sat on the other side of the desk, running down the list.

"Do you want me to let everyone here know what's happened, Meredith?"

"Yes, please, Suzy. I am not quite up for that just now. Thanks."

Suzy went back into the general office and spoke quietly to everyone about the tragedy that happened. Tom felt particularly bad about his flippant comment regarding Foster.

Meredith gave Suzy the contact details for Foster's company, and when she first spoke with his boss to tell him that something had happened to Foster, he made the comment "We wondered where he was. Has he done a runner?"

Suzy said, "It's nothing of the sort. Mr Browne was killed in a motor vehicle accident last night. I am his wife's PA, and she is in no condition to speak with you, so I am advising you in her absence." Suzy hung up the phone with a bewildered expression on her face. She had no idea what was behind the comment of Foster's boss. *What did he mean "has he done a runner?"* Suzy decided not to tell Meredith what had been said as she didn't want to add to her stress.

Over the next few days, Suzy took charge. She organised for Foster's body to be taken to the funeral home and made all the arrangements that she thought were right as Meredith had sunken into the depths of despair and could hardly be relied on to answer a simple question. This was so unlike the woman whom Suzy had spent more than five years working for, a woman who was always on top of what was happening, giving orders, pulling events together at the last minute while managing to look impeccably groomed. The woman in the inner office was none of these things now. Suzy saw a bit of the old Meredith when she asked her to make an appointment for her hair and nails to be done before the funeral.

The day of the funeral dawned fine and sunny, but it was doubtful if Meredith took any of this in. She had asked Suzy to ride with her in the mourning car mainly because she had no one else she could ask. Her parents were in some godforsaken spot in the Northern Territory, and they had never met Foster. She had grown apart from them since they had "gone bush" as she liked to tell people.

There were a few representatives from Foster's company and several of the staff from MC Events Management Company but no friends or relatives. The funeral service was quite short, and Suzy had been asked to do the eulogy. It was a small gathering, and Meredith moved amongst everyone with a dazed look on her face. She was, of course, impeccably groomed.

Meredith had not wanted a wake. She just wanted the whole thing over and done with so she could go back to the apartment and grieve in private. She was just holding herself together, and onlookers thought she was so cold about this tragedy that had befallen her. She was upset, but deep down, she was very angry – angry that Foster had done something so stupid, angry that he had wrecked her car, and even angrier that he had been so ungrateful about their European adventure. As usual, it was all about Meredith.

Eighteen

Two weeks after the funeral, Meredith was contacted by the CEO of Foster's company, who asked her to come into their office at her earliest convenience. When she said that it wouldn't be convenient for some weeks, he made it quite clear that they would expect her within the week. "There are some very pressing financial issues that we need to talk to you about, and sooner would be better than later." Meredith incorrectly assumed that it had to do with an insurance payout on Foster's death or perhaps back pay or commissions that he was owed. On that basis, she reconsidered, phoned the CEO back, and made an appointment for the next afternoon.

Meredith arrived a few minutes after the agreed time for the meeting as she didn't want to seem too keen to have whatever the company was offering. The receptionist greeted her with "Mrs Cunningham-Browne, welcome. The partners are waiting for you in the boardroom just along the corridor and to your left." Meredith just nodded in acknowledgement of the directions. The door to the boardroom was open, and several men were standing by the windows chatting, but others were seated.

"Come in, Mrs Cunningham-Browne," the chairman of the board said. "On behalf of the company, we are very sorry for your loss."

Meredith just inclined her head and answered, "Thank you for your condolences. Foster's death has been a great shock to me, and I am not sure how I am going to cope." Meredith was an astute businesswoman and didn't miss the looks that passed between a few of those present, although she couldn't readily identify the sentiment behind them.

"Please sit down. Would you like tea or coffee?" Meredith declined, and the rest of those present picked up their cups from the tray provided and took their places around the oval table.

"Mrs Cunningham-Browne, we have some serious issues to discuss here today, and some of them may come as a shock to you."

Meredith lifted her face. "Shock?" she said.

"Yes, I'm afraid so," replied the chairman. "When you were on your 'European adventure,' I think your husband called it, we had an unscheduled audit of our clients' accounts. Some of those clients had raised issues about money they thought should have been in their accounts, and it seemed to be missing. Foster had left several notes on their files about the funds being invested elsewhere, but their exact location was not recorded. Also, he noted that he had had several conversations with some of them to reassure them that the amounts were not exactly 'missing' per se but that transfers had been made to areas, some in foreign countries, where they had a chance of earning more money on their investments. However, he had not actually spoken to these clients, and they were unaware of any changes. In fact, the majority would not have authorised him to go ahead."

Meredith sat there with a closed expression on her face. The chairman continued, "Now we are not accusing Foster of any wrongdoing, but we do have to explain his actions to our auditors and clients to establish where almost one million dollars is at this point in time."

Meredith jumped to her feet to defend her deceased husband. "My husband was a very honest person, and I take great offence at your accusations. I will not sit here and listen to this assassination of his character. Goodbye, gentleman. I will let myself out." And she left the room. She almost ran from the building and couldn't wait to get in the chauffeur-driven car she had organised for this meeting.

If what they say is true, then I will be in financial difficulties. How could he be so stupid to do that, if indeed he did? Maybe it all got away from him while we were out of Australia, and he couldn't keep up with the money markets because of the time difference, and we were moving from one place to another. I will just ignore them until they contact me again.

She only just managed to hold back the tears until she re-entered her apartment. She threw herself down on the lounge and sobbed until she thought she would be sick. She also knew that she could not go into the office for the rest of the day and sent Suzy a text letting her know she wasn't well and would be in tomorrow. Pamela could see that Meredith was upset, so she tried to snuggle up next to her but was pushed away, so she went back to the second bedroom and got up on the single bed, where she knew she shouldn't be.

If it was proved that Foster had embezzled money from his company, Meredith was worried about how much of that mud would stick to her and what the repercussions would be. Then like a bolt from the blue, Meredith realised that all her money had been invested by Foster, and she had no idea how much there was or even where he had put it. She had never asked and had brushed him off when he wanted to talk about how they were spending too much money and living above their means. She also knew that she had forced him into the very expensive holiday they had recently returned from, and she had not held back on her shopping for the months before they left and while they were away. She was extremely concerned about her future.

Upon returning to work the next day, she went straight to her office and shut the door, buzzing Suzy's phone on the internal system. She couldn't face anyone until she knew just where she stood financially. Suzy came through the door with a cup of coffee for Meredith and was shocked at the dark circles under Meredith's eyes and the worried look on her face. "Should you be here, Meredith? Are you still sick?" Suzy enquired.

"Please sit down, Suzy. I have something to talk to you about." Suzy sat quietly on the chair opposite Meredith and waited for her to start.

"I have been told by Foster's company chairman that there is money missing from a number of accounts that my husband was handling before we went away. I have to get to the bottom of it because I don't believe Foster would be so stupid as to embezzle money from the company that employed him. They are talking in terms of millions that they know of."

Suzy just sat and stared at her. "Millions? What are you going to do?"

Meredith just put her head in her hands, and when she lifted her tear-stained face, she shrugged. "I have absolutely no idea, Suzy, but I'm very scared about what lies ahead."

Suzy reassured her she would not say a word to anyone. "I will help you any way I can, Meredith. You have only to ask."

"Thanks, Suzy, but first, I have to find out exactly where I stand, and being here crying isn't going to achieve that. I'll have to go back to Foster's company and see them again, although I'm not looking forward to that experience. I'll let you know how I get on."

Suzy left the office and dropped into her chair with a stunned look on her face. If Meredith's future was threatened, then hers was too. If MC Events Management Company folded because of Foster's embezzlement, then she would be out of a job. It was time for her to reassess her position and maybe look for ways to improve her employability out in the marketplace. She had experience working for Meredith but no formal qualifications. She was a single parent, which some employers thought was a handicap, and she had minimal savings. She wouldn't leave Meredith's employ unless she had to, but she certainly needed a plan if everything collapsed.

Meredith made an appointment to go back in a few days and see Foster's employers, but in the meantime, she had to find out where she stood financially. She made a list of what she thought her situation was. She was aware the apartment was rented. Her car that Foster had managed to write-off was leased, and that would be a debt as no insurance would be forthcoming since the toxicology tests had proved a very high blood alcohol reading. There were three credit cards in Foster's name, and she had the second card on them but no idea what was owed. Foster paid those bills. Two years ago, she had sold her own property and thought that Foster had invested their 'nest egg' money. Did she still have that money somewhere?

As the list increased, so did her feeling of foreboding. She was coming to realise that she had – at her peril, it would seem – ignored their financial situation as she didn't like the idea of cutting back on any of her spending. Her parents had provided for her up until they left to travel around Australia, and when she married Foster, he had kept up their good work of smoothing the path of spending for Meredith. She had never wanted to discuss money with him and had brushed aside any of his concerns. This was not looking good.

Meredith was feeling ill with worry. She had been searching through the filing cabinet at home for some evidence of where her money had been invested. After several hours, all she had come across were meticulously filed receipts for rent, household expenses of food and wine, utilities, lease payments on both their cars, and then the folder of credit card statements. The three cards totalled almost $200,000 owing with only the minimum amount being paid for almost a year. The monthly interest was sending the balances steadily skywards, and not all the charges for the last week of their holiday had appeared yet. Meredith still held on to the hope that perhaps Foster had the investment paperwork in his office safe. It was time to face the lions in their den.

An appointment was made for 2 p.m. on Thursday, in two days' time. Meredith put this time delay to good use by phoning every bank they had ever dealt with to try to track down the "missing" money. She asked each manager to carefully check their accounts and establish if they had a safety deposit box, but all her attempts were unsuccessful.

With a heavy heart, she arrived for her meeting on Thursday in a very different frame of mind than when she had last appeared in the boardroom. As before, the chairman was courteous and asked her to come in and sit down. Other members of the board were present, and all looked very grave. She hid her hands under the table as she was having trouble stopping them from shaking.

Before the chairman could start the conversation, Meredith asked, "Do you know if Foster had any investment details of our joint money stored in his safe? I am looking for the money from the sale of my property that I asked him to invest for me. I never did find out the details." She said this with a small smile. The chairman was very sombre when he informed Meredith that they had gone through Foster's safe, filing cabinets, and computer to try to clear up the problem of the "client's missing money," but there were no such documents in there.

"Are you sure?" Meredith asked in a trembling voice. "There was two million dollars from that sale."

"I am sorry, Mrs Cunningham-Browne, but there doesn't appear to be a record of such an amount."

In the next thirty minutes, Meredith's world as she had known it imploded. She was informed that Foster had fraudulently removed amounts from his clients' accounts that were now estimated to be approximately two million dollars, and they were still looking for more. Very little of it was deemed recoverable as he had used the money to fund their lifestyle, and he was now deceased. The chairman informed Meredith, "We are seeking legal advice to have you make good this debt, Mrs Cunningham-Browne, as your name was on many of the documents." Meredith was stunned, but when the meeting ended with no good news forthcoming, she stood up from her chair; and with as much dignity as she could manage, she courteously thanked the directors for their time and quickly left the boardroom.

Nineteen

Meredith returned home, again in her chauffeur-driven car. *It will probably be public transport for me from now on. The days of living high are well and truly behind me, thanks to Foster.*

She had been focusing on where the sale money from her apartment was located but had overlooked the sale of his apartment. She didn't even know how much he had sold it for because of her disinterest in their finances. There were a lot of questions that needed answers. Meredith had just been brought down to earth with a thud. She sent Suzy a brief email to say that she wouldn't be in on Friday as things hadn't gone well with Foster's company, but she would tell her more on Monday.

Meredith knew that Jacinta had married a well-known financier whom she had met on one of the long-haul flights to the United States. Putting pride aside, she rang her. "Hi, it's me, Meredith. How are you?"

The voice on the other end of the phone asked in polite tones, "I'm fine, thanks. What do you want?"

"Is that any way to speak to an old friend? I just thought it was time we caught up again." Jacinta was under no illusions that there wasn't something in this for Meredith. After all, they went back a long way, and she knew that it would be to Meredith's benefit to call after so many years. "I was just wondering if Jack was home."

"Why, what do you want to speak to him for? You've never even met him because of your incredibly busy life, I believe."

"Well, I have a bit of a problem he might be able to help me with. I am willing to pay for his time, but I want our conversation to be private."

"Just a minute, and I will see if he's able to come to the phone." She disappeared into the home office, leaving the phone on the kitchen bench so Meredith couldn't hear her conversation.

"Jack, Meredith is on the phone and wants to speak with you."

"Who's Meredith? Is she that high-flyer company owner whose husband died a while ago?"

His wife answered, "She has a problem, and she is willing to pay for your advice. Here's my advice – charge her the maximum rate as she owes me for all the horrible things she said and did to me when we were younger." Her husband just grinned and walked to the kitchen to pick up the discarded phone from the bench.

"Hi, Meredith," he started off. "I hear you have a problem that needs sorting. What can I do for you?"

Meredith gave him a brief rundown of her situation, and after a few minutes, Jack put the phone on speaker so his wife could hear what was going on. "How about you come into the office next week? Ring my secretary, and she will give you a time. Ask her to log in two hours or so to ensure we have plenty of time because this sounds like a very complex issue. Okay, bye, Meredith. Nice to chat."

By this time, his wife had almost collapsed into a chair with shock at the mess Meredith had found herself in. She couldn't help remarking, "Well, the higher they fly, the farther they fall." And she raised her glass of wine as though in a toast.

Meredith went back to work on Monday and asked Suzy to come into the office. By now, most of the staff knew there was something going on, but Suzy – ever the professional – didn't mention a thing. "If you want to know something, ask Meredith" was her advice to anyone who approached her, and that was the end of his or her enquiry. It was more than their life was worth to question TOB about her personal life.

Suzy got a brief rundown of what had happened in the boardroom at Foster's company, and Meredith reassured her that she was going to fight to keep whatever she could from the wreckage that Foster had created. She told Suzy she was going to get legal and financial advice and wasn't going to go out with a whimper. Although Meredith was pale, had dark circles under her eyes, and was anything but her usual self, Suzy could still detect a steely undercurrent in her boss.

"I promise you, Suzy, that I will keep you up to date with everything that happens. I don't want you to think that I am abandoning ship, so please, I am begging you, stay with me until I get this sorted. I really appreciate your loyalty over the years, and when this is over, I hope I can still be your friend." Suzy was stunned. She had never considered Meredith her friend, but people can change, although Suzy was very much of the opinion that a leopard doesn't change its spots no matter what.

"Thanks, Meredith. I will do whatever I can to help, and I hope it sorts itself out for you."

When she had settled Larissa down for the night, Suzy logged onto her computer and started to source online courses, preferably for very little cost given her financial situation. There were a few that would diversify her skills and linked in nicely with the events management industry, especially on the financial side of running such a company. If everything went pear shaped with Meredith, Suzy wanted to have skills to get herself another job as quickly as possible. She was also aware of the possibility that Meredith's company may be liquidated or sold off if Foster's debt had to be repaid. It was a worrying time for Suzy, and she had given her word to Meredith that she would stay with her, but that was no reason not to improve her marketability.

The meeting was set up with Jack for Thursday, exactly one week after the disastrous news from Foster's company. Clutching a folder with as much paperwork as she thought relevant and could find in the filing cabinet at home, Meredith tentatively approached the building. She had not met Jack as she had been overseas when he and Jacinta had married; however, she remembered that Suzy had organised a very nice gift for them, so that should get her on his good side – if he remembered what she had given them.

She announced herself at the reception desk and was then ushered into a beautiful office with a view over the harbour. *He must be doing all right for himself, but I hope he keeps his wife's friendship with me in mind when he does his invoice.*

"Hello, Jack, thank you so much for seeing me at short notice. Sorry, I couldn't come to your wedding, but I wasn't in the country at the time. I hope you liked my gift."

"Er, yes, thanks, Meredith. It was lovely." Meredith could tell he had no idea what she had sent, but in her mind, she had established that she had cared about their wedding day.

Niceties aside, Jack motioned for Meredith to take a seat on the opposite side of his desk. Within moments of seating themselves, Jack's secretary, Imogen, knocked gently on the door and, upon opening it, enquired, "Would you like tea, coffee, or a cold drink, Mrs Cunningham-Browne?"

Meredith replied, "Perrier if you have it, please, Imogen, and a slice of lemon with it would be lovely. Oh, and just a shaving of ice. Perfect." Imogen just raised her eyebrows at Jack and closed the door. Shortly afterwards, she returned with a tray holding a coffee for Jack and the requested combination for Meredith served in a beautiful cut crystal glass.

What a princess, Imogen thought as she again closed the door.

"Now, Meredith, how can I help you with this dilemma you have gotten yourself into?"

Meredith visibly bristled and rather curtly said, "I didn't get myself into this dilemma, Jack. Foster did it for me, thanks very much, and I want to get that straight right at the beginning."

Jack was rather taken aback by her tone, but his wife had warned him about the beautifully manicured claws of this particular lady, not to mention her acid tongue. "Okay, Meredith. I didn't mean to offend you, so let's get down to the nitty-gritty and see exactly what we have to deal with here."

Meredith had sorted the paperwork out as best she could, given that she had never seen the majority of it before because of her complete lack of interest in anything that required her cutting down on her expenditure. There were receipts for rent, car leases, and credit cards with various banks and very high limits, most of which had been taken to that limit.

Early in their marriage, Meredith had never bothered with cash and had just used whichever credit card Foster told her to use for that week or month. After a short time, Meredith had found it annoying trying to work out which card she should use for the nail artist, the hairdresser, the day spa, the boutiques, and the long lunches. Foster had given in to her tirade about the inconvenience and had managed to get her a card of her own in a colour that immediately showed those receiving it that she was a woman of wealth. Foster then spent the following years shuffling money from one of his accounts to Meredith's often used credit card so that she would never be embarrassed that it would be declined. He was well aware of how that would turn out – for him.

After two hours in Jack's office, it was time to apprise Meredith of her financial situation. "Meredith, I don't know how to tell you this, but here goes. You are broke. Not only are you broke but you also are in serious debt. Your financial situation is dire, and I have no idea how you are going to get yourself out of this and have anything left. And bear in mind this is outside of what Foster's company may require of you. Do I have your permission to talk with them in the near future so we can come to an equitable resolution?" Meredith just sat there, and Jack could see the colour drain out of her face.

"I have nothing?" she whimpered with tears in her eyes.

"Worse than that, Meredith. You are in terrible debt and facing the possibility of bankruptcy. It is also probable that you will have to sell your company."

"Just give me a minute, please. It's a lot to take in, and I had no idea it was this bad. I'm grateful for your offer to speak with Foster's company and will sign whatever release or agreement you need." The room was warm, but her future was bleak. When composed, Meredith rose from her chair, reached across the desk, shook Jack's hand, and then with regal bearing walked from the room, softly closing the door.

Jack just sat in his chair with paper spread all over his desk and muttered, "This is going to end badly for her. I know Foster's board members, and they will go for the jugular. They will show no mercy as they have to keep their clients happy."

Upon returning to the office the following morning, Meredith called Suzy in and gave her a brief rundown of the meeting but omitted the very real possibility of her company being sold. Suzy had managed to hold it together while Meredith was telling her the edited version of the bad news. The repercussions of possibly losing her job saw Suzy in the stairwell at lunchtime crying her eyes out and hoping nobody saw her. She didn't know whether to take Meredith at her word that she would be okay as far as a job went; however, during her lifetime, Suzy had learned that if you were going to row a boat, then it was better if you were the one with the oars. At least that way, you could decide the direction of the boat.

Twenty

Meredith took a taxi home, but when she put her key in the door, it was all she could do to not collapse in the foyer with shock. Never in her life had she felt so uncertain about her future. She had never had money problems. First, her parents had topped up her bank accounts and paid down her credit cards. Then when she married Foster, he had taken up where her parents left off when they abandoned her to go on some ridiculous lifestyle change in a metal can on wheels. She was furious with everyone else whom she thought had put her in this position, conveniently forgetting that she had a major role to play in this whole disaster.

There was a bottle of Scotch in the cabinet that someone had given them one Christmas, and it had remained unopened. Meredith usually drank champagne, but the one bottle in the fridge was not going to get her to the comatose state she was looking for on this wet, windy night in Sydney. She only put on one lamp in the lounge area, which was just enough to see the level of Scotch in her glass. Pamela wisely stayed out of her way on the bed in the second room.

Morning arrived much sooner than Meredith's aching head was ready for. Her mouth felt like the bottom of a birdcage, and her neck ached from falling asleep on the lounge. There was no food in the fridge, which was not unusual, but going out for breakfast in her present state was a bridge too far for Meredith.

She dialled Suzy's extension at the office and informed her she would not be in as she was unwell and spending the day at home. Her voice sounded strange, and when Suzy asked her if she was okay after the meeting the previous day, Meredith burst into tears. "Oh, Suzy, it was so humiliating. It's much worse than I ever thought possible, and it is only going to go downhill from here. I can't talk now. I'm too upset."

"I'm coming over, Meredith. Leave the door unlocked, and I'll bring you some coffee and something to eat. I'm on my way." And with that, Meredith dropped the phone back onto the coffee table.

Thirty minutes later, Suzy was opening Meredith's door. It was all she could do to hide the shock that she felt when she saw the state of her usually impeccably groomed boss. Meredith's eyeliner and mascara made black streaks down her face, her hair was all over the place, and her lipstick smeared to one side of her mouth. Her breath stank of alcohol, and she was wearing yesterday's clothes and no shoes.

"Hi, Meredith. I brought you some coffee and pastries for breakfast as you couldn't make it in today. I hope that's okay with you."

"Suzy, you are a lifesaver. I drank too much Scotch last night, and I'm not capable of going anywhere today."

At the sound of Suzy's voice, Pamela came trotting out of the bedroom; and immediately, Suzy bent down to ruffle her curly head. "Hi, Pamela," she said and then had her fingers licked in greeting. Suzy played with her while Meredith ate half the breakfast Suzy had brought and made an effort to have a shower and sort herself out. An hour later, she emerged from the bathroom looking almost like her usual self, but her eyes were dull, and she still looked hungover despite the application of make-up and freshly shampooed hair.

Meredith sat down on the lounge and motioned for Suzy to sit in the other chair, whereupon Pamela immediately jumped into the visitor's lap, did a few circles, and settled down with a contented sigh. "She never does that with me," complained Meredith, "and

I am the one who feeds her." Suzy had her own thoughts on that subject but wisely kept them to herself.

"Suzy," Meredith started off, "I have no idea what I'm going to do. The meeting with Jack was just awful. I gave him permission to speak with Foster's board members and try and sort out this mess Foster has gotten me into. I am so angry with my husband because I've been left in a situation I had nothing to do with." Again, Suzy wisely just nodded in a sympathetic way but kept her own counsel. For a woman who was such a business whiz and had built a successful company from the ground up, Meredith had the ability to compartmentalise who was at fault in any given situation; and in most scenarios, it was not her.

"What does this mean for your company, Meredith?" Suzy ventured. "Will you be able to keep going?"

Meredith just shrugged and replied, "At this point, Suzy, I have no idea. Jack is going to try and get me the best result possible, but I won't know for several weeks where I stand. I may have to downsize from this apartment and perhaps lease a less expensive car, but I'll let you know as soon as I know. I just ask you, Suzy, please don't desert me now. It would be more than I could cope with."

Suzy nodded. "I'll stay with you, Meredith, for as long as I can. That's all I can promise you."

"Thanks, Suzy. I really appreciate your honesty."

A few weeks later and just when Meredith thought nothing else could go wrong to make her life any more stressful, there was a knock on the door. Again, there were two police officers waiting there who asked if they could come in. Meredith thought they were coming to arrest her for embezzlement and went to shut the door in their faces, but one of them had the toe of their boot in the doorjamb. "Please, Mrs Cunningham-Brown, we need to speak with you about your parents." She slowly let the door open and stepped aside, and they came into the foyer, where they stood until she asked them to come into the lounge room. "We're sorry to have to tell you that your parents had an accident yesterday."

Meredith just stared at them. "What happened?" she managed to ask.

"They were killed in a hot-air balloon crash up in the Northern Territory yesterday. We're sorry for your loss. Is there anyone who can stay with you at this terrible time?" one officer asked.

"You don't know how bad their timing is," she replied to an astonished constable. "As if I don't have enough to worry about, and they go and do something stupid. No, I don't have anyone to stay with me. I'll be all right as I always am." Neither police officer could think of anything to say.

"Mrs Cunningham-Browne," one of the officers ventured to say, "what do you want done with their belongings and the Kombi van?" These last two words got Meredith's attention.

"What Kombi van? They left here in a quarter-of-a-million-dollar Winnebago several years ago. Where has that gone?" The officers were astonished at this woman's attitude towards the news of her parents' deaths.

"I'm sorry," the senior officer replied. "We don't know anything about a Winnebago, only that they owned a Kombi van, and we need some direction about where you would like it to be sent. Also, we need to know what you would like to do about transporting your parents back to Sydney. As you're in Sydney, the Northern Territory police have arranged for a close friend of your parents to identify their bodies. We know this is a difficult time for you, but we need to ask these questions. If you are unable to decide now because of the shock you must be suffering, then I will give you my card, and perhaps you could come to the police station tomorrow, and we can sort it out then. Would that be okay?"

"Well, I don't have many choices, do I?" Meredith snatched the proffered card from the police officer and threw it behind her on the coffee table. "You can go now. The door's over that way."

When they got outside, they couldn't believe what they had just heard. They knew from their training that people reacted in different ways to grief, but her attitude was definitely a first. "Not looking forward to her visit tomorrow," one of them remarked.

After the police left, Meredith threw herself down on the lounge in temper. *Just what I don't need. Now I must organise to get them back from the Northern Territory and make funeral arrangements.*

And where the hell has the Winnebago gone? They probably sold it and "downsized" to a Kombi so they could stay on their ridiculous never-ending holiday. As if I have time for this now with all the rest I've got going on. They make me so angry. Up there having a wonderful time, no thought of how my life is turning to mud. And what am I supposed to do with a beat-up Kombi van? Will look lovely out the front of this apartment – not.

Once again, Meredith called on Suzy for help. "Hi, Suzy, I was wondering if you could do me a favour."

"Yes, sure, Meredith. What do you need?"

"My parents managed to get themselves killed in a hot-air balloon accident yesterday, and I have to get them and the stupid Kombi van they were driving back from the Northern Territory. Have you any idea how to go about that?" There was silence on the other end of the phone. "Suzy, are you there?"

"Yes, Meredith, I'm here. I'm just shocked at this terrible news. Are you okay? Is there anything I can do for you?"

"No, thanks. I'm okay, but this is an inconvenience I don't need right now. Could you see what is involved and let me know? I'm going down to the police station to see what I have to do. Get back to me, please?"

"Sure, Meredith, as soon as I know something." Suzy hung up the phone with a dazed look on her face.

Suzy went out into the main office, and after asking for quiet, she announced that Meredith's parents had been killed in a tragic accident in the Northern Territory, and they would all need to pull together to keep things going for a while. Nobody spoke for a moment at this unexpected news, but they assured Suzy they would do whatever they could to help her.

Thanks to Suzy's efforts, Meredith reluctantly left Sydney to fly to her parents' funeral in Darwin. She assumed the service would be sparsely attended but was surprised to see the small chapel full of people she had never seen before. A man approached Meredith and held out his hand to her. "I'm so sorry about your parents. I'm Bill, and I've been travelling with them in our group for a few years. I realise this is difficult for you, and I've prepared a eulogy, if you would like me to speak on your behalf. Would that be okay with you?"

"Yes, thank you. That will be fine." Meredith sat in the seat the funeral director indicated. She just stared ahead at the two coffins in front of her. She had no idea who had paid for this, nor did she care. She was, however, horrified at the bad taste shown by the number of travel stickers plastered all over each coffin.

Her parents had sent emails or postcards over the years and mentioned names, but Meredith had never taken much notice of where her parents were and whom they had met. She still harboured resentment that they had gone on this trip, which Meredith considered ridiculous. It was a mystery to her why her parents had gone off on the grey nomad's trek around Australia, even if they had started out with a luxury vehicle.

After the service, several people came up to Meredith and voiced their sympathies about the tragic accident and how much they missed Ken and Margaret's company, the laughs they used to have with them, and how life on the road wasn't going to be the same without them. Meredith was being given a different version of who her parents had been. She had only known them as two people who granted her every wish when they had lived in Sydney and then sold their home and abandoned her.

Suzy had organised a buffet lunch at one of the hotels in Darwin for those people who wished to talk about Ken and Margaret and share some anecdotes. Meredith was horrified when she saw the type of people who arrived and the weird variety of vehicles that were pulling up in the driveway. The valets were certainly earning their money trying to figure out how to drive a Kombi van that obviously had several thousand kilometres on the clock. It took a while for Meredith to realise that this vehicle decorated with a banner that read "Farewell, Ken and Margaret" and A4 size photos of her parents' holiday snaps was what she had now inherited – a far cry from the shiny white Winnebago they had set out in several years before.

Bill, who had given the eulogy, seemed to be the leader of this ragtag group of people dressed in clothing that Meredith found visually offensive. She approached him with a forced smile and said,

"Thank you for the kind words you said about my parents. I hardly recognised them from your description of the life they led."

"Your parents talked about you a lot, what a wonderful life you were having in Sydney, and your successful events management company. They were very proud of your achievements and your marriage to that handsome husband of yours." Meredith realised that her parents hadn't spoken about Foster's death or posthumous fall from grace with his company, and there was no way Meredith was going to inform this stranger.

"I met up with your parents when they were travelling the Strzelecki track on one of their early adventures, and we stayed in touch. Every so often, we would team up with other groups, and it was a fabulous life. They were great people, Meredith, but I'm sure you already know that."

"Mmm, Bill, can I ask you something?"

"Sure, Meredith, what do you want to know?"

"Well, I was wondering what happened to the Winnebago and why they were driving a Kombi van."

"Pretty simple really. The Winnebago was too big and cumbersome for some of the more rugged outback that Ken and Margaret preferred, so they sold it a few years back and bought the Kombi. Gave them a bit of change to keep travelling the back roads and was easy to pull up beside the road or a river. They loved that little van, and I guess now it's all yours."

To Meredith, the prospect of owning the ugly little vehicle was not on her bucket list, and she planned to get rid of it as soon as possible. But first, she would have to get it back to Sydney. "Bill, could you tell me how I am going to get this thing back to Sydney? There is no way I am going to drive it."

"Well, I can help you out there, Meredith. My campervan needs repairs, and it'll take two weeks to get the parts up here to Darwin. If you trust me to drive it back to Sydney and pay for a one-way plane trip from Sydney to Darwin, I'd be happy to do that for Ken and Margaret. I'll take good care of it, I promise."

"Okay, it's a deal. Here's my mobile number. If you could give me a call when you're a day or two away from Sydney, I'll get Suzy to organise a flight back to Darwin for you."

"Oh, I might stay a few days in the big smoke while I'm down here, catch up with friends and family, but I'll let you know when I'm ready to go back. Thanks, Meredith. Happy to help out Ken and Margaret's daughter. Just sorry that it is under these circumstances."

"Me too," Meredith replied but for very different reasons to Bill's.

The Kombi arrived ten days later, and Bill phoned Meredith's mobile as instructed. "Hi, Meredith. Your mum and dad's van travelled really well, and I parked it out the front. Hope that's okay?"

It wasn't okay as far as Meredith was concerned, but she had arranged to park it in a back corner of the underground garage of her building and directed Bill to the entry. Minutes later, Bill was at her front door again with a package held in front of him. "You needn't have brought a gift, Bill. I'm grateful that you agreed to drive the van to Sydney."

"Ahh, it's not a gift, Meredith. Your parents arranged with a Darwin solicitor a few years ago to give me enduring guardianship in case it was ever needed. They didn't want to bother you. It's two urns with your parents' ashes in them."

He solemnly handed the box to Meredith, and she almost dropped it when she was told about the contents. "Um, thanks, Bill. I hadn't even thought about anything past the funeral. It was a big shock."

"Yeah, it was to all of us. It was a good thing the travel company who owned the hot-air balloon paid for the service and cremation. None of us could have afforded it, just in case you were wondering. Well, I'd better go. I'm meeting some mates at the pub. Thanks for organising the flight back. Look after yourself, Meredith." And he turned to go down in the lift.

Meredith was still standing holding the box containing her parents' ashes and had no idea what to do next.

Twenty-One

Meredith returned to work on Monday morning physically and emotionally exhausted. She hadn't realised how much her parents' deaths would affect her. They hadn't been in Sydney for a long time, and although she had emails or postcards from them over the years, she had never been interested in where they were headed next. Now they were gone from her life forever, and she had nobody in the world she was related to. For the first time in her life, Meredith knew how loneliness felt, and she didn't like it one little bit. The staff offered their condolences and couldn't help but notice that Meredith's usually glossy appearance was certainly lacking.

On her return from Darwin, she had once again contacted Jack to see if he had any news, good or bad, about her financial situation. He first suggested she sit down and then brought her up to date with conversations, personal and by email, with Foster's company directors and accountants, and it was not good. They were conducting a thorough investigation of all the transactions Foster had been involved in for the past five years. His company was also going to go after Meredith's assets to make good Foster's debt. When she received this information, she knew she was in real trouble financially.

"Jack, why do I have to make restitution for what Foster embezzled? I don't think that's fair. I didn't have anything to do with our finances. I have enough to worry about with my company, let alone our domestic situation. I left that up to Foster."

"Meredith, the really bad news is that several of the documents they have clearly show your signature."

"But, Jack, I only signed whatever Foster put in front of me. I didn't know what they were for. He just told me they were transfers of our money to get a better rate. I am so angry with him."

"Sorry, but ignorance is no excuse here, Meredith. Your signature is on the documents, and that is all his company cares about. They know you have a business that can be sold to help clear Foster's anticipated debt, and all they are interested in is keeping their clients happy. Your future is of no interest to them whatsoever. I'll get back to you when I know some figures. Bye."

Meredith sat with her head in her hands in complete despair, with angry tears sliding down her cheeks. *Sell my company? I have worked so hard for two decades to build it up into what it is today, and now it will be taken out of my control? Surely, there must be another way.* But for the life of her, she couldn't think of one.

Suzy knocked gently and opened the door a little. She could see Meredith sitting at her desk, and she could hear her crying softly. "Meredith, are you okay?" Suzy quietly asked. Her boss' reply surprised her.

"No, Suzy, I'm not, and I may never be again. I think I'm in more trouble financially than I could ever have imagined. I may even have the company taken from me to settle Foster's debts. I just have to wait and see what his company comes up with, but Jack said they will go for the jugular, and I don't know if I can survive it. Please don't say anything to the rest of the staff until I know what those vultures are going to do."

Suzy promised to keep quiet until her boss was ready to make an announcement, but she also knew it wasn't going to be good. She wouldn't leave Meredith in the lurch, but she had to ensure she had employment and a steady income given her own financial circumstances. Meredith had suggested it could take between three and six months for "those vultures," as she termed the investigators at Foster's company, to come up with a final figure. Suzy had looked at online courses to improve her employment prospects for her next career, although she had not signed up for anything as the cost was often a deterrent. She had managed to keep the majority of the money that Meredith had given her over the years for house-sitting or pet-sitting. It was now an investment in securing her financial future. Evening study and online assessments were the way to go, and that would be the first thing she would do when she got home tonight.

After dinner, Suzy turned her computer on; and the next minute, Larissa was right beside her, wanting to know what was going on. Her daughter was very smart and knew her way around basic computer programs such as Word and Excel and was well informed on social media requirements. Suzy knew she would be a big help to her.

"Well, my darling daughter, I am going to future-proof us. I'm signing up for an online course in business management. Would you like to help me?"

"Sure would, Mum. I love computers, and maybe I can learn too. After all, I'll be trying to get a job in a few years, and every bit of knowledge helps as you always say."

"At least it proves you listen to me sometimes, Larissa, although I'm not always convinced that it goes any deeper than into your ear. Okay, let's get this show on the road."

Over the next few months, Suzy worked hard every evening with Larissa's invaluable assistance into the mysteries of computers. Although Suzy had a computer at work, it was a set program where she entered the information required which resulted in organising the whole function. The financial side of MC Events Management Company was taken care of by faceless accountants in a building somewhere in Sydney. Suzy's job description did not include how to run a business from the ground up, and that was the gap in her knowledge she had to fill. The scores given on her assignments were high, and the comments were positive and encouraging.

While Suzy was doing her online course, Larissa was learning a lot and was very keen to help her mother. "Gee, Mum, who would ever have thought we would be doing this sort of stuff on the computer? It's heaps better than the stupid things my friends put up on social media. The math part of it is helping me at school too." Suzy couldn't help but be thrilled her daughter was so eager to learn. She was in year 8 at the local high school and was a keen student.

The dreaded day finally arrived, and Meredith knew the news wasn't good as soon as she heard Jack's voice. "Hi, Meredith, how are you?"

"Terrified about what you have to tell me, Jack. Could I come to your office later today? I would rather not be in my office if I have a meltdown, and I suspect that could be the case."

"Okay, I'll see you here at about four. I'll have a strong drink ready for you. I think you're going to need it."

This was not sounding good, but then again, Meredith had never expected it to be. When she had returned from Jack's office the first time and looked at the approximate figures he had generated on his computer, she knew she was in trouble. Over the past six months, she had tried to curb her spending, but it was too little too late. Her previous carefree and extravagant lifestyle had ended with Foster's death. A few years of marriage, and what did she have to show for it? A well-travelled Kombi van that she hated the sight of and a mountain of debt.

Meredith arrived at Jack's office and was fearful of what her situation was going to be. She was met by Imogen and directed straight into Jack's office. Once seated, she was aware of the grim look on his face and asked, "Okay, Jack, give it to me straight. How bad is it?"

"Well, Meredith, the situation's this. Foster's company wants your blood, and that is not being dramatic. They want everything repaid."

Meredith's face paled, and her voice was almost a squeak when she murmured, "Everything?"

"Yes, Meredith, every last cent, and they won't negotiate on that."

"How much?"

"Two million three hundred and fifty-five thousand dollars."

"How on earth am I going to raise that much money? I don't own the apartment, I don't have a car, and all the credit cards are maxed out."

"You'll have to sell your company, Meredith, and probably walk away with nothing. If you're to get a good price, you'll be able to clear the debts to Foster's company. You'll probably be bankrupt."

"Oh god, I need a stiff drink." Jack quickly poured her a very hefty Scotch and placed it in front of her.

After he watched her take a few sips, he said, "Okay, Meredith, we need a plan and timeline to get this disaster sorted out because they'll be tacking interest onto the debt owed, and it won't be at the lowest rate either. I'll bring my laptop over to the sofa, and you can sit beside me to see what's on the screen. Let's get to work."

Over the next two hours as the early evening dusk turned to inky-black sky, Jack typed figures into a spreadsheet and, along the way, explained to Meredith what the numbers represented. He had taken the liberty of having her company valued for sale as he suspected it was going to come to this, given the attitude of Foster's company executives. As time passed, Meredith could see that she would be lucky to come out of this with anything at all. If she was declared bankrupt, she would not be able to start up another company in the foreseeable future, and she didn't know if she had the heart to do it again anyway.

All that work for two decades, and I'll have nothing to show for it. I won't have a business, an apartment, or a car and will be lucky if I can ever borrow money again. Foster, if you weren't dead, I would kill you for what you have done. Meredith realised what she had just thought and laughed out loud.

"What on earth could be funny about all this?" asked Jack with a bewildered look on his face, so Meredith repeated to Jack what she had thought about Foster, and he laughed along with her.

That same night, Jack sent off an email to Foster's company with the figures that he had worked on with Meredith and made an offer of repayments and the timing of them. He was trying to buy a few months for MC Events Management Company to be on the market for a good price rather than sacrificed to settle a debt. Within twenty-four hours, he received a short email rejecting the repayments schedule and demanding that the debt be settled within thirty days, and there would be no further negotiation on the matter. He knew that there was no way Meredith's company could be advertised and sold within thirty days for the price it should bring on the open market. She needed to settle the debt, pay off the entitlements of her staff, and move from her luxurious apartment to something smaller and affordable within a month.

There were those companies who were on the constant lookout for businesses in trouble and offered a figure that was way below market value. Once they had secured a bargain, they kept it for a short while and then sold it on at market value in the future or used it as a tax write-off. Jack went home that night very despondent because he couldn't help Meredith out of the hole she was in. He had done all he knew to try to maximise her ability to come out of this situation with at least something to start with again. He knew there was going to be nothing left over, but he didn't think the reality of that had hit Meredith yet. The life Meredith had lived was nothing like her future was going to be.

Twenty-Two

Monday morning dawned after Meredith had spent a weekend with almost no sleep because she was so worried about how she was going to cope. Her company would be sold, her staff entitlements would be paid out, she would have to move out of the apartment into something smaller, and she would have no job. Meredith had finally come to grips with the whole nightmare of her future. She had been drinking heavily over the past two days and looked less than her glamorous self when she called a staff meeting to be held on Tuesday.

Suzy was very concerned about her and knocked gently on Meredith's door about an hour after she had arrived and made the announcement about a staff meeting. "Hi, Meredith. Are you okay?" asked Suzy with a worried look on her face.

"Thanks, Suzy. No, I'm not all right on any level. Tomorrow I am going to announce to the staff that the company is being sold and everyone will receive their entitlements, but it means that there will be twenty good staff out of work."

"Oh, Meredith, I didn't realise that things were that bad. Is there anything I can do for you?"

"Yes, Suzy, a good strong coffee would go down well about now, and hold all my calls, please, unless it is Jack or my accountants."

"Will be back in a minute." Suzy closed the door with tears in her eyes. It had finally come down to what Suzy had feared the most. She would be out of work and competing with the rest of the staff for a position with another company, if she could not stay on with whoever bought Meredith's company. She was glad that she had done her business management course and passed with good grades and comments on her work. That should stand her in good stead, but after ten years with one company, it would be a huge change and not one she was looking forward to. At least now Larissa was in high school; she could get herself to and from school.

The staff meeting was very difficult for Meredith, and there was shocked silence while she spoke, and then everyone started talking at once, asking questions and expressing their dismay about the imminent loss of employment. Meredith reassured the staff that they would all receive references and severance pay. They would have these figures by the next payday, but in the meantime, she asked them to try to keep things going for as long as possible. Given the dislike most of the staff felt for her, it was unlikely that they would stay on this sinking ship. It was every man (or woman) for themselves. Meredith noticed that Suzy hadn't said a word during all the noise after the announcement and had quietly left the room. Meredith didn't know if this was a good or bad sign, but she had never needed Suzy more than she did now.

In the meantime, she was working with her accountants to work out staff entitlements, and this figure was frightening in itself. She had to let her clients know that the company would be changing hands very shortly, and she released a press notice. It was brief and stated that, owing to health issues, she would no longer be the CEO of MC Events Management Company and that they should contact her accountants for refund of monies paid for future events. She knew that those in the marketplace would be fully aware of the situation, and a "fire sale" would be the end point for MC Events Management Company, and there wasn't a thing she could do about it.

The thirty days to settlement were already ticking by when she received a phone call from her accountants to inform her that they had received an offer for the company. When the amount offered was mentioned, she collapsed back into her chair. "But it's worth twice that!" she screamed into the phone. "They know I'm down, and they want to kick me as well." After slamming the phone down in the ear of her long-time accountant, she put her head on the desk and cried in frustration.

How dare they do this to me? This company is worth twice that amount, but they know I'm on the ropes and can't do anything about it. I don't have time to negotiate and play the waiting game. I'll just have to go with it.

She rang her accountant back and apologised for slamming the phone down in his ear. He was more amazed by the apology than the deed as it wasn't the first time Meredith had hung up on him, but this was a very different Meredith he was dealing with now. "I suppose I have to accept their offer, don't I?" she queried. "I don't have any other offers on the table, and I'm running out of time. So what do I do now?"

"You'll have to come to the office and sign some papers for the sale. For what it's worth, Meredith, I'm really sorry it's come to this. It must be a terrible blow for you."

"Thanks. Yes, it's probably the most awful thing that has ever happened to me, and the worst part is I had nothing to do with it."

The accountant wisely kept his mouth closed. He knew that Meredith had lived the high life without any thought of where her next dollar was going to come from. No wonder her parents had cashed in their assets and taken off on their trip around Australia. At least they had enjoyed their later years without having to pay off Meredith's debts, but he felt they would have been disappointed at this outcome for their daughter.

She had never had the need to learn financial responsibility for herself, and now it was too late. She would be lucky if she had any dollars at all to worry about once the sale went through and all debts were paid. This would be a very different world that Meredith would be living in, and he doubted she would have any idea how to go about the daily business of surviving on a severely reduced income. This was not going to end well for her.

By the time the sale went through, most of the staff had left for other positions, but Suzy stayed until the end. She had been offered a position in a totally different field and a smaller company but wasn't due to start for another month. School holidays were coming up, so she and Larissa were going to spend ten days in Bali, paid for out of her severance pay. Her daughter was thrilled about a trip as their holidays had been few and far between, but this was a dream come true for her. Neither of them had a passport as they hadn't been out of Australia, so that was first on the list of things to do.

In the meantime, she was helping Meredith pack up the apartment, ready to move to somewhere smaller, although she hadn't even looked at any yet. Suzy was aware that it was a huge blow to her pride that she had to give up her luxury lifestyle, but there were few dollars in the kitty, and this was the way it had to be. After looking at places to rent online and spending hours looking at small two-bedroom units in suburbs with postcodes that Meredith would never have visited, Suzy was at the end of her tether and decided to tell her boss where it was at.

"Okay, Meredith, you need to hear this for your own good. You are only days away from the expiration of your apartment lease, and you don't have any money to extend it. You don't have enough to put down a bond and two weeks' rent on anything you would consider living in. I have tramped around with you looking at places, usually from the outside, because you won't get out of the car and even go inside. I can't do this any longer, Meredith.

"I'm taking Larissa on a well-deserved holiday in ten days, and then I'll start my new job. You need to get yourself organised and rent something before you are on the streets. You don't have to stay there forever, but for goodness' sake, make a decision. That's all I'm going to say. Now do you want a coffee?" Meredith was a bit taken aback by Suzy's outburst but knew that she was right. She couldn't afford to live where she would like to and couldn't find anything she would live in where she could afford.

When Suzy returned a few minutes later with a coffee, Meredith motioned with her pen for Suzy to sit down. "You are absolutely right, Suzy. I'm letting my pride get in the way of making a decision. If you could give me just one more day, I promise I will find something somewhere. I know I am not going to find the luxury I have had, but if it is quiet, clean, and pet friendly, I will take it. Could you do that for me, please?"

"Okay, Meredith, this Saturday is the last available time I have. I'll pick you up at 8 a.m., and we will get your next home organised. You may not like where you have to live, but that's life." Suzy left the office.

Saturday was a real eye-opener for Meredith. She had to go into areas where she had never been before and had no desire to live, but Suzy had issued her with an ultimatum. She had to decide today. One of these rundown dog boxes was to be her new home, and she was having trouble getting excited about that prospect. They took a coffee break at about two thirty, and Meredith was getting more and more despondent. She knew she only had until four o'clock to find something as Suzy had made it quite clear that was the deadline.

As they passed a real estate agency on the way to the coffee shop near to where Suzy lived, there was a handwritten sign just being put in the window.

Neat one-bedroom property to rent.
Partly furnished. Available immediately.
$350 per week. Apply within.

They forgot about the coffee and went into the office. The property was above the real estate office and had been let to an overseas student who had finished his studies and gone home. Meredith and Suzy were given a key to go upstairs and have a look to see if it suited. Of course, Meredith was less enthusiastic than Suzy; but with a bit of extra furniture, it would be okay until she got another company up and going. "If they let me have Pamela," she told Suzy, "I will take it. I noticed a small backyard, so maybe they won't mind."

When they reappeared in the office, there was a young couple talking to one of the salesmen, who then turned to Meredith and Suzy and asked, "Are you going to take it because this young couple want it?"

Meredith looked at Suzy, who was out of direct sight of the salesman, and Suzy mouthed, *Don't mention the dog, or you won't get the flat.* Meredith turned back to the salesman and told him she would like to take it on a six-month lease, and she would sign up now. She emphasised the fact that she was a company director and was looking for somewhere to stay while her own apartment was being renovated.

She went into an office away from the front desk and filled in the appropriate paperwork. She had bedazzled the young man so much with her loaded charm that he didn't even bother to do a credit check. Meredith's expensive clothing, handbag, and bling were enough for him. Little did he know that it was all window dressing. As usual, Meredith thought someone else would take care of the money to be paid; so with a smile, Suzy put forward her credit card for the bond and the two weeks' rent in advance.

"Thanks, Suzy. I was in such a rush this morning that I forgot to put my credit card in my bag." Suzy knew different. There was no credit card available to proffer for the bond and rent. They had all been stopped because of the debt and a perceived lack of ability to pay the balance.

Suzy had organised for the majority of Meredith's furniture to be sold on eBay to give her some extra cash but also because trying to find a unit or villa that would be able to house a seven-seater Italian leather lounge with a chaise on one end would be impossible. The huge wall-mounted TV was happily rehoused in a family with teenage boys, who were delighted to watch sports on it. The king-sized bed was sold long ago as Meredith refused to sleep in it after Foster died, so she used one of the single beds in the second bedroom. Pamela usually occupied the other, and Meredith had enough on her plate to scold her dog to get down off the furniture.

Twenty-Three

Moving day for Meredith and Pamela was predictably fraught with difficulties. The removalists had insisted on being paid before they would load one carton, so of course, Suzy was asked to fund this. The real estate agent was closed on Sunday, so she chose that day to move as she didn't want anyone to see Pamela. She was a little quiet dog, getting on in years now, but she wasn't supposed to be in the unit. She asked Suzy to mind her for the day, and Larissa was delighted. She had always loved Pamela and enjoyed every opportunity she got to play with her.

There was very little furniture to move from her apartment, but Meredith had refused to even consider giving away her clothes to charity, although she had no idea how to go about selling them online. She still hung on to the illusion that she would once again be a successful businesswoman, completely ignoring the fact that it was very likely she would be declared bankrupt and unable to start another company for quite some time. Suzy came to help on the day, and she was horrified about how many portable wardrobe boxes were supposed to fit into the removalist truck, not to mention where they would go once they got to the rather compact unit Meredith had rented. "Where on earth are you going to put all those wardrobe boxes?"

"Well, if they don't fit, then I'll hire a storage unit close by. I can't give away a fortune in clothing. It took me too long to buy it all, and some of the shoes and bags aren't even out of their wrapping. It would be a crime to just give them away to a charity shop," Meredith lamented.

"Meredith, do you know how much a storage unit costs each month?"

"No, should I?"

"Well, yes, you should because you are going to need a fairly big one, and it could cost you up to $400 a month, which is money you don't have."

"Yes, but I might have some soon when all the dust settles from the sale."

Suzy just shook her head and walked away. Repaying Suzy for the bond, two weeks' rent, and removalist costs should be her first priority; but in reality, her now ex-boss had absolutely no idea about the practicalities of life. Suzy despaired of how long it would take Meredith to run out of money completely, and she suspected it would be sooner rather than later. *You can dream, but dreaming won't pay the bills.*

By 8 p.m., Suzy and Meredith were exhausted. The wardrobe boxes took up nearly all the bedroom, so only one single bed could be fitted in along the wall. Pamela immediately took up residence, but Meredith was too tired to worry about her. She would just curl up alongside her sometime in the next ten minutes and fall asleep. Meredith had never worked so hard in her entire life, and it had taken its toll.

She had asked Suzy in the early evening to ring up and get some gourmet pizzas and a bottle of very nice red. "Spend anything up to $100 for the lot," she instructed.

Suzy just looked at her in amazement. "We won't be having gourmet pizzas and a very nice red. Firstly, you owe me a few thousand dollars. And therefore, you don't have a spare $100, which incidentally I need repaid when I get back from our holiday. I'm not paying a ridiculous amount of money for one meal and a bottle of wine, which neither my daughter nor I will be drinking. I'll send Larissa down to the shops, and she can bring back some fish and chips. That'll do for dinner. I'm too tired to worry about what I eat, and I have to drive back home, so 'a very nice red' is out of the question."

With that statement, Suzy turned on her heel and went back into the kitchen to try to get some order into the chaos. Suzy and Larissa were leaving for their long-awaited holiday in a few days, and Meredith was left to unpack what remained of her previous gold-plated lifestyle. Suzy was starting her new position straight after their return from Bali and wanted to be organised for that before they left Sydney. Hours had been spent doing things for Meredith to get her settled, and time was now in short supply for Suzy.

The Kombi van sat in the lane beside the real estate agent's office, and Meredith was hoping she wouldn't have to be seen in it. The shops were just down the end of the street for day-to-day shopping. If there was something she needed that wasn't locally available, she would get it delivered. This was, to Meredith, a simple problem with a simple solution. She still hadn't figured out that nothing would get delivered without a credit card, and she was unlikely to have another one for quite some time. The money in her bank account was the sum of her wealth, but most of that, she owed to Suzy.

She slept the sleep of the exhausted, and when her phone rang at nine on Monday morning, she didn't even hear it. Eventually, after about thirty minutes when the phone rang again, she reached over and answered "hello" in a sleep-thickened voice.

"Hi, Meredith, I hope I'm not disturbing you."

"No, that's fine, Jack. Moved yesterday, and it was a big day. What can I do for you?"

"Ah, I just wanted to let you know by phone before you get the email that your net worth, as we speak, is just under $5,000, not including any personal effects such as jewellery. Also, your credit rating is not even worth talking about, and you are really in the bad books with that one. My email will set everything out, but the most devastating part for you, Meredith, is that it will be unlikely you will be able to start another business in the foreseeable future because of Foster's embezzlement and your part in that."

"My part in it!" she yelled down the phone. "I had nothing to do with it. I've told you that before. Whose side are you on anyway?" And she slammed the phone down.

Considering all the work Jack had done for her, he felt insulted. Typical Meredith – me, myself, and I. Jack just shook his head and hit the send button on the email. He was expecting another furious phone call once that hit her inbox – if she had paid her Internet bill.

Twenty-Four

The second night Meredith and Pamela spent in their new home was more than memorable. There were scratching noises in the roof, which made Pamela growl, something she had never done before; but then again, their past luxury apartments did not have cavities for unidentified animals to make their home in. The next morning, Meredith was too tired to worry about what had been making the noises and went to the fridge to inspect its contents. Suzy had brought her some groceries, but Meredith was more interested in the whereabouts of the expected champagne bottle. She was surprised at its absence as she hadn't realised she had consumed the last bottle, so she rang Suzy. When the phone was answered, Meredith started in with "Did you forget to buy champagne?"

The immediate reply came back "No, Meredith, I did not forget to buy champagne. I chose not to buy it. You can't afford it anymore, and I don't have sixty extra dollars to spend on one bottle of it. Simple. Is that all you wanted? I have a lot to do today." Meredith was rather taken aback by the sharpness of Suzy's reply and could, for once in her life, think of no retort.

After a small pause, Suzy spoke again. "Goodbye, Meredith, and good luck in your new life. Give Pamela a hug from Larissa and me." Meredith just stood there staring at her phone in her tiny rented apartment above a shop. This was not working for her.

Meredith did not relish the thought of going job hunting or, as she thought of it, position acquisition. Surely, a company out there had need of her business acumen, her knowledge of what it took to keep several staff members on their toes, and her considerable book of contacts, the latter being out of bounds according to the terms of the sale. She had decided that she would only get in touch with someone who would be sympathetic to the position that Foster had put her in before he managed to kill himself while being drunk. Very few of the people in her black leather-bound book of contacts actually cared what happened to Meredith Cunningham-Browne, and most would not be forthcoming in offering her a position, especially if they valued the staff they already had.

After several weeks of interviews arranged by various agencies and polite phone calls and emails with basically the same message – "We're sorry, but we cannot offer you a position at this time but will keep your résumé on file" – Meredith was becoming dispirited. She could not understand why nobody was knocking down her door to offer her a middle-management position at least, even with a reduced income.

Now when she looked in the mirror, the reflection was not quite as glossy and well cared for as it had been three months ago. She had filed her nails down and removed the polish coat as she could no longer afford the fortnightly infill. She purchased a pair of tweezers from the local chemist so she could shape her eyebrows, and the mousy brown roots of her true hair colour were starting to show through. This was not the face she wanted to see in her mirror. Her sun-kissed, glowing skin had reverted to its rather pale appearance and not evenly so. Her immaculate pedicures had long ago disappeared along with her manicure and regular facials. She had used up every bit of moisturiser, eye cream, cleanser, toner, exfoliant, and assorted other beauty products that had been purchased in her other lifetime. She was depressed about the prospect of cheaper brands, the names of which she had never bothered to learn or considered buying.

Her biggest concern right now was the mousy brown regrowth. She walked into the local salon, which was full of clients at the time, and gave the bemused stylist quite a rundown on what she required to restore her hair to its original condition. The girl had been in business a long while and really did not want this troublesome woman as a new client. She knew she would never be able to please her and correctly assessed her to be high maintenance and one who would never be satisfied no matter how good the finished colour was. She quoted a minimum of $400 for what Meredith required, and after the raising of the possible new client's eyebrows, she suggested that perhaps, as she was fully booked for the next two weeks, that "madam" might look around for someone who could fit her in sooner. Meredith nodded briefly and left the salon.

Upon her departure, one of the long-time clients said, "Natalie, you don't charge $400 for colour no matter how long it takes."

The hairdresser replied, "Yes, you and I know that, but I couldn't face doing her hair as she would never be satisfied, so I quoted a ridiculously high price and hoped she would go away. Mission accomplished."

When Meredith was back home, she checked her emails to see if there was a position offered yet and then looked at her bank balance. This was getting seriously worrying, even for her. To replace her skin care and cosmetics, even with cheaper brands – the thought of which made her shudder – and have her hair restored to its former glory would take every dollar she had and then some. She still owed Suzy money, and the rent was due at the end of the week. Reality was finally making its appearance in Meredith's world, and she didn't like the feeling one little bit.

She had no business to go to each day, no friends, no income, no job offers, and her future looked extremely bleak. Her last conversation with Suzy about the "missing" champagne had really shocked her. How could she live without champagne? It was part of her lifestyle – or at least her previous lifestyle. The thought of having to buy dreadful, cheap sparkling wine made her feel ill. *Who could possibly drink that sort of thing? If I can't have what I have been used to drinking, then I won't bother at all.*

The idea of no champagne lasted only a few days. Meredith had to come to the heart-wrenching decision that she needed to drink something alcoholic, or she would go mad sitting in her tiny rented apartment, surrounded by wardrobe boxes, with only a small dog for company. She felt quite safe going into the local bottle shop, again another unknown territory for her as cases of her favourite alcohol had always been delivered. Fortunately, she was now living in an area where nobody knew her and would see her going into a bottle shop. She moved along to the section where her usual champagne was housed and was tempted to take a bottle out, but she knew her bank balance was precariously low, and she still had to eat. Searching the refrigerated cabinets where the dreaded sparkling wine lived brought her no joy. She stamped her foot in annoyance, and a voice behind her asked, "Can I help you with anything, or are you just browsing?"

"Just trying to find something that is similar to the usual Moët I drink but half the price. Where would I find that?"

"There is no such product, I'm afraid. Moët is Moët. There are some sparkling wines I can show you that are around twenty dollars, if you are interested."

Meredith was not sure she could bring herself to do this, but she reasoned that alcohol was what she needed at the end of the day. "Okay, I'll try one bottle, but I can't guarantee that I'll like it. My palate is rather used to a more superior product."

The sales assistant was amused by her attitude, but frankly, he didn't much care whether she liked it or not. A sale was a sale. He handed over the chosen bottle in a paper bag, and the look of revulsion on Meredith's face did not go unnoticed by him.

Back at the apartment, as Meredith liked to think of the tiny rented flat, she put the bottle in the fridge and decided to try it a little later with dinner. However, one look at the contents of the fridge was enough for her to know that dinner was likely to be cheese and biscuits and not good quality either, if the generic labels were anything to go by. *Good heavens, fancy Suzy thinking that I would eat this cheap stuff. But then again, I didn't pay her for it either, so I can't complain. At least there's some dog food for Pamela. I'll have to find the nearest gourmet supermarket as soon as possible, if I am to survive. But worst of all, tomorrow I will have to go to Centrelink, no matter how much I loathe the idea.*

The next day and with a cheap wine hangover, Meredith set off on the adventure of taking a bus, a mode of transport she had not used since she had left school. In her mind, the bus was a superior option to climbing into the VW Kombi, which was still in the side lane and she hadn't yet driven. It was Monday morning, and Meredith arrived at the Centrelink office, where she was taken aback by the types of people waiting in a queue. She was conspicuous with the immaculate hair that could be seen below the hat she wore to hide her mousy brown regrowth, perfectly applied make-up, knee-length red leather coat, black leather bag, and high-heeled shoes worn with sheer charcoal-toned pantyhose.

The first thing Meredith was aware of was the amount of people nudging one another and whispering while looking at her. Usually, she enjoyed being the centre of attention, but the behaviour of these people felt threatening to her. It wasn't long before the comment came from behind her. "Are you in the right place, love? Youse don't look the sort who needs Centrelink, or have you come to make a donation?" This last comment brought snorts of laughter from others waiting in line. Meredith turned around and glared in the direction the voice had come from, but nobody stood out as the comedian everyone had laughed with.

The queue slowly moved forwards, and after almost an hour, Meredith arrived at the counter, where she was asked why she was there. "Well, I need to see someone about having my bank account topped up. It is dangerously low, and I have expenses."

"I see," replied the assistant. "Well, there are several ways we may be able to help you, but a lot more detail will be required before we can 'top up' your bank account. If you could just go over and see that lady at the third desk across, she will assess you and see if you qualify for benefits."

"Of course, I will qualify for benefits," replied Meredith in her usual haughty tone that she used when dealing with people she felt inferior to her. "I have been a taxpayer for many years and probably more so than the rest of the rabble you let in here." She left the counter and made her way to the third desk, where she was asked to take a seat.

"Good morning. My name is Daphne. How can I help you?"

"Well, I've come here about Centrelink providing me with some income. What do you need to know?"

Daphne was amused by Meredith's approach and expectations and felt that this lady was a long way from even understanding what was in front of her and what was available if her clothes and manner were anything to go by. "There are some forms that would need to be filled in so that we can assess whether you are entitled to any benefits and, if so, what those might be. There are several levels that may be accessed depending on your circumstances. So let's start with your name and address, date of birth, and so on, shall we?"

Meredith thought the interview would go on forever with the amount of details required for her to access government money. Daphne informed Meredith that it would take up to a fortnight before she was contacted as the information she had given had to be checked and verified, to which Meredith replied in a sarcastic tone of voice, "Well, I wouldn't want you to rush." She had never felt so humiliated in her whole life having to lay bare the details of her sad and sorry story to this person, Daphne, who looked like she needed benefits herself.

Twenty-Five

After two weeks, Meredith received an email from Centrelink requesting her to phone their office. In the meantime, no management position had been offered to Meredith, her bank account was almost empty, and she was in danger of slipping behind in the rent. All she had left were her clothes, jewellery, and – if you could call it an asset – the 30-year-old VW Kombi still parked in the side lane.

That could be a short-lived situation too as the real estate agents had made it clear to her that the van needed to be moved as soon as possible. In their opinion, it was occupying valuable kerb space for clients coming to their office. So far, Meredith had ignored their requests as it was still registered for a few months more, and she loathed to even get in the thing. She had never driven a manual car and wasn't about to start with this ugly duckling full of her mother and father's camping equipment and mementos from a trip that had ended with their deaths. At least it was somewhere she could keep the urns containing their ashes until she decided their eventual fate.

Centrelink was contacted, and after Meredith supplied more details, she was informed that she would receive rent assistance and a widow's pension, the sum total of which would just cover the rent and about two days' worth of food. It was becoming increasingly clear to Meredith that she was facing severe financial difficulties.

Suzy was very happy in her new job and was not surprised to receive a phone call from Meredith, who started off with, "Suzy, I need your help."

"What can I do for you, Meredith? I'm at work so can't talk for long." Meredith had obviously forgotten that personal calls were something she had not allowed at MC Events Management Company and was happy to take up Suzy's time with a personal call when she wasn't paying her salary.

"Centrelink are going to pay me some money each fortnight, but I can't live on it!" she wailed down the phone to Suzy. "How am I going to keep myself looking presentable in case I am offered a job? I am reduced to drinking revolting, cheap twenty-dollar-a-bottle sparkling wine and am consuming quite a lot of noodle dishes from the local takeaway, which cost me about ten dollars a day. I'm putting on weight, and I look awful. What am I going to do?"

"Meredith, this is too much to deal with over the phone, and I am really busy in this new job. I'll meet you after work in the coffee shop just down the road from you, and we'll try to come up with a plan. What do you think?"

"Thanks, Suzy. I'll see you tonight about 6:30."

Suzy hung up the phone and shook her head. *Will this woman ever learn that the whole world does not revolve around her? Probably not, but she obviously is in a lot of financial trouble. I'll try and help, but really, she is her own worst enemy.*

Just after 6:30, Suzy entered the coffee shop and was surprised to see that Meredith had bought two coffees and was waiting for her to arrive. "Hi, Meredith. Sorry I'm a bit late, but there was a lot of traffic from the city."

"That's okay, Suzy. It's not as though I have somewhere else to be. Thanks for coming at such short notice because I really need your advice." Meredith then showed Suzy a piece of paper with handwritten notes of income and expenses, and unsurprisingly, the last amount showed a deficit each fortnight.

"What am I going to do? I haven't got enough to live on, and I can't get a job. The only assets I have are those wardrobe boxes of clothes that cost me such a lot of money originally, my jewellery, and that blasted VW Kombi van."

Suzy went over the expenses and pointed out to Meredith, once again, that buying wine of any price was out of the question. The rent assistance would help, but until Meredith came to grips with the idea that she was no longer rich and powerful, there was little that Suzy could do to convince her that her previous lifestyle was dead in the water. Selling the clothes to a boutique designer recycling outlet was suggested but immediately rejected by Meredith with the comment "I'm not going to go begging into those places for a few dollars to see me through. What about if they know me? I would die of embarrassment."

"Well, Meredith, you might have the choice of dying of hunger or embarrassment if you don't do something soon. If the clothes are more than one season old, as some of them are, you will get hardly anything, even though you originally paid hundreds and even thousands of dollars for them."

Meredith just sat and looked across the table while her coffee slowly cooled. Suzy could see she certainly didn't have the same attitude as she did six months ago but was still unrealistic about her financial situation. If this downward spiral of income and upward trend of spending continued, it would only be a matter of weeks before she was out on the streets, and the rent assistance would not be required then. Suzy knew the lease on the unit was almost up, and given the few times that the rent had been in arrears, only to be paid when it was made clear that this could not continue, it was doubtful if her lease would be extended. There were too many other people who would be happy to rent the unit and with stable jobs to support their application, unlike the poorly groomed woman sitting across the table from her.

"Meredith, do you realise how dire your financial situation actually is?" Suzy asked.

"I think it's worse than I realised, Suzy. I have ignored what I didn't want to know, and now I'm almost destitute. Selling the clothes will buy me some time, but how am I going to get them to the places that might take them? I can't drive that ugly thing my parents left me, and besides, it is full of their stuff – and them."

Suzy's eyebrows went up. "What do you mean and them?"

Meredith's reply stunned her. "Well, I put their urns in there because, after all, that was where they were happiest, and I don't really want them sitting in my place, do I?"

It had not been mentioned to Meredith that Suzy had a new man in her life mainly because Suzy knew she would not be in the least bit interested. She had met Brady at a work function one night in the city, and he happened to be the organiser of the event, so they found they had a lot in common. He was a few years older than her and had been married before but had no children. Brady and Larissa seemed to get along well, and Suzy was smitten with him. It had been more than a decade since Suzy had had any inclination to go out with a man, but this one ticked all the boxes. He was well mannered and intelligent and could discuss almost any subject they cared to talk about.

He also had the use of a rather large company van that Suzy was sure could accommodate a good deal of Meredith's wardrobe to transport the unwanted clothing to a new destination. Suzy just mentioned that she would see what she could do about the clothing problem and get back to her. She wasn't sure if Brady would agree to do this for Meredith, having heard a few tales about her previous behaviour, but he would most likely do it to help Suzy.

A few days after their coffee meeting, Suzy could tell Meredith that she had been able to get the use of a van and driver to take the clothes that were surplus. She asked Brady not to say that they were "an item" as she liked her private life to be just that. She also told Meredith that she would try to get the best price possible without letting her know that she had quite a good knowledge of these shops, given her previous employer's insistence that all her staff be well groomed. It was just another example of Meredith being out of touch with how the other half lived.

When loading up the clothes, Suzy was appalled at the number of beautiful dresses, suits, pants, coats, shoes, and handbags that still had their price tags attached. At least it might help with bargaining power when she took them to the designer recyclers because they could see they hadn't been worn and what the original price had been. When she tallied up the dollars of just the items with the price tags, Suzy could not believe that a new medium-sized car could be bought with the money.

The clothes and accessories in their wardrobe boxes were stored in the garage of Suzy's neighbour as there was not enough room in the small place she rented. The plan was to take some of the most recent purchases first and see what she could get for them. By the end of the first week, she had $2,500 to give Meredith and was stunned when she was handed back $500 for all the work she had done and the groceries she had bought but never been paid for. You just never knew what Meredith would do next.

Clearing the wardrobe boxes and their contents from the unit had given Meredith much needed space. The $2,000 should keep the wolf from the door for a while, but Suzy suspected that, with Meredith's previous spending habits, some of it would be wasted on gourmet pizza and a bottle of Moët. After all, it was her money, but she didn't have a clue how to make it go the distance because she still hadn't accepted that she was not yet destitute, but it was lurking just around the corner if she didn't change her ways. In Suzy's opinion, Meredith coming to grips with her situation was as likely as her swimming around the entire coast of Australia.

Even though it was a company van that had been loaned free of charge, Suzy made sure that it was filled up with fuel before it was handed back and used some of the money Meredith had given her. Brady would not take a cent for his help and reassured Suzy he would do anything for her as he had never had a woman as wonderful as she was in his life. Over the next month, Suzy spent a considerable amount of time on weekends going to designer recycling shops all over Sydney. Brady happily accompanied her, and they were always able to fit in lunch or a few drinks at the end of the day.

The money was accumulating from the sales, but Suzy was reluctant to hand it over in a lump sum given Meredith's freewheeling spending habits, which were still not expunged from her mindset. She suggested to Meredith that she would deposit half the money with the real estate agent to give her a paid-up roof over her head for at least the next few months. Predictably, Meredith was reluctant to do this, but Suzy was determined in her efforts to try to delay as long as possible the looming homelessness of her former employer. Budgeting was still a foreign language, and cutting down on her cosmetics from luxury to everyday brands had not yet happened. When the last of the money was handed over, Suzy was alarmed to see the "gleam of spending" in Meredith's eyes.

"This is all there is, Meredith. You have a roof over your head for the next few months, and you need to put some of this cash away to pay for your phone and electricity bills and stock up your cupboards. Also, you need to make sure Pamela's vaccinations are up to date while you have some money. Are you listening to me, or are you planning how many bottles of Moët this will buy?"

Rather shamefacedly, Meredith admitted that the latter option was more attractive than the boring first part of the conversation. "I'll do my best, Suzy, but I can't promise there won't be some Moët in there somewhere. It's very hard being short of money, you know."

Suzy found it hard to not reply, "And you don't think I am aware of how hard it is to budget, rent, and be a single parent with a teenage daughter?" But she knew it would fall on deaf ears, so she just let herself out of the apartment after giving Pamela a hug and ruffling her rather unkempt fur.

Twenty-Six

By the end of the next six months, Meredith was broke. Rent was due, the electricity bill was unpaid, and her mobile phone was about to be disconnected for the same reason. The Kombi had to be registered and the green slip paid for. She had been on her own for nearly a year, and the only person she kept in contact with from her previous lifestyle was Suzy, whom she suspected was getting a bit fed up with her. When she didn't think things could get worse, she was served with a notice from the real estate agents that she had one month to vacate the premises or bring her rent up to date immediately. Facing homelessness was her new reality.

She had no money for a bond, even if she could find another property for an affordable amount, and it was unlikely the real estate agent would give her a good reference. She was unemployed and living on Centrelink benefits, not quite where she thought she would be at this stage in her life as she had been the owner of a successful company, married to a good-looking and successful financier, and regularly appearing in the social pages. She was angry with her parents for spending her inheritance but ignored the fact that they adopted her so she would not be put into foster care. She was angry with Foster for killing himself but avoided any anger directed at herself for her part in her own downfall. She chose to forget about the lavish lifestyle she had demanded they lead and the extremely expensive overseas tour that had brought about Foster's downfall and subsequent death.

She had one last chance to put some money in her bank account, and that was to sell her jewellery. She still had her diamond engagement and wedding rings, several pairs of earrings, bracelets, and necklets set with different precious stones. She also had Margaret's engagement and wedding rings. The first things to go were her own engagement and wedding rings, but the sale didn't go quite as Meredith had planned.

Ever conscious of presentation, Meredith dressed in her best leather coat, knee-high boots, and a leather bag that held part of her last saleable possessions. She took a train into the city to an area where the shopfronts promised "Jewellery bought and sold. Fair prices guaranteed."

She approached the first doorway, which was barred for security reasons with a sign instructing "Please ring bell to enter," which she did. Meredith entered the store and, for once in her life, was nervous about conducting this transaction. She was aware of how much the two rings were insured for and knew she would be lucky to get half their value, but it would be a start.

"Good morning. I'm Gerard, the store owner. What can I help you with today?"

"Oh, hello. I have some very expensive jewellery I would like you to have a look at for me. I'm thinking of selling it but only if I get what I think it's worth. Do we understand each other?"

"Perfectly understood," he replied as a felt mat was placed on top of the glass counter. "I'll have a look at the pieces and give you my estimation of what I'm prepared to pay for them. However, I must warn you that it will be nowhere near the purchase price. Do we understand each other?"

"Perfectly understood," she replied as she sat down on the chair opposite the jeweller.

After looking at the engagement and wedding rings with his jeweller's loupe and under a strong light, he asked Meredith, "You do know these are not diamonds, don't you?"

Meredith replied, "What kind of jeweller are you? Of course, they're diamonds. They have been insured for a number of years. My deceased husband bought them for me."

"Madam, I have been a jeweller for forty years, and I know a diamond when I see one, just as I know when a stone is not a diamond. However, as you are unhappy with my opinion, I suggest you take them elsewhere and have someone else look at them. I would not be offering any money as I only buy and sell jewellery set with precious stones."

He held the two rings out to Meredith, and she snatched them out of his hand and approached the door. "Let me out. I won't be coming back here with the rest of my collection."

Meredith walked a few blocks and found another shop. She entered and spoke to the wizened elderly man sitting on a stool behind the counter. She gave him the same spiel that she had given Gerard about the expensive jewellery she was thinking of selling. He didn't say a word, but again, a felt mat was placed on the counter, and he suggested that she should put her items on it. He went through the same process as Gerard and, unfortunately for Meredith, expressed the same opinion. The stones were not diamonds but a man-made imitation worth only the value of the gold in both rings. The price was a far cry from the many thousands of dollars Meredith had been expecting and had already earmarked for some beauty treatments and a case or two of Moët.

She hadn't even bothered to take out any of the other earrings, necklets, or bracelets as she was in total shock. She had the awful feeling that the rest of the jewellery he had bought her over the years was also in the same category. She scooped up the two rings and threw them back in her handbag. She was so angry with Foster that he had allowed her to be subjected to this embarrassing situation.

Money in her bank account was the driving force of her day, so after two glasses of champagne in a dimly lit bar, she once again sought to sell some of the other pieces. She was not going to produce the "diamond" rings on this occasion. The next jeweller carefully examined each piece one by one, putting them in two separate piles, and then scribbled figures down on a pad that was on the shelf behind him, out of Meredith's eyesight. As he placed the last piece on the mat, he handed one of the piles back to Meredith.

"These bracelets and earrings aren't worth anything, I'm sorry to say. They are gold plated. However, there are some nice pieces over here." He pointed to the smaller pile of earrings and necklets. "I can offer you $3,500. Do you accept the price?" he asked.

Meredith felt she had no choice but to accept the offer. She was dispirited and knew her back was against the wall. She had come into the city today thinking that she would possibly be $30,000 richer by the end of the day, and instead, this man was offering to transfer just over 10 per cent of that amount into her bank. It was a take-it-or-leave-it situation, and she had no more energy left to be going around the city trying to better the price. She handed over her banking details and left the store with two fake diamond rings, a handful of gold-plated trinkets, and a receipt for $3,500.

Once home via the boutique wine shop for a bottle of Moët, she rang Suzy and started complaining about how Foster had bought worthless jewellery and how she now only had $3,500 to last her seemingly forever. Suzy suggested she pay off all her bills, get ahead with her rent, and save the rest for a rainy day. All these sensible suggestions fell on deaf ears. The main point of the conversation was that Foster had tricked her into believing she had valuable jewellery and that she had had a tiring and extremely embarrassing morning being told her rings weren't worth anything. "How would you feel about that, Suzy?" moaned Meredith down the phone line.

"Well, unlike you, I would be looking at it in the light of the $3,500 that you now have to help you survive as the pieces of jewellery are not going to house and feed you, are they? All you have left now is this money and the Kombi, so I wouldn't be wasting it if I were you, especially on Moët." Meredith had the uncomfortable feeling that Suzy could see into her rented flat as she held a glass of champagne to her lips.

How long could she make the money last? Her choices were fast becoming the streets or living in the VW Kombi van, the thought of which made her shudder. She couldn't even drive it anywhere and would have to call on Suzy or Brady to help her – once again. She was depressed and, for once in her life, thought that some of it might have been her fault, especially the regular bottles of Moët that she had previously purchased until Suzy had firmly removed them from her fortnightly shopping allocation. Meredith knew she had a lot to do with her budgetary dilemmas mainly because, in her previous life, she had spent hours in front of the mirror primping and preening, but now the mousy brown hair and the unflattering haircut (acquired cheaply at a local salon) were just more than she could bear.

Some months later when her bank account was once again becoming seriously close to zero dollars, she called Suzy for help. She explained that she needed to learn how to drive that "revolting thing outside" as she had been given notice to vacate the flat, and it looked like she would be sharing a home with her parents again, the irony of which was not lost on Suzy. Brady offered to teach her how to drive, and Meredith was a bit taken aback to learn that Larissa and Suzy were planning to move into his apartment. She had no idea that their relationship had reached that level. She was pleased for Suzy but apprehensive that her support system might be otherwise occupied in the future.

While they were having coffee one day, paid for by Suzy, Meredith broached the idea that perhaps if she and Larissa were going to move in with Brady, they could rent a bigger place, and she could share. Suzy was instantly averse to this idea as she knew that Brady had worked Meredith out very early in their relationship. In his words, "I have never met a more self-centred person in my life, and I don't know how you put up with her."

The driving lessons proceeded as promised, even though Meredith hated the vehicle with a passion and still couldn't come to terms with the fact this was the new roof over her head. It was either this, under a bridge, or in a tent as Brady had pointed out.

"Your choices are limited, Meredith, so you may as well get used to the idea. You can't afford private accommodation. The social housing list is at least fifteen years long, and refuges for single women are few and far between. You might need to start thinking of the Kombi as a plus, not a minus. Now let's start again with the clutch and gears."

After searching the Internet, Suzy discovered that Meredith could park the van in several caravan parks around Sydney's suburban areas; but of course, it was going to cost money – an item that was in short supply. The other alternative, much less attractive, was to move the van around suburban streets and only use the van parks one or two days a week for showers etc. This should be financially doable, providing the tiny fridge did not contain an endless supply of Moët. Predictably, Meredith was horrified at the prospect of living in suburban streets. "I have always lived in the city. I have no idea how to live in the suburbs."

"Well, Meredith, it's the only alternative. You can park on the streets of a suburb provided you adhere to the times shown on the parking signs. You must be legally parked and have your vehicle registered. It is registered, isn't it?"

"Yes, that's one thing I managed to do while I still had money, but I don't know how I am going to come up with the money for a green slip next time. Just another problem I have to cope with."

Suzy thought but didn't say, *You have no idea what you are going to be up against, Meredith, but most of your present situation is of your own making.*

Meredith had asked Brady if he would help her move out of the flat and if Suzy would try to sell whatever she could on eBay, hoping for a few more dollars to keep her going. Meredith had transferred only a few of her possessions into the Kombi, given that there was very little room. Larissa was coerced into looking after the ageing Pamela while this all took place. It was no hardship for her as she had always loved the little dog, but she was worried about what would happen to her in the future. She just hoped that Meredith looked after Pamela if she got sick and needed treatment of any kind, putting something or someone before herself for a change, although that theory hadn't been tested yet.

Twenty-Seven

Meredith drove the Kombi van behind Brady and Suzy until they found a suitable spot in an inner-city suburb not far from them that looked reasonably safe for her to spend the night. It had finally dawned on her that this was the first day of the rest of her life, and she was terrified. Pamela picked up on Meredith's anxious vibes and softly whimpered as she tried to get close to her on the front seat.

Suzy suggested to Meredith that they take Pamela with them. There wasn't much room in the Kombi, and Meredith would have to get up in the night if Pamela needed to go to the toilet. The idea of getting out of the Kombi, parked by the kerb in an unfamiliar suburb, had no appeal. Meredith was more than happy to hand the little dog over. After a few hugs, Meredith was left alone standing beside the Kombi, watching her only friends and her dog drive off into the distance. She had never felt so alone in her whole life and really frightened about what the future held for her.

The refrigerator in the Kombi was battery powered and quite small but would hold enough for a few meals. The cooking facilities were limited, equally matching Meredith's skills in that area. During the time she'd lived alone, she hadn't bothered to learn how to cook very much and had relied on the noodle shop down the corner and gourmet pizzas being delivered when she had too much Moët on board to go out. Lunch seemed like a long time ago, so Meredith ordered a meal and coffee which cost her twenty-five of her diminishing dollars. She finally realised that eating out or buying takeaway was no longer an option.

Brady had advised her that she could only stay a day or so in any one place if she didn't want to bring attention to herself living in the van. There were a lot of stickers on the van representing places her parents or the previous owners had been. This would draw enough attention from curious people, seeing the same person emerging from the vehicle at different times of the day. She also had to be somewhere close to a park so she could access public toilets or those located in cafes, where she might buy coffee and a cake. Reality check – coffee and cake were no longer in her budget.

After two days, she moved on to another street in another suburb. On the third day, she phoned a caravan park a few kilometres from the city and discovered it would cost her about $40 per night for a powered site, so she booked in for the next day. Upon arrival, she packed some clean clothes, toiletries, and a towel and headed for the shower block. She was refreshed after her shower and went back to the van to lie down for a while.

After only four days of being without a permanent address, she was finding that the effort required just to feed and keep herself clean was already too much. She didn't know how to use the stove in the kitchen and suspected it had something to do with a gas bottle that appeared to be attached to it. While she was on the powered site, she could use the microwave, which was within her range of domestic skills, limited though they were. The park shop had ready-made meals with prices that were much higher than she had anticipated, but she bought one anyway as she had exhausted the food supplies in the cupboard, and the fridge only contained cheese and milk.

She felt quite safe in the park, and the site she was on had plenty of shade, so she paid for another night. She was reluctant to leave the park and move back into the streets, but at $280 per week, it was far too big a chunk to come out of her pension, and now she didn't have the rent assistance to help. She still had to eat and buy fuel for the van. At the end of the first week, Meredith had spent five nights in suburban streets and two in a caravan park. This would be her life unless the gods of employment smiled on her, which she felt was an idea without much hope of fruition.

After three months of this life, she was exhausted and dispirited, felt grubby, and was fed up of constantly moving every few days. Even though Brady had advised against it, she drove to a beachside suburb with an amenities block. The local council was quite strict about vans being parked overnight, but Meredith decided to ignore Brady's warning. In her mind, he thought he knew everything, but she didn't have to take his word for it.

There seemed to be a few people around, but it was getting late in the day, so she hurriedly showered as the amenities were empty. When she emerged after a lovely though brief hot shower, the car park was empty. Her van was missing. At first, she couldn't believe her eyes. Even though she initially hated the Kombi, it would be nice right now to see it where she had left it. Fortunately, she had her mobile in the amenities block with her, so she phoned Suzy.

She was hysterical on the phone, and after Suzy told her a few times to calm down because she couldn't understand what she was saying, Meredith related what had happened in the last thirty minutes. It was almost dark, she was in a deserted car park, and her van was missing. Suzy suggested she phone the police immediately and report the van stolen. In her panic, Meredith couldn't remember the licence plate number and had to go to the entrance of the car park to be able to tell the police which beach she was at.

Within twenty minutes, a police car pulled up, and two officers emerged. "You reported a missing vehicle?"

"Yes, Officer. My Kombi van was stolen. I parked it right over there and went into the amenities block to have a shower. When I came out, it was gone." And she then burst into tears.

"Okay, come and sit in the car, and we'll take down some details and put it out over the network."

After they had taken down all the information, they asked Meredith if there was somewhere they could take her. She tearfully explained she had no relatives and only one friend who might be able to put her up for a night, but she would have to check first. Once again, she called Suzy. But this time, Brady answered the phone. "Hi, Meredith, what's happening? Have the police arrived?"

Through her tears, Meredith explained that she now had no home and was wondering if Suzy could come and pick her up from the park and let her stay with them for a few days. There was a pause and an audible sigh from Brady. "Well, under the circumstances, we can hardly turn you away, but it can only be until you find somewhere to go, Meredith. We don't have a spare room, so it will be the couch, I'm afraid. Tell me where you are now, and I'll ask Suzy to come and get you when she leaves work."

Meredith thanked him and waited at the park entrance for Suzy to appear and take her back to their place. After speaking with him, it was obvious that Brady called the shots in that household, and she didn't want to stay there any longer than she absolutely had to. Once again, she was oblivious to the challenges that would be facing her in the weeks and months to come.

She had never been to Brady and Suzy's home and was surprised to see just how small the inner-city terrace was. Fortunately, there was a backyard for Pamela to get out in. However, according to Brady, the little dog would have to sleep in the laundry, but he hadn't reckoned on Larissa's long-time attachment to Pamela.

Dinner was already under way when Suzy and Meredith came through the front door. The couple worked different hours, so it was Brady's job to start dinner before Suzy got home, and she was surprised at how good a cook he was. Meredith was not used to men cooking. Her father had never done so, and Foster – well, the only thing he ever made was reservations wherever and whenever Meredith decreed.

The dinner was delicious, and Pamela was happy with the leftovers put down for her. There were moments of awkward silence throughout the meal, and it was obvious that the couple needed to talk about this latest catastrophe in the life of Meredith. At about nine, Suzy brought out a pillow, sheets, and quilt and then converted the couch to a bed with some tugging of levers. All that Meredith had with her was her toiletries bag, a damp towel, and the clothes she had taken off before her shower and the ones she had on. It was the least amount of possessions she had ever had in her life.

Suzy gave Meredith a hug and reassured her, "We'll talk in the morning and work out the next step if you don't get the Kombi back, okay?"

"Thanks, Suzy. I really appreciate you coming to help me out once again. Hope this isn't going to be a habit."

So do I, thought Suzy, *although I can't see an end to the trials and tribulations of Meredith Cunningham-Browne anytime soon. Her situation is just getting worse with every passing day.*

Twenty-Eight

There was tension in the household the next morning when Meredith emerged from her cocoon on the couch. Brady was having coffee out on the back terrace, reading the paper, and he didn't look up as he greeted her with "Hope you slept well."

Meredith replied, "Yes, I did. Thanks, and I appreciate you putting me up for the night."

"When you check out places today for a more permanent accommodation, you are welcome to use my computer. I think the sooner you get started . . ." He left the sentence hanging.

It was not lost on Meredith that her staying with Brady and Suzy was seen as a rescue mission for the short term rather than indefinite. She had no idea where to even start looking on the Internet, but Larissa offered to help her on the computer. Pamela had been taken across to the park for her morning toileting and was sitting quite comfortably in Larissa's lap while the computer was booted up.

"Maybe get a coffee, Meredith, and we'll get started on the search." It was becoming all too real for Meredith that she was expected to move and soon.

"But what if I can't find something? What will I do then?" It was obvious from the tone of her voice that moving to an unknown destination was quite frightening and not something she was keen to even start contemplating.

"Well, there must be somewhere that a single woman can find to stay, so we'll start with boarding houses first. What do you think?" asked Larissa. Meredith wasn't brave enough to voice what she thought, which was that Brady was being selfish and Suzy had become spineless since she had met him.

Larissa set to work trying to find long-term accommodation for Meredith. Boarding houses, if there was a vacant room, would take two-thirds of her pension, and then she had to feed herself without the benefit of a kitchen. The latter had never bothered Meredith in the past, but now that she had limited money, she knew it was going to be difficult. Private rental was out of the question with Centrelink benefits as her only income. She had no money for a bond of four weeks' rent, which was standard, and two weeks' rent in advance. Her credit history would not stand up to scrutiny, and there was very little rental accommodation at the low end of the market.

Nearly all the places that Larissa found would not allow animals, so that was the first hurdle. Larissa had already asked her mother if they could keep Pamela if Meredith couldn't find somewhere to live that would allow animals. Brady and Suzy agreed that the old dog would be fine with them but had not mentioned it to Meredith yet.

There was one vacancy at a hotel a few suburbs away, and Larissa asked them to hold the room until her mother could get over there later and let Meredith have a look at it. Suzy drove them to the Emperor Hotel, and one look at the facade was enough to make them both think this was not going to end well. Meredith didn't even want to get out of the car; Suzy was just as determined that she would.

Brady and Suzy had had a long talk about what Meredith's future was likely to be and agreed that it was going to be nothing like her past. Whether she was equipped emotionally to cope was something they could do nothing about. She had led a privileged life, taken no responsibility for her present financial circumstances, and felt that the world owed her. Entitlement had been her attitude for most of her life, but what neither of them wanted was for her to be a permanent resident on their couch.

"Meredith, I know this must be very scary for you and not where you thought you would be at this time in your life, but this is your reality. We'll go and have a look at the room and then sit somewhere, have coffee, and talk about your options, okay?" Meredith just nodded dumbly, and Suzy could see the fear in her eyes.

They walked from the car to the office area, and Suzy asked if Meredith could see the room available. The manager informed them in a no-nonsense voice, "The tariff is $280 per week, payable in advance. And if in arrears, then tenancy would be terminated. The bathroom is shared between four rooms, and it's expected that it would be left clean and tidy after each tenant's use. It's first in, best dressed and no arguments about how long someone has been in there. It's queue up and shut up. No animals allowed. No smoking in the rooms, and no cooking appliances in the room other than a kettle. No visitors to stay after 10 p.m. and noise to be kept to a minimum. Keep your door locked always. Those are the rules. Do you want to see the room or not?"

"Er, yes, I suppose so," stammered Suzy while Meredith just stood there like a deer in the headlights.

She tugged on Suzy's sleeve as they walked up the stairs and whispered, "I don't know about sharing a bathroom. Haven't they got one with an en suite?" Suzy just rolled her eyes and continued up the stairs without answering.

The room was at the front on the first floor, and it had been decades since its original dark wood picture rails, hanging light with deceased insects trapped within, peeling yellow floral wallpaper, and clashing rose-patterned carpet had been the decoration of the day. It was clean, and the bed was covered in another type of floral quilt. It gave the impression that someone had thrown a bouquet of mixed flowers into the room, and they had stuck on the walls, floor, and bed. Meredith was speechless when she saw the pink-and-black-tiled bathroom with a shower curtain covered in blue fish.

Suzy spoke to the manager. "Thanks for letting us take a look. We'll just go downstairs and have a chat over a drink. We'll get back to you in about half an hour. Is that okay?" The manager just nodded and walked back in the direction of his office.

"I need a very stiff drink, Suzy. That is horrendous, and they want to charge almost two-thirds of my pension every week to stay in it?"

"I'm afraid that it's very difficult to get a room that you can afford, and at least this one was clean and tidy, although old-fashioned in decor. Your choices are limited, Meredith, and you must realise that by now."

"Well, could I just stay with you until I find out about the Kombi? The police haven't been in touch yet, and I don't want to move in here if I have to move out again." Suzy knew that this was not going to sit well with Brady at all.

"I don't think that would be acceptable to Brady, but perhaps a week wouldn't be so bad. Meredith, just a word of advice, you can't just leave the couch in a mess like you did this morning. After all, it is our living area. You aren't living in a hotel yet, and we aren't the staff. I'll talk to Brady and get back to you, but whatever he says goes, okay?"

No, not okay, Meredith thought. *Bossy Brady telling her the rules. Who does he think he is anyway?*

That night, Suzy told Meredith that she could stay for a week, but that was all, whether the Kombi was found or not. Meredith had a sullen look on her face, but Suzy chose to ignore it. Brady was more important than Meredith's hurt feelings or selfishness. Suzy was sure that a week was going to be more than enough to have their household turned upside down. Going to work for five of the next seven days was going to be a blessing.

Three days later, the police contacted Meredith on her mobile with the news that the Kombi had been found in northern NSW but had been burned out. They said the details of the police report would be forwarded to her email address for the insurance company. She thanked them for their efforts and collapsed onto the couch. No need for an email for the insurance company – she had never insured the "ugly thing," as she had referred to it, and now she had no home and a very short tenancy on the couch. Four days to go, and she was out on the streets.

That night after dinner, she told Suzy that the Kombi had been found but had been burned out. She didn't mention the thought that her parents had been cremated once again. "Well, at least you'll get insurance, Meredith. That will help in your present circumstances, won't it?"

"It wasn't insured. I couldn't afford it at the time, so I let it lapse."

Suzy was not surprised that insuring a vehicle had not been on Meredith's must-do list. She had only ever leased cars, and someone else had taken care of those details, usually Suzy when she had worked for Meredith and then Foster after they married who also arranged cars through his company. What a mess! No Kombi, no insurance, and no roof over her head with only a pension to live on. All her clothes, bags, and shoes were in the Kombi, which was now a burnt-out wreck somewhere in northern NSW. A shopping trip would have to be organised but not to the high-end boutiques Meredith usually frequented but to one of Suzy's favourite charity shops just down the road. That was certainly going to be a new experience for one of them – and it wasn't Suzy.

The next morning, Suzy told Meredith that they needed to go shopping but made it clear that it wasn't going to be the usual experience she had had in the past. "You need clothes, underwear, shoes, toiletries, and make-up and maybe a coat for when it gets colder. After breakfast, we'll go to Salvos at Tempe first and then try a couple of Vinnies shops. You can get most of what you need at those places, and it's going to be the cheapest way to replace your lost clothing. We'll leave at ten o'clock, okay?" Suzy left Meredith with a dumbstruck look on her face.

Shopping in charity shops? What do they think I am? Poor? "I can't go in there," Meredith whined as Suzy took her firmly by the arm towards the entry to the Salvos. "It smells of old stuff."

"Meredith, this is your one chance to replace your clothing and other things you need. I only have today, and you know that Brady is expecting you to move out in two days' time, so you have to buy things to set yourself up wherever you go. How much money do you have to spend?"

"I only have about $200," replied Meredith.

"That should be enough. You'll also need a large suitcase to put it all in." At the mention of a suitcase to "put it all in," Meredith felt quite ill. This was what she had been reduced to – a bag lady.

Suzy had developed a no-nonsense attitude, which Meredith attributed to being with Bossy Brady for too long. She would never have been like this had she not met him. Maybe she could even have talked Suzy around to letting her stay more permanently but totally overlooked the fact that it was Brady's house they were all living in, including Pamela.

After two hours of wandering up and down aisles of clothes, shoes, underwear, cosmetics, and all that the Salvos had to offer, Suzy had to tell Meredith that she had better start finding something that fitted, even if it wasn't this season's fashion. She was getting fed up with the constant rejection of quite good clothing because of Meredith's constant complaining about how she wouldn't be seen dead in that. Suzy did her best to hold her temper but was determined that she would find at least some tops, pants, underwear, and shoes that Meredith could be seen alive in.

"How do people live like this and have to buy this awful clothing?"

"It's not awful clothing, Meredith. It's just not designer label, like you're used to. How do you think I used to manage as a single mother to come to the office well dressed as decreed by you, pay rent and childcare, as well as feed myself and Larissa? Did it ever occur to you that this might be the way I managed that?"

Meredith just shook her head. "No, I never really thought about it," she admitted. "It wasn't something I ever had to do."

"Well, you were the lucky one then, weren't you?"

Twenty-Nine

When Suzy and Meredith eventually arrived back at the house, the bags were unpacked on the couch, which had been cleared of the previous night's bedding. Brady was again out in the terraced area, having coffee, and didn't show any interest in what had been bought. He was just glad that it was another step in the outward journey of Meredith, and he looked forward to that happening in two days.

The longer Meredith stayed, the more Suzy agreed with him that a week was more than enough sharing their space with her. She occasionally made coffee, but where she finished it was where the cup stayed. The couch was not cleared off until late afternoon, and that left very few areas that the other three could use. Fortunately, the terraced area outside was large enough for a table and outdoor chairs, and Pamela had laid claim to a folded-up old rug under a cane lounge. She wasn't nimble enough anymore to jump up onto the chairs, and if Larissa lifted her, it was obvious that it hurt the little dog when she had to get down. As no accommodation had been sourced that would allow Pamela to stay, it was mutually decided that she would continue to live with Larissa, who had always loved the little dog.

Suzy encouraged Meredith to use the washing machine and freshen up all the clothing she had bought so it felt more like it belonged to her. No amount of washing was going to give her that feeling, but she went along with the suggestion anyway. She knew time was running out, and moving day was approaching at a faster rate than she had thought possible. With reluctance, she had agreed to stay at the hotel for the short term until she found somewhere better. Unbeknown to Meredith, Suzy had paid a week in advance to make sure that the hotel kept the single room for her as they had not managed to find anywhere else that was available at such short notice. She had discussed this move with Brady, and he agreed tongue-in-cheek that it was the best investment she would ever make.

The next morning after a slowly eaten breakfast and other delaying tactics by Meredith, Suzy packed the meagre belongings of her former employer into her car and drove the few kilometres to the Emperor Hotel. Suzy had instructed Meredith to make sure that she had the $560 required for the first two weeks but didn't mention that she had already paid one week to hold the booking. Suzy looked on the $280 she had paid as insurance against Meredith needing to come back to live with her and Brady again.

When she got back home, Brady had a bottle of wine and two glasses set out on the table. "What are we celebrating?" asked Suzy, although she suspected it was the relocation of Meredith.

"Having our space back," replied Brady, "even though it now includes an arthritic old dog."

Suzy's mobile rang before she had even lifted the glass to her lips, and when she saw it was Meredith, she commented to Brady, "Gone but obviously not forgetting us." And she showed him the screen. "What could possibly be wrong now?"

"Whatever it is, it's probably not life threatening. Drink up. You deserve it."

"I just want to really thank you for what you've had to put up with since you've known me. Meredith was good to me, in some ways and only if it suited her, when I was working for her. I know her present situation is mostly her own fault, but I couldn't just abandon her. I really appreciate you giving over our home to her, though I'm glad she's moved on. I thought, at one stage, I might have to get a bulldozer to move her out, but she went quietly enough – for Meredith. I love you, Brady, and thank the powers that be we crossed paths and are so happy together. I hope you don't mind too much that Larissa wanted to keep Pamela. She is a sweet little dog and doesn't take up much room."

"Would rather have her on the couch than her mother," he replied in his dry wit way.

"I suppose I had better return her call, but I might need another drink before I do."

"No problem. One white wine coming up." And he leaned down and kissed Suzy on the forehead before he disappeared inside to refill their glasses.

"What's the matter, Meredith?" enquired Suzy when her call was answered.

"I didn't buy any bath towels. I thought they would be supplied like all hotels do."

"Well, if you go down to the local shopping centre, I am sure there will be a Kmart, Target, or Reject Shop that can help you out with that. You might want to work out where the nearest laundromat is for your usual washing too."

"Oh." Meredith hesitated. "I thought I could perhaps bring that to your place when you aren't using your machine."

"I don't think that would work, Meredith. You don't have a car, and I work irregular hours, so it wouldn't be convenient. Check out the laundromat. It will be closer for you," stated Suzy firmly before she terminated the call.

Brady heard the end of the conversation and handed Suzy her glass. "Thanks, darling. Meredith didn't buy any towels and thought that all hotels supplied them. They might if they have a few stars after their name, but I don't think the Emperor Hotel quite runs to even one star. This is going to be a steep learning curve for her, I'm afraid."

"She'll survive, but it won't be a life she has been used to, that's for sure. I don't think waiting patiently to use a bathroom is in her DNA. I think the manager was quite adamant when he said the tenants had to queue up and shut up. Meredith is only marginally good at queuing, and as for the other instruction, that's going to cause her a lot of grief, I feel."

"Stand by for the next exciting episode" as they say on television.

Meanwhile, Meredith had followed Suzy's advice – unusual though that was for her to do – and walked down to the local shopping centre and located a supermarket. Not far away was a laundromat, and Meredith was anxious when she looked at how much it cost to wash and dry clothes. Most of the clothes from her previous life were dropped off to the dry cleaners by Suzy and collected at a later date; the cost was added to Meredith's credit card, paid for by Foster. It was a system that worked well for Meredith but for neither of the other two.

Meredith slowly walked back to the hotel. She now had less than $100 in her purse and another ten days to go before the Centrelink benefits appeared in her bank account. How was she going to live on $10 a day? She had no microwave to heat anything, and it was strictly forbidden to have an electric appliance other than a kettle. The small fridge provided in the room would hold milk and a few other things but nothing she had to cook. She was sure the manager would not hesitate to check this detail when the cleaners did their rounds, whenever that was.

Later that day, she used the cheap towels after her shower; and because they were new, they hardly dried her off. This put her in a bad mood for the rest of the day, and as evening approached, she had to give thought to what she would have for dinner. She checked the menu in the dining room downstairs that advised her that steak, chips, and salad would be eighteen dollars; chicken schnitzel, chips, and salad sixteen dollars; and so on. Every price was above her ten dollars allocated for the day. It eventually dawned on her that she also had to supply herself with two other meals within that amount.

How does the government expect anyone to survive on this ridiculously small amount of money? I have paid taxes – and a lot of them – all my life, and now I get reduced to poverty because of my parents and stupid husband. Oh, I could just scream.

Fortunately, she had passed a noodle bar when looking for the supermarket, so she walked back to check on their prices. There were quite a few people there, and as it was almost closing time, a takeaway container could be bought for five dollars. Meredith stood in line and handed over her money. Noodles were becoming part of her diet, it would seem. Thank goodness Larissa had wanted to keep Pamela, or she wouldn't have been able to feed her too. At least tonight she wouldn't be hungry, but tomorrow was another day.

Thirty

Meredith was not happy in her hotel room. The traffic noise from the main road kept her awake at night, and a woman who had a room at the other end of the corridor walked up and down the hallway incessantly. Meredith could hear the slap-slap of her slippers and the woman's mumbling every moment that the traffic kept her awake.

She complained to Tom, the manager, about the noise of this woman mumbling and stumbling along the hallway, and she had caught her using "her" bathroom. Tom listened to what she had to say and then explained that Sylvia had mental health issues, slept all day, and walked all night. She didn't have any friends or relatives and had lived in the hotel for a few years. He also explained that she liked to use the pink bathroom at Meredith's end of the hall as the other one was green, and she didn't like that colour.

After listening to Tom's explanation of the nocturnal wanderer, Meredith told him, "Well, I'm paying good money to stay here, and I think you should do something about her disturbing my sleep. It's driving me mad."

Tom gave her a steely glare and delivered the message. "Listen, Meredith, this is not a prison, and you are free to go anytime you like. It wouldn't hurt if you had a bit of compassion for the poor soul as well." He just turned his back and went into the room behind the bar.

Meredith could not believe that her request to do something about the wanderer had been ignored. If he wasn't going to do something about Sylvia, then maybe she had to consider her options and move somewhere that had a better level of clientele. She decided she would speak to Suzy about this problem at the next opportunity. It just wasn't good enough to have her sleep disturbed nightly.

A few days later, after sleepless nights of tyres squealing outside the window and slippers slapping along the hallway, Meredith was fed up. She phoned Suzy at work, totally ignoring the fact that she had a very busy job and that personal phone calls were to be kept to a minimum. Suzy had just answered the call when Meredith started her list of complaints about the hotel and the resident down the hallway. Before Meredith managed to get into full stride, Suzy interrupted her with "This is not a good time to chat, Meredith. I will ring you tonight after dinner, but frankly, I don't know what you expect me to do about it, okay? Call you about 7:30. Bye for now." And the call was terminated.

This was not working out at all for Meredith. She had expected some empathy from Suzy, not to be cut off mid-sentence. *Just goes to show how selfish some people can be. It's all right for her with her new life and Bossy Brady to keep her company. Here I am in an inner-city hotel and too scared to go out any farther than the local shops. Well, tonight I will just let Suzy know how inconvenient it is for me living here because they wouldn't let me stay with them. I didn't mind the couch, and at least there was decent food to eat.*

Meredith's phone rang at 7:40 that night, and she let it ring a few times before she answered it in an attempt to have Suzy worry that something had happened to her. When she finally accepted the call, it was with a hurt tone in her voice. "Hi, Suzy. I thought you had forgotten about me. You said 7:30, and it is ten minutes after that now."

"I did say I would ring after dinner, and I have done so. What's the problem now?"

Meredith launched into her string of complaints about the traffic noise and Sylvia walking up and down the corridor, mumbling to herself all night, and using "her" bathroom rather than the one at her end of the floor. And eventually, she ran out of problems to tell Suzy about.

"Well, Meredith, you don't have to stay there if it doesn't suit you. Look for somewhere else and see if you can do better is my suggestion. Anyway, I'm sorry it's not working out for you, but maybe you could make a friend of Sylvia. She certainly sounds like she could do with one."

"She's not my sort of person with her mumbling and shuffling. And you should see what she looks like. Her hair hasn't seen a comb or a decent cut for a long time, so I don't think we would have a lot in common really. Anyway, I might have a look for somewhere else that has a better class of resident. Bye for now. I'll let you know how I go." And with that, she finished the call.

On her end of the phone, Suzy had a bemused look on her face; and when Brady asked what was wrong in Meredith's world now, Suzy sat down and gave him a brief rundown of the call. "She just doesn't get it, does she? She has no money left in the bank, lives on Centrelink benefits, is in one bedroom of an inner-city hotel, and is annoyed that the woman at the other end of the hall walks all night and talks to herself. She's also critical of the woman's appearance, but has she really looked in a mirror lately? If she moves out or is asked to leave by the manager, she will be sleeping all day and walking at night because that's what a lot of homeless people do apparently."

Brady replied, "It's hard to feel sorry for her when most of this is her own fault because she has always had an inflated sense of her own importance and place in the world. Maybe we could have a look on the computer and see if we can find her a placement in a refuge. At least she would have a bit more money each fortnight. What do you think?"

Suzy cuddled up to Brady. "You're such a caring guy. I know she drove you crazy when she was here with her messiness, and we don't have the space or the inclination for her to return, but if we could get her a place, that was more to her liking."

Brady burst into laughter. "That's what I love about you, Suzy, your eternal optimism. Somewhere more to her liking, did you say? How about we just cut to the chase and ring the best five-star hotels in town and see if they have any vacancies?" For this comment, he got a sharp dig in the ribs from Suzy's elbow, and they both burst into laughter.

After checking the Internet for information on refuges, they learned that Meredith would have to apply to some agencies to try to get a placement. She was not a victim of domestic violence, did not have drug or alcohol dependency, did not have diagnosed mental health issues, and had no accompanying children to accommodate. Suzy contacted Meredith over the weekend to let her know that she and Brady had been trying to find a place for her in a women's refuge and didn't receive the response she expected.

"Suzy, I appreciate the work you have done, but I'm not sure I want to mix with people like that."

"What do you mean 'people like that'?"

"Well, you know, people who are mentally ill or drink too much. Some could be on drugs, and they might smell. I don't see that working out. I saw Sylvia outside my bathroom the other morning and told her to kindly keep to her end of the hallway, but I don't think she had any idea who I was or what I was talking about. She seemed a bit out of it to me, probably on drugs or something. I think, for the moment, I will stay put and give it another few weeks."

A few days later, Meredith heard the hapless Sylvia wandering up and down the hallway, mumbling to herself. She judged when Sylvia would be almost outside her doorway and stepped quickly into the corridor in front of her quarry. "I want to speak to you, Sylvia. You can't keep wandering up this end of the building. Your noise and mumbling keeps me awake, so if you don't mind, stay down your own end, all right? If you don't, I will have to report you to the manager. Do you understand?"

Sylvia's eyes widened in fright, and she took off at a shambling run back to her room just as Tom appeared at the top of the stairs. "I heard raised voices," he said. "What's the problem?"

"Well, as I mentioned before, Sylvia's wanderings, mumblings, and slipper slapping are very annoying, and I have told her she should stay down her end of the corridor. I don't want that kind of person down my end."

"Well, as I mentioned before, Sylvia is a long-term resident and has never been a problem to anyone else until you moved in. You have two choices. First one is to leave Sylvia alone as she isn't hurting anyone and is mentally unwell but is of no danger. Second, I won't have tenants harassing anyone else who lives here. If that doesn't suit you, the door is always open for you to leave through. Do I make myself clear?"

Meredith gave a haughty toss of her head. "Perfectly clear, thank you. Given your attitude, I may look for somewhere else more suitable."

On his way down the corridor, he turned to Meredith and said, "Would be happy to help you relocate." But it was said in such a tone of voice that Meredith didn't know if Tom was having a go at her or would perhaps help.

The nocturnal wanderings of Sylvia continued. Meredith had decided that, given Tom's attitude and her present financial predicament, it might be a better option if she bought some earplugs and tried to ignore what went on outside her door. A few good nights' sleep improved her energy levels but not her attitude.

Thirty-One

Meredith was invited by Suzy to come for lunch on Sunday as there was something she wanted to talk to her about. "Well, I hope it's something better than noodles, Suzy. I am so tired of them."

"Yes, Meredith, I'm sure I can come up with something between noodles and lobster."

Brady hadn't heard Meredith's response on the other end of the phone and, with a puzzled expression, asked Suzy, "Why are we having something between noodles and lobster? We don't eat either of those things."

"Well, Meredith requested that we don't have noodles on Sunday for lunch as she's a bit sick of them."

"That woman is the limit. Talk about bite the hand that feeds you. What time are you going to pick her up?"

"I thought about twelve, so we can have an early lunch and give me time to let her know what sort of life she would have if she decides to move out of the hotel, or more likely evicted, and into a refuge. She'll be shocked, I'm sure, but she needs to know what is likely to be in front of her if the hotel manager decides she has to leave. She might not be happy there, but from what I have read about refuges, she's a lot safer where she is. But as we both know, Meredith won't be happy wherever she is."

Suzy arranged to meet Meredith on Sunday and was shocked at her appearance. A diet consisting mostly of noodles obviously put on kilos. The clothes that had been sourced from the charity shop only a month or so ago now needed replacing with a bigger size, but Suzy wisely said nothing to Meredith about her appearance. She was rather surprised to see that she was wearing a trendy style of hat with her hair tucked up underneath, something she had never done before.

"Hi, Meredith, good to see you again. We'll be home in fifteen minutes, so buckle up, and we'll get going," Suzy cheerfully instructed.

"Good to see you too, Suzy. I'm looking forward to a nice lunch. I know you two are pretty good in the kitchen."

Fifteen minutes later, Brady, Larissa, and Pamela were greeting them at the gate to the terrace house. "Come in, Meredith. Have a seat on the back terrace, and I'll get you a drink. What would you like?"

True to type, Meredith replied, "I would love champagne if you have one but only if it's a good one."

"As we don't buy expensive champagne, what would be your second choice?" asked Brady as he went back into the kitchen with a smile on his face. *Some things just don't change.* "I can offer you a nice chardonnay, if you like."

"Oh well, I suppose that will do under the circumstances," Meredith replied with a sigh as she sat down on one of the chairs.

Suzy was surprised to see Meredith's hair when she removed her hat. It was much longer than it had ever been, pulled up into a ponytail; and the colour, without chemical enhancement, was now a dull mousy brown. Meredith caught the look of amazement on Suzy's face and announced, "It's like this until I can find a suitable salon somewhere close by. One of them wanted to charge me an exorbitant amount of money for very little work."

A lovely lunch had been prepared, and as they all took their places around the table, glasses were raised to celebrate a promotion for Suzy and new employment for Larissa with an international importing company. Pamela was quite happy on her rug, curled up under Larissa's feet, and took no notice of her former owner at all. Meredith also took no notice of her former pet. When lunch was over and coffee was brought out from the kitchen, Larissa said goodbye to Meredith and left to go out with friends to celebrate her new job.

It was time for Suzy to inform Meredith of what she had found out about women's shelters and what other types of accommodation were available in a crisis. She handed Meredith a piece of paper with information on how to source crisis accommodation and suggested that she keep it somewhere easily accessed or even enter the details in her mobile phone.

At the end of Suzy's information session with Meredith, there was silence in the room. Suzy had presented a picture of life that Meredith had never envisaged she even needed to know about. The scarcity of places to stay, even in a crisis, had never occurred to her.

In some recesses of her mind, she knew there were homeless people. She had seen them down near Circular Quay while she sipped champagne in one of the harbourside restaurants in her former life. She had never really given a thought about how they got to be without a roof over their head. Like most of the population, she had assumed that they got that way through their own fault by taking drugs, drinking too much, gambling, and so on. She was firmly of the belief that it was their choice to be living on the streets as, in a country as wealthy as Australia, there should be no need for the bundles of humanity living on the streets in full view of people walking by, going about their daily business. In her former life, she had found it offensive to have to walk around these people who took up pavement space with their rug spread out and handmade cardboard signs asking for money.

She had seen signs that said they couldn't get work, but if they tried hard enough, there was work for everybody in this lucky country, wasn't there? Surely, if they slept through the day, they weren't going to find work. They were obviously just lazy and couldn't be bothered, but then again, who would employ them with the way they looked? They were scruffy with dirty clothes, no shoes, and missing teeth, and some of them had pets that looked just as bad as the person they sat beside. She ignored the thought that she had not been able to secure another position after her company was "stolen" from her as she thought of the forced sale.

Most of the homeless she had seen were men, so she had no idea that a lot of the transient population were single women aged 55 and over. They were less visible because they were more likely to be living in their car, a caravan parked in a backyard somewhere, a garage roughly converted to a bedsit at a friend or relative's place, in a couch of someone else's home, or in a refuge for the short term, if they could find a place to take them. She no longer had a vehicle or a friend with a garage, and a couch had been denied her on a long-term basis. She was almost out of options. She could stay in the hotel even with the stumbling and mumbling Sylvia to put up with or try to get a place in a refuge. Neither of these options gave Meredith any hope that her future was about to get better.

After an extended and shocked silence, Meredith asked, "Well, what am I going to do, Suzy? I am so frightened of where I am going to end up."

"I didn't want to spoil your day with us, but you need to know what your options are, and unfortunately, they are very few. It's always good to have a plan if things go pear shaped and if you must move out of the hotel in a hurry, don't you think?"

"Well, if I have to move out," retorted Meredith, "it will be Sylvia's fault with her shuffling and mumbling. Even with earplugs in, I can sense her out there."

Suzy had long ago given up the idea that Meredith would ever take responsibility for her situation in life. Now it was the harmless Sylvia's turn to be blamed. Suzy drove Meredith back to the Emperor Hotel, where she disappeared inside the doors without so much as a wave goodbye. Suzy correctly assessed that Meredith was in a shocked state and would perhaps reassess her treatment of Sylvia, given that one more tirade directed towards this poor lady would result in Meredith's eviction. Suzy did not hold out much hope that Meredith would show any empathy towards the wandering resident of "her" floor in the hotel.

It wasn't many more weeks before Tom was fed up with Meredith and her constant complaints about the state of the bathroom, Sylvia's nocturnal activities, and anything else she felt wasn't up to standard. It was time for the Emperor Hotel to be rid of its annoying tenant. Tom caught up with her as she was about to go up the stairs. "Meredith," he called out, "could I have a word, please?"

Meredith retraced her steps and, when she was facing him, said, "So are you going to tell me that you are doing something about Sylvia?"

"I have thought of a plan to solve the problem," he replied. "You won't have to worry about her in two weeks' time."

"Oh, that is good news. Thanks for sorting that out. I knew you'd think of something." She was about to turn and continue up the stairs.

Tom stopped her with "Meredith, I haven't finished my conversation yet. It is not Sylvia that will be leaving, but I am terminating your tenancy. You need to be out of here in two weeks."

Meredith scowled at Tom. "That's not quite the solution I had in mind, but if you prefer a disruptive tenant over me, then perhaps I need to move on somewhere that is more to my liking, so I will accept your offer."

Tom just watched her go up the stairs and thought, *That woman is something else.*

Thirty-Two

It was all Tom could do to not stand on the footpath outside the Emperor Hotel and clap when Suzy picked up his least favourite tenant in the morning of her departure. In the hotel business, there were plenty of difficult people to deal with, and she was certainly one of them.

"Thanks for coming to my rescue again, Suzy. It's all because of that woman Sylvia. But then again, the place could do with a bit of a spruce up, and the bathrooms haven't been redecorated since the 1950s."

"Now you know we can only put you up short term, don't you, Meredith? A month at the most until we find you somewhere else to live, which may not be easy, but we will try. You can stay in Larissa's room."

It wasn't long before they pulled up outside the terraced house that Brady and Suzy lived in. Larissa had moved into a large rented house on the north side of the harbour, which was shared with eight others. She had a few friends who lived there, and it was close to her work at North Sydney. Larissa was happy with the arrangement as it gave her freedom to come and go as it suited her lifestyle. Also, Brady was a bit old-fashioned when it came to boyfriends sleeping over; and as it was his house, he had enforced this rule on more than one occasion. Larissa didn't like putting her beloved mum in the middle of an argument, so it was better for all concerned that she moved out and started her grown-up life, just a thirty-minute car journey from Suzy.

Brady was sitting out on the back terrace when they arrived, and once settled, he asked their guest what she would like to drink. Meredith replied, "A white wine would be nice, thanks. I have given up champagne as it is too expensive for my budget, and I can't stomach that cheap sparkling substitute."

Well, that's an improvement on her attitude from when she was last here.

After serving the drinks, Brady went back into the kitchen to start getting lunch ready so Suzy and Meredith could chat. Earlier in the week, Suzy had contacted most of the refuges and explained Meredith's situation. None of the people she spoke with gave her much hope of a placement as she didn't meet most of the criteria except facing homelessness. She was an unemployed woman who had no income and relied on Centrelink benefits. She was at the end of a very long queue of people needier than her.

This information was given to Meredith, who hung her head and muttered, "I'm in real trouble, aren't I? I don't know what to do after I leave here."

"Try not to worry. We'll phone again tomorrow and see if there's any crisis accommodation available for short-term stay. It's a sad fact, Meredith, that over 100,000 people each night in Australia are living on the streets, and they are just the ones who appeared in the last census. The truth of numbers is unknown, but women over 55 years of age are amongst the fastest growing group, and little, if any, provision is being made for them. Tomorrow is a new day, so we will see if we can get you in somewhere."

"Can't I stay a bit longer with you?" she asked in a tearful voice. "I'm so afraid of being out there on my own."

"That's not possible now. Since Larissa is not home anymore and lives her own life, we've put the house on the market and are moving to one of the regional cities. We don't know which one yet as it depends on how much Brady gets for the house, but he can work from home, and I wouldn't mind a bit less stress in a new job. We may go into business together, but again, the house sale will decide a lot for us. We might even travel for a little while until we make up our mind where we want to settle. I'd like to help out, Meredith, but you can see it's not possible once the sale goes through."

Tossing and turning all night did not put Meredith in a good temper the next morning, but she had learned to be wary of Brady because it was obvious Suzy deferred to his decision on almost everything. Phoning the refuges again did not bring forth any joy at all. It became obvious that there was considerably more accommodation available for men than there was for women, even though men represented 60 per cent of the single homeless population and women 40 per cent. It was a very disheartening morning for Meredith and Suzy, and little could be done to alleviate the feeling of hopelessness to find somewhere for her to go.

"Well, that didn't go too well, did it, Meredith? Maybe we need to contact some of the bigger organisations such as the Salvos as the centres in this area can't help. We'll try again tomorrow. In the meantime, let's go out for a coffee – my shout."

A week later, Suzy managed to find a two-week placement for Meredith in a women's shelter, but at least it was something. She was advised that it would be in a shared room as that was all they had, and if Meredith didn't accept today, they couldn't give Suzy any idea how long before something else came up. Suzy accepted the offer immediately and told them she would bring her friend over there that afternoon. Meredith was unhappy about having to move out, but Suzy had been firm that, if it wasn't this placement, there mightn't be another for a long time. They had sold the house within a week of it going on the market, and because the buyers had wanted a short settlement, Brady and Suzy would be moving out in a month. That would leave Meredith with nowhere to go – at all.

Reluctantly, she packed her bag and was ready at 3 p.m. to be taken to the refuge. She knew that there was no alternative other than the streets. Suzy had spoken to the refuge supervisor, Alana, who was there to greet them. She entered Meredith's particulars and then asked for her next of kin's contact details. Meredith looked bewildered, glanced at Suzy, and asked, "Can I put your name and mobile down? I don't have anyone else." Suzy agreed, and they were shown to a twin bedroom that she was to share with another woman, a bit younger than Meredith but with the similar future of facing homelessness quite soon.

Her roommate looked up from the book she was reading and, with a shy smile, said, "Hi, I'm Sally. What's your name?" Meredith introduced herself and Suzy, and after a few minutes, Suzy left.

There was an awkward silence in the room between the two women, and they spoke at the same time. "How come you're in this place?"

Meredith asked Sally if there was somewhere she could get a cup of coffee or if she would have to go out to a cafe. Sally told her where the shared kitchen was but warned Meredith that she should clean up any mess she made and then offered to go with Meredith and show her the ropes. "Thanks. That would be great. So which way do we go?"

Sally set off down the corridor to the kitchen, and they returned to their shared room with a cup of coffee each. Meredith asked, "What do you do all day, Sally? You don't stay in this room, do you?"

"No, I don't. I found Patti's Place just a bus ride away where I can go and have breakfast and lunch, but they are only open from 8 a.m. to 2 p.m. most days. They have classes there where you can learn to cook, sew, paint, or other things to make your life better. I tried yoga but couldn't get the hang of that because my pelvis was fractured in a car accident. They also have people come in who will do a résumé for you. I take my washing there and have a shower. It's really important to be clean, Meredith, or people look at you like you are scum. It's humiliating, and they stand in judgement when they don't know the circumstances that brought you to live this way. I'm going to Patti's Place tomorrow. Do you want to come and meet some new friends?" Meredith agreed because she had nothing better to do, and lying on a bed for the day to read a book didn't appeal at all.

The next morning, she was ready at eight with her washing in a bag that she had borrowed from Suzy, and they set off for Patti's

Place. Sally was easy to talk to, but she didn't ask Meredith any questions about why she was in a women's refuge.

Sally volunteered the information that, at the time of her car accident five years ago, she had a good job, was in a relationship with a man she thought she was going to marry, and had money in the bank saved for a trip overseas. Costly medical procedures, physiotherapy, and rehabilitation had taken most of the money. She lost her job because she couldn't do the work due to her injuries. The company was unable to offer her an alternative position given her limitations in their workplace. The love of her life found it all too hard and left her. She couldn't keep paying the rent on her apartment, and her goods were all put into storage. Her car was sold when the registration was due as it needed repairs she couldn't afford. It wasn't too long before the cost of the storage shed became impossible, and she sold everything except her clothes, mobile phone, and a few suitcases. She had slept on the couches of friends, but that often didn't work out.

She cheerfully ended the conversation with "So here I am, without a home or job and relying on Centrelink disability benefits, not quite where I thought I would be at 40 years of age, that's for sure."

They were almost at Patti's Place, and Sally said they should get off at the next stop. They carried their suitcases a short way down the road to the destination and rang the doorbell. "Hi, Sally, come on in. You've brought a friend with you. Welcome to Patti's Place" came a pleasant voice from the other side of the screen door.

Sally introduced Meredith to Louise, who smiled pleasantly and stood aside so the two women could enter. "How do you know Sally?" Louise asked Meredith as she walked in front of them down the carpeted hallway of a grand old home.

"Well, I'm her roommate for a short while until I find something else."

"Well, you're more than welcome here. We're just about to serve breakfast, and if you want to do your washing, Sally will show you the laundry, and you can get a load started before you sit down. Just come out to the back courtyard when you're ready."

Meredith followed Sally to the laundry area at the back of the house. It was set up with several washing machines and dryers. "How much does this cost? The laundromat I used cost me a fortune each week," asked Meredith.

"It doesn't cost anything. Patti's Place is run by a charity, and they do a lot of fundraising to keep this place going. It was donated to the community by a family many years ago and was specifically to be used as a women's safe place to come to through the day, have a meal or two, and maybe learn a skill while they were here. It has certainly saved my sanity, I can tell you. Since I've been coming here, I don't feel so lonely, and there is always someone to talk to.

"We don't always discuss our past, but everyone has a story. Some of the women are from overseas and have been deserted by their husbands, perhaps have no family support, or have been unable to find work. And so the downward spiral of no job, no pay, and no future starts. Also, a lot of the women here haven't had a good education, and they struggle with day-to-day living, but you can learn a lot from the volunteers who come and teach us how to cook cheap meals, where to get free toiletries, how to budget and just look after ourselves to the best of our abilities. I think you'll like it. I have always felt quite safe here, and it gives me the courage to go back to the refuge each night. Let's go and meet the other girls."

Meredith followed Sally out to the courtyard, where there were about twenty women sitting around tables and starting to eat breakfast. Sally took Meredith over to a table with two spare seats and introduced her to the women there. Some of them just nodded; a few said, "Hi, welcome"; and others averted their eyes. As Sally said, everyone had a story, and Meredith thought that some of these women looked like they had been to hell and back.

Sally beckoned to Meredith to come with her to where breakfast was being served, and she was amazed to see fresh fruit, juice, and a variety of bread with lots of different spreads to go on them. There was another section with jars of cereals, next to which tea and coffee were set out. "Help yourself, Meredith. You can come back if you need something else, but breakfast only goes until nine thirty."

Meredith took her advice and followed Sally back out to the courtyard, where she seated herself between two women and nodded at each of them. They dropped their eyes, firmly staring at the plate in front of them, and it didn't seem that they wanted to speak. After Sally's explanation of how she might be greeted, Meredith didn't take offence but didn't offer a greeting either. She had dealt with enough people in her business life to know when an approach was not welcome. She ate quietly and answered anyone who spoke to her but didn't ask any questions either. She would just wait and see what happened throughout the day. Sally had told her that lunch was served at twelve thirty, but she would look at the timetable to see what was on in the classroom that day.

Sally came back to Meredith and told her they had a choice of sitting in the lounge area to listen to a volunteer play the piano for an hour, attending a sewing class, or just relaxing out in the courtyard. Meredith decided the latter option would work for her, but Sally was going to the sewing class. She told Meredith she had not had any sewing skills before she came to Patti's Place, but now she could take up a hem and do minor repairs and had even tackled altering a top she had bought for two dollars at Salvos. The last time Meredith had sewn anything was for her year 12 exam. It was a ghastly creation that she had never worn and consigned to the rubbish bin the minute she got home.

There was a small library in one of the rooms, and Meredith found a book that interested her and took it out to the courtyard. She sat quietly in the shade for a while, went back inside to get coffee, and returned to the area she had been in before. She passed a pleasant hour reading while Sally was at her sewing class, and by then, it was nearly time for lunch. Louise came to the door leading into the courtyard and announced in her cheerful voice, "Lunch is ready, ladies. Roast chicken and veggies today. Come on through those of you who're interested." And she disappeared back inside. Roast chicken and veggies – it had been a long time since Meredith had eaten something so nice, except when she had been at Suzy's. This was turning into a good day. Breakfast in the courtyard, washing done and dried, lunch about to be served, and she had found a book as well.

When 2 p.m. was approaching, Sally came back and told Meredith that they needed to catch the next bus back to the refuge. "Did you enjoy your day?" she asked Meredith.

"I did. I can't believe what a beautiful place it is. How often do you come here, Sally?"

"Every day if I can. It only costs me $2.50 per day for the bus fare, and going there stops me from being lonely and depressed. The bus fare is an investment in my mental health, Meredith. Money well spent, I feel. There is always something going on here and a few women who will sit and chat, although a lot of them are struggling with life. Some of them have lost children in dreadful circumstances, been abused by violent partners, or are just generally down on their luck – a bit like you and me. Do you want to go again tomorrow?"

"That'd be great. I really enjoyed today and spoke to a few of the women, but others, as you explained, are more solitary. But that's okay. We don't all want everyone to know all the gory details of our previous life, do we?"

"I don't talk too much about my previous life either, Meredith. It drags me down every time I repeat it, so I just skim over the details and leave it at that. I don't need people who are strangers picking apart my life and telling me what I could have done better. I made choices in the circumstances I was in at the time. Not all of them worked out in the end, but one thing I have learned, Meredith, is that we don't set out to fail. It just sometimes happens through circumstances beyond our control.

"Anyway, that's enough misery for today. Let's get back to what I call 'home' for the time being. My stay is nearly up there, and I don't know where I'll be able to get in next. I hope it will be a transitional house, but most of them go to women with children, and you and I don't qualify. No point worrying about it, is there? There's nothing we can do about it. Might as well enjoy the safety while we can."

When they got back to the refuge, they discovered that someone had been in their room and taken some of their clothes. They reported the theft to Louise, and she said she would take down the details, but it was unlikely they would see the clothes again. She asked them why they hadn't locked their door before they went out, and Meredith replied, "I didn't realise we would have to, and I was last out of the room. Sorry, Sally. I won't forget again."

"That's all right, Meredith. What I had wasn't all that great, but it just means I need to replace them from the charity shop and spend money I wasn't expecting. What have you lost?"

"My warmest coat has gone, but at least it's summer now, so I can replace it before winter comes. I just hope whoever took it needs it more than I do."

"Well, at least we each have a bag of clean clothes to wear, so it's not a complete disaster."

"Do you always look on the bright side, Sally?"

"I try to as often as I can, but I don't always have the energy to smile."

Thirty-Three

Meredith and Sally continued to visit Patti's Place mainly because it was so pleasant there but also because it got them out of the refuge for a few hours each day. Sally was informed that she only had ten more days to stay, and Meredith wasn't too happy about sharing the room with someone else after Sally left. They decided that two together was better than going it alone, but there was nothing being offered to them when their time at the refuge finished.

Later that week, Meredith mentioned, "One more day to go, Sally. What are we going to do? I'm really scared about my future."

"I know someone, Meredith, that might put us up for a night or two, but I haven't been able to contact them yet. I guess it's under the bridge for us."

"What do you mean under the bridge? That sounds terrifying. Are we going to have to rough it?" Meredith had a horrified look on her face, but Sally just laughed at her.

"It's not that bad, Meredith. I've done it before, so I know some of the tricks. Stick with me. We'll be all right," Sally said. "Unfortunately, that is the life that faces us, Meredith. We can't get into another refuge yet. We can't afford private rental, even if there were any available to us. At least the weather is warm, and we won't freeze to death."

"Oh, that's so reassuring, we won't freeze. But what about being robbed or mugged or something even worse?"

"I'll look after you, Meredith. I was joking about under the bridge, if that makes you feel any better. We can find a squat somewhere, and we'd better start looking for our next night's accommodation sooner rather than later. Grab your stuff, and let's get out of here."

From experience, Sally knew her way around the inner city. It wasn't long before they stopped at the side of a boarded-up warehouse. Sally informed Meredith that she had stayed here before and that it was dry with not too many rats.

"What do you mean not too many rats? One rat is one more than I want to have to deal with. Anyway, how do we get into it?"

Sally walked along the side of the warehouse, testing the timber nailed to the window openings. She finally found one towards the back that was not secure over a door and managed to pull it away far enough to get inside. Meredith hadn't seen where Sally went to and was really scared standing by herself when she saw Sally beckoning to her from the end of the lane. "Down here, Meredith, and be quick about it," called Sally as Meredith dragged their suitcases behind her.

Sally held the makeshift door open enough for Meredith to slip through and bring the suitcases inside. One look around in the dim light was enough for Meredith to want to get back outside, but Sally had a firm hold on her arm. She knew this was a different way of life for Meredith, but she was confident they would be reasonably safe in the building. It was dry and didn't smell of anything revolting, but it was dark. They needed some light before they tripped over and injured themselves.

"How much money do you have with you, Meredith?" asked Sally. "I have about eighty dollars, but we need to stock up on some supplies if we are going to shelter here for a while. We can pool our money, and we'll be okay."

"Oh, that's great. We'll be okay. I feel very reassured that this beautiful building we have just broken into will be our home for who knows how long. Maybe we can get some decorators in to make sure it is on trend," Meredith said in a sarcastic tone.

"Don't be such a snooty bitch, Meredith. Without me, you'd really be on the street, so cut the crap, okay? Now drop the attitude because we need to do some shopping, so let's go." She turned around and headed for the loose piece of timber, now serving as their illegally gained entrance to a possibly condemned building.

Sally instructed Meredith to look as clean and tidy as possible so as not to attract unwanted attention from either other shoppers or the management of the centre. On their way to the nearest supermarket, Sally was telling Meredith what they would need to buy, and one of the first things was a closed-in shopping trolley. The rest of the list sounded so extensive that Meredith was sure it would exceed their combined funds.

"We'll just buy our most urgent supplies today, such as a torch and some food we don't have to heat up. We need either pull-top cans or a can opener, long-life milk, juice that doesn't need refrigeration, some plastic cups, plates, and cutlery, plus a dish to wash up in. We also need a groundsheet or some large plastic bags to put on the earth floor and insect repellent in case there are cockroaches or fleas. Are you taking all this in?" Sally asked. Meredith just mutely nodded. In her previous life, she certainly had never needed to decide between a pull-top can and a can opener.

"What are we going to do for blankets or pillows?" queried Meredith.

"There's a charity shop just up the road that's open until 3 p.m. so we'll have time to go there after we drop our shopping home. Hope we still have some money left by then."

Meredith was incapable of speech by this time and just nodded when Sally made a comment. This was a whole new world to her and one she hadn't even known existed. Plastic bags big enough to lie on? "Come on, Meredith, pick up the pace a bit. We'll never be settled by tonight if you don't get a move on."

Sally had brought a small calculator with her, and each time an item went into the shopping cart, she tapped the amount in. Not having enough money at the checkout would only draw attention to them. Sally knew from experience that this was not a good thing to happen in front of a crowd of other shoppers. It was not only embarrassing but made the management suspicious as well if they had to go into that supermarket again.

Meredith's learning curve was going to be steep. She picked up the premium brand from the shelf, which Sally gently removed from her hand and, without a word, exchanged it for the generic brand instead. Gourmet red salmon was not on Sally's shopping list. Sally spoke quietly to Meredith in one of the less populated aisles. "Meredith, don't be offended, but let me do the shopping, okay? We'll get more for our money that way. Agree?" And Meredith just nodded.

They had a full trolley by the time they reached the checkout, but with Sally's careful shopping, they had enough money. There was some leftover for the rest of the items they needed from the charity shop later that day. Sally knew, but didn't tell Meredith, that they were likely to be in their new-found "home" for some time, if they managed to avoid detection. Them entering or leaving the building would raise suspicions of illegal squatting and could lead to an unwelcome visit from the police. Sally knew she would have to give Meredith many lessons in being inconspicuous in their new location. They had to be very careful not to be noticed for as long as possible.

By the end of the day, they had a dry place to sleep, a suitcase full of groceries which they could keep closed to keep out any unwanted creatures, and a torch. Their recently purchased shopping trolley housed some of their clothes. Sally was trying hard to keep Meredith's spirits up, but it wasn't working. Time for some tough love. "Meredith, do you know how lucky you are?" she ventured.

"Lucky? Are you serious? I have never felt less lucky in my whole life."

"Okay, here's the story. If you and I are going to stick together and be as safe as we can be given our circumstances, you need to get your act together. You're lucky, Meredith, because, firstly, you have good health. Secondly, you have people in your life who care about you. Even though Suzy is not living in Sydney, you can contact her if you need help. I have poor health and not one soul in the world who would mourn my passing." And with that, Sally pushed a packet of crackers and cheese at Meredith and commented, "Dinner is served, madam."

Always wanting to have the last word, Meredith asked, "Is the Moët chilled enough yet, Sally?" And she grinned to show all was okay between them.

Thirty-Four

Meredith had spent a mostly sleepless night, tossing and turning, constantly worried about something attacking her. Sally, however, slept quietly and seemed very peaceful. *How does she sleep so soundly? I don't know if I will ever sleep again. I hear every scuffle and tiny noise. I'm going to ring Suzy tomorrow and demand she come and get me out of this situation.*

With a breakfast of cereal, milk, and a piece of fruit presented to her by Sally, Meredith was very quiet. She was tired and grumpy, and when Sally enquired if she had slept all right, Meredith replied that it was a stupid question. Of course, she hadn't slept all right. There were noises, scuffling, and wind blowing through the cracks of the building. Complaint after complaint spilled from Meredith's mouth while Sally quietly ate her cereal, peeled her banana, and drank her juice. Meredith eventually ran out of words.

"Well, it's nice to know, Meredith, that you appreciate my company, the ability to put a roof over your head and food in your stomach. There's no ropes or chains keeping you here, so feel free to leave anytime you like." Sally got up off the upturned milk crate she had been using as a seat and walked away from Meredith.

By the time Meredith decided to apologise, Sally had gone from the building and left Meredith to think about what she had just said. For the first time in her life, Meredith felt ashamed of what she had done. This was an entirely new feeling to her. Meredith curled up in her makeshift bed and let the tears fall. She had possibly lost the only person who was willing and able to keep her safe, and she had abused her efforts.

When Sally returned an hour later, Meredith was still asleep. Sally sat with her back against the wall of the building and contemplated whether her new-found friend was worth the trouble. She decided that, although Meredith was hard work, they would do better together than apart, but she wasn't going to put up with being taken for granted and verbally abused for her efforts. It was time for them to come to an agreement on their lifestyle if they were going to try to help each other through this tough time. To start with, Meredith needed to learn how to be grateful. A few nights without Sally's support should achieve this.

When Meredith finally roused herself from sleep, she was surprised to see Sally sitting just a metre away. "What are you doing here?" asked Meredith quietly.

"Well, it's where I live, isn't it?" Sally replied. "You and I need to have a talk, and you might not like some of what I have to say. It's up to you to decide if you want to stay with me wherever our journey takes us or move on now, okay?"

"Okay, firstly, I want to apologise for being so horrible to you. When I get scared, I lash out at whoever is closest. Unfortunately, that happened to be you, and I won't do it again. I'm really sorry, Sally. Can you forgive me?"

"It's not about forgiveness, Meredith. It's more about putting another person before yourself, and I suspect that's not a skill you've ever learned. You're selfish and think you are the centre of the universe. However, you're not the centre of my universe. You need a lesson in survival to cope with the situation you're now in. I guess it's a sort of crash course in homelessness, but I think it will make you appreciate what you have, not worry about what you don't have, okay?"

Meredith had a worried look but nodded in answer to Sally's question. "What do I have to do?" she asked quietly.

"I want you to spend five days away from here with our last twenty dollars in your pocket. You'll have to find shelter, but you can take the plastic bags and blankets from here. You need to keep yourself clean and tidy, find meals, and stay out of trouble. You can take some of the food from here as you've helped pay for it. I'll still be here if you make it back after five days. You had better start getting organised."

Meredith put her face in her hands, and her shoulders shook as she cried. Sally just ignored her and started putting some food aside for Meredith to take with her. She didn't want to see her starve, but she certainly needed to be brought down from her high horse and drop her princess attitude. If she couldn't manage that, then she would be on her own. Her suitcase was finally packed, and she was out the makeshift door and on her way. Sally was worried for her, but it was a lesson that Meredith had to learn.

During the time it had taken Meredith to pack her suitcase, Sally had been giving her some tips on how to survive as a homeless person. She was hoping that Meredith had been listening, but given her reluctance to accept her situation, Sally doubted she had taken much in. A few days on the streets should sort her out.

Finally, it was time for her to leave, and she was certainly in no hurry. It was not in her nature to beg for help, so feeding herself with only twenty dollars in her pocket was going to be her priority. She was standing out the back of the building, looking up and down the lane, trying to work out which way to go. She wasn't familiar with this part of the city, but Sally had written down the address of their squat in case she got completely lost and couldn't find her way back. First thing she needed to do was work out where she was going to stay that night.

Sally had told her that it was safer to sleep through the day and walk during the night. Meredith had never slept in the daytime in her entire life, and the concept was foreign to her, but if Sally said it was safer, then for this first night she would give it a try. But where to sleep? It was midday, and she had been walking for about an hour. She came to an area near a city railway station where there were benches in the shade. Most of them were occupied by men stretched out asleep, with their belongings in duffel bags tied to the seat. Now

Meredith remembered why Sally had packed a very robust belt to be tied to the handle of the suitcase and secured to something to stop an easy theft.

I've got the rest of today and four more days to go, and I can't even find somewhere to rest now. How on earth am I going to make it to the end of this week? I'm thirsty, hungry, and tired because I didn't sleep last night. Sally is angry at me because I was horrible to her, but I must make this work, or I'll really be on my own, and that scares me witless.

Meredith walked slowly a bit farther along the path and found a bench against the railings surrounding the park. The bench was in the shade, and she planned to tie her suitcase to the railing, but she wasn't happy about being so exposed to people walking past. She sat on the bench for a while to see if anyone approached her, smiling or otherwise. Sally had warned her to avoid eye contact as some people may see that as aggressive. It occurred to Meredith that when she was running her company, in her other life as she thought of it now, eye contact was one of the things she was especially good at. Now it was a minus, not a plus.

Within a few minutes, a thin scruffy-looking woman with a beer can in her hand approached from Meredith's right. Meredith heard her before she was aware of her presence. "Hey, you!" she yelled in a rough voice. "Get your arse off my bench and make it quick!"

Meredith got such a shock that she stood up quickly and tried to move away from this aggressive woman but tripped over her suitcase and fell on the grass. "Serves you right, you bitch. People have rights, you know, and this is my bench. Go find one somewhere else."

Well, that was a great start to my search for somewhere to sleep. How am I supposed to know who sleeps on which bench? Maybe I'll try to find a spot behind that small shed. It might be safer to be out of view, or is it? This is much harder than I ever thought possible, but if I don't do this, Sally will definitely not be teaming up with me. She's made that very clear.

Meredith crossed the park to the small shed with a sign that said it was for the use of authorised personnel. At least it was in the shade, nobody seemed to be around, and she could anchor her suitcase to the bolt on the bottom of the door. By then, she was becoming anxious that she needed to sleep soon because, after dark, she would be trying to find somewhere to eat while walking the streets, dragging her suitcase – not quite like other times she had a suitcase behind her, travelling first class around Australia in search of new business.

She took out her plastic bags to put on the grass and then her blankets. She had a drink of juice, ate some cheese and biscuits, and then settled down in her makeshift bed. She was so tired that she was unaware of the noisy birds in the trees, the office workers talking on their mobiles while they hurried up the path near her, and dogs barking. She awoke at about 6 p.m. and had to find a toilet. She remembered passing a sign pointing to toilets near the entrance to the railway station. She wouldn't be conspicuous in the station as there were platforms for country trains, and a woman with a suitcase was not unusual.

Sally had warned her not to leave her suitcase outside the toilet cubicle as there was a high chance it would be stolen. She had advised Meredith to use the disabled toilet so she could take her suitcase in with her, have a wash, comb her hair, dust any leaf litter off, and look like any other traveller. Meredith was becoming more grateful by the minute for all the survival skills Sally had told her. After tidying herself, Meredith felt it was time to start looking for food before she started on her nocturnal wanderings.

Again, it was Sally's information to the rescue. She had mentioned a few places where they served food from a mobile van each night. Meredith's knowledge of city streets was less than vague. While she sat in the back of a chauffeur-driven limousine and spoke on her mobile phone, she had never taken one scrap of notice of street names. Now she needed to find out where these vans were located but was hesitant to ask anyone. She decided to put forth the story she had come down from the country and wasn't sure where to find these streets. She was directed towards a map of the city by an information person at the railway station. Sally had told her to take a photo on her mobile phone so she could find the van.

It took Meredith nearly an hour to find her way to the mobile van, where they started serving from 6 p.m. It was now

7.30 p.m. and she was hoping they hadn't run out of food by the time she arrived. She turned a corner and could see the lights of the van beside a park. Several people were milling around, some were standing in line, and others were sitting with their backs against trees.

She was nervous about approaching them. She was a woman on her own, but she was becoming increasingly desperate about surviving in her present life. The weather was still mild at night, but winter was on its way, and the cold would be another challenge to being homeless. Meredith decided to give the food van a try but would stay well back out of sight until she felt comfortable approaching it. This whole scenario was her new reality.

As the night sky darkened, Meredith made her way across the street to the van. After waiting a few minutes and reassuring herself the people who had been served with food seemed a harmless lot, she tentatively approached the front of the van. A voice to her left said softly, "Hello, love. Haven't seen you here before. Make sure you get enough to eat before they run out, hey?" And his skinny hand clasping a cup of hot liquid appeared from the ragged end of his coat, and the other reached for the contents of a paper bag. He quietly moved away and disappeared into the dark.

"What would you like?" questioned the young man at the counter of the van. His appearance of facial tattoos, multiple piercings, and missing teeth were at odds with his gentle voice and manner. Meredith had no idea what to say as she didn't know what was on offer, so taking the advice of the man who had preceded her, she tentatively asked, "What do you have? I haven't done this before."

"Well," the young man replied and pointed towards a menu board behind him, "you can have whatever is up on that board that we still have available. You can have soup, a hot drink, and a meal or sandwiches for later." The menu board bore no resemblance to any Meredith had seen in the French or Italian restaurants she had frequented. She decided on soup and a meal as she had not eaten much today. He smiled and said "enjoy" before he served the next customer.

Well, you certainly can't judge that book by its cover.

Meredith walked away from the van and found a quiet corner to have her food. She had dined well tonight, and tomorrow was another day. She still had the idea that she was "not one of them," even though she now was. They were homeless, and so was she. They were short of money, and so was she. They looked as though they could do with a shower and a washing machine for their clothes, and then she realised her appearance was very similar to theirs. Reality bit hard.

Thirty-Five

She had never felt so ashamed in all her life. The smell of the dumpster located just outside a Chinese restaurant made her gag. Prawn heads, slimy vegetables, and greasy leftovers formed a kind of moving soup as Meredith tried to extract something that she could eat. She sensed rather than felt someone touching her coat and turned around quickly.

"Nice coat. Stole it, did ya?" enquired a rough female voice behind her.

Meredith still retained a certain amount of dignity even in these dark days of her street life. "No, I did not steal it," she replied haughtily. "I bought it years ago. Cashmere wears well, you know." She had bought it at half price from a charity shop the day she had left the squat and Sally.

"Don't look too good with that cabbage leaf stuck on the sleeve and sauce down the front of it," the woman persisted. "Anyway, this is my dumpster you've stuck your nose into, so piss off before youse gets hurt."

"Don't tell me what to do. And if it's your dumpster, you're welcome to it. You smell almost as bad as it does," Meredith retorted as she turned and walked away. She was shaking with fright but had learned not to let anyone see how scared she was feeling. After turning the corner out of the alley, she leaned against a wall and tried to gather her wits. She had been unsuccessful today in getting food and wasn't sure what to do next. She had only a few dollars left and wouldn't have any put into her bank account by Centrelink for another three days. Maybe she would try the food van again.

She moved farther along the alley and saw an open door leading into the back of a restaurant. One of the cooks was standing outside, having a sneaky cigarette. Meredith quietly approached the cook and asked him, "Do you have any leftovers I could have, please?" The cook was surprised to see her standing there but knew it was more than his job was worth to give food to homeless people. His boss had made it quite clear that he didn't want those "useless hobos" hanging around his restaurant, and it was instant dismissal if the staff were caught.

"Where did you come from, and what are you doing in this alley?" Guido asked. "You don't look like the usual sort that hang around here."

"I was chased out of an alley by some woman a few minutes ago. She said it was her dumpster and I should move on – but not exactly in those words. She looked a bit deranged, so I took off and finished up here. I saw the restaurant door open and thought I might be able to get some leftover pizza or something. Can you help me, please?" Guido felt sorry for her as she seemed to be a lady with class who had fallen on bad times.

"Wait here. I have to go back into the kitchen, but if you hang around for another ten minutes or so, I will quickly open the door and put some food outside for you, but don't eat it here. If I get caught, I'll be dismissed. My boss doesn't like us feeding homeless people. He would rather put it in the bin so nobody can have the leftovers."

As good as his word, fifteen minutes later, Guido quickly opened the back door, a cardboard box with "pasta sauce" written on the outside appeared on the top step, and the door was closed. Meredith picked up the box and made a hasty exit down the alley away from the restaurant. She was very grateful to the unknown Guido and even more so for the freshly made pizza and garlic bread the box contained. There was also some leftover pasta in a container and another one of what looked like veal scaloppine. It made Meredith smile to see the plastic cutlery and paper serviettes that he had included. It was only minutes before Meredith found a quiet doorway and, with relief, slid down the wall and devoured this welcome food.

When the box was devoid of its very tasty contents, Meredith saw that there was some writing on a note taped to the inside of the lid. Guido had written that he worked Tuesday, Thursday, and Saturday nights from seven to midnight and took his break at about nine thirty, if she happened to be in the neighbourhood at that time. *Oh, Guido, you are a godsend. Thank you for your kindness and letting me know you are willing to help. I never thought it would be this hard.*

Day three arrived of Meredith's five days living alone and on her wits. She was tired from only sleeping a few hours each day, walking for most of the night, and trying to keep clean and tidy. It was certainly a challenge. Sally had packed some baby wipes in Meredith's trolley, and these were very useful for a quick sponge down in the toilet cubicle wherever she was. She had also packed her a plastic cup which she could fill with water and use to wet a toothbrush and clean her teeth. Meredith was very glad she had someone to show her the ropes of living rough.

Even with all of Sally's good advice, she was finding it particularly hard to get food. She was surprised at how much even the cheapest fast food cost, and she only had a few dollars left with two days still to go. It was not Guido's night to work, so she decided to go back to the food van she had visited on her first day away from Sally. The menu was much the same as it had been, but Meredith was beyond caring about such minor details.

The same young guy was serving the customers, and he introduced himself as Tom. He asked her, "What can I get you today? We have vegetable soup, baguettes with different fillings, and half a small pizza."

Meredith chose the soup and baguette so she could keep the baguette for breakfast. "Thanks so much," she replied. "I really appreciate the food, and I'm so glad you're here." Meredith found an upturned milk crate close to a tree but still within the light provided by the street lamps. She was spooning her soup while keeping a close eye on her suitcase, which she had tied to the bottom of the crate, when a young woman approached her.

"Hi, haven't seen you here before. What's your name?" she questioned.

Meredith looked up in surprise as she hadn't heard her approaching, but she could smell the alcohol on the stranger's breath. "Oh, hello. I'm Meredith, and this is only my second night at the van. I don't know my way around very well. What's your name?"

The newcomer answered, "I'm Angela. I've lived around here for years since my parents kicked me out. The food not's bad, and it's free. Where are you sleeping tonight? Around here somewhere? I've got a place if you want to come with me."

Meredith's newly emerging danger radar started to send her messages, so she answered, "Thanks for the offer, but I'm staying with a friend a few blocks from here. She forgot to leave the key out for me, so I said I would wait until she got home from work and walk to her place." With that, Meredith put the baguette in her bag. "Nice to meet you."

Receiving no reply from Angela, Meredith made her way to the edge of the road and turned left away from the food van. She stopped a few times, bent down to look as though she was adjusting something on her shoe, and kept walking. There was no sign of Angela following her, so at the next corner, she started to make her way back to the park, where she hoped she could find a spot to sleep for a few hours.

Thirty-Six

Meredith was roused from her sleep by someone tapping her on the arm. She wearily opened one eye and asked, "Who are you?"

A kindly face looked back at her and answered, "I'm Belinda from the Sisterhood Day Shelter just near here." And she produced her identification for Meredith to check. "Would you like to come and have a meal with us today? We try to help the women sleeping rough with a meal and somewhere to shower and rest up in safety."

Meredith tried to sit up a bit but was tangled up in the plastic bags under her and the blanket that had wrapped around her in the night. "Oh, thanks. Just let me get myself untangled."

Belinda helped her up from her bed and, when she had repacked her suitcase, handed her a cup of hot coffee delivered from a thermos she was holding. "Here, drink this down. You must be a bit chilled this morning. It was colder last night than it has been for weeks." Belinda kept up her amiable chatter, and when the coffee was gone, they walked towards the women's shelter she had been promised, and what a welcome sight it was.

She was shown into a large room that had once been a church hall. There were long tables with bench seats and plenty of food on the table. There were fresh fruit, muffins, bread rolls, and plenty of spreads for the toast popping up from toasters set on tables against the side wall. Belinda took her over and showed her where there were tea, coffee, and fresh fruit juices. Meredith couldn't believe her eyes, but her grumbling stomach gave her away.

Belinda smiled at her and asked, "How long since you've eaten?"

Meredith replied, "Last night, but I only had soup, and I saved the baguette for later. That was it for the day."

There were several helpers in the hall moving around, clearing plates, and quietly asking each woman if they would like something else to eat. There was soft music playing, and Meredith noticed chairs were arranged in groups at the back of the hall. Some had small coffee tables between them, and others were in a row. Meredith noted that Belinda referred to the women as "clients."

The women seemed to be of all ages. Some looked desperately poor, dishevelled, and dressed in mismatched clothing, and their footwear had definitely seen better days. Others were dressed in tracksuits, casual pants, and tops but looked to be in better physical condition. *Oh my god, those poor women could be me if I don't behave myself with the way I speak to Sally. I'll be so glad to go home.*

Belinda guided Meredith over to a group sitting around a coffee table and introduced her. "This is a new client this morning, ladies. Please make Meredith welcome. Show her around our lovely shelter, and if one of you would like to take her on a tour, that would be appreciated." Belinda smiled at the group, patted Meredith on the shoulder, and left her with the five ladies, who were all staring at her.

One of the more forthright clients asked, "So what's your story, love? Everyone has one."

"Shut up, Milly. She's hardly put her bum on the seat, and you now want to know the ins and outs of her life. Let the poor girl catch her breath, will ya?" Meredith learned later that Lexie and Milly always went on like this, but it was all in good fun.

Lexie offered to show Meredith around after she had eaten. She was desperate for a shower and to wash her hair. She mentioned to Lexie that she only had one clean lot of clothes left in her suitcase, but they would have to do. As they walked towards the part of the building that housed the toilets and showers, Lexie commented, "We have a clothing pool here, Meredith. Some of it's quite good, and it won't cost you anything if you can't afford it. I'll show you where it is when we go back into the main hall. I'll get you a towel, and when you've finished your shower, just put your towel in the bin over there."

"I hate to ask, but could I have two towels, Lexie? I need to wash my hair, and it has grown quite a bit longer than I'm used to since I've been on the streets."

"No problem. I'll get you another one, and in the shower, there are dispensers of shampoo and conditioner. Will leave you to it. Just come back into the main hall when you're ready, and I'll save you a seat at our table."

"Thanks so much, Lexie. See you soon." And Meredith stripped down in the cubicle for a much-needed shower. On Sally's advice that you can't be too careful, she took her suitcase in with her and hung her discarded clothing on the hook. Twenty minutes later, she felt like a new woman. She went back into the main hall and was surprised to see how many more women had arrived in her short absence. Meredith was glad Lexie was saving her a seat because they now seemed to be in short supply.

Meredith had noticed Belinda circulating and speaking to the women as they arrived at the hall. She always had a smile on her face and gestured to where they could get food and a drink if they hadn't been there before. Lexie noticed her watching Belinda and leaned over to tell Meredith, "She's amazing, isn't she? So cheerful all the time and never seems to tire. We're so glad to have her running this shelter. She does it for free. When someone asked her why, she just replied for family reasons. We found out later that she lost her only daughter at just 18 years of age to a fatal bashing when she was sleeping rough in a park. What made it worse for Belinda was that the last words she spoke to her daughter were harsh and cruel, so this is how she tries to make amends for other women."

"Did she find you in a park, Meredith?" asked Lexie. "She goes around some of the city parks in the early morning. She's come across some awful sights when doing this. She has found women dead from drug overdose, alcohol, or murder."

"Yes, she found me this morning sleeping behind the gardening shed in the park just up the road," replied Meredith. "I think it might be my lucky day."

"More than you know," replied Lexie. "That was where the murdered woman was found only a few weeks ago. It's hidden there, so it might seem safe to you, but predators know where to look."

The look on Meredith's face was full of horror. She stammered, "I didn't realise. I just thought I would be out of the way and nobody would see me."

"Exactly the point," remarked Lexie. "Now let's see if we can get you some clothes. They've all been washed, so you needn't worry on that count."

Meredith quietly followed Lexie up onto the stage at the front of the hall to the clothing racks. She could see some cubicles for the clients to change in, and mirrors were also set up. Lexie showed her that the clothes were in sizes and separated into tops, pants, and tracksuits, and there was another area for shoes. Underwear was in bins, and all of it seemed new, some even with price tickets still attached. This was a whole new world to Meredith but one she was grateful to have entered today.

Lexie informed her that clothing came in weekly from all over Sydney. A lot of it was manufacturer's overproduction, some of it was clothing that didn't pass stringent quality control, and a smaller amount was sourced from charity bins. In another section were sample bottles of shampoo and conditioner, moisturiser, toothbrushes, and toothpaste in new packaging along with boxes of feminine hygiene products.

As Meredith was looking around, Belinda came up and spoke quietly to her. "Hi, Meredith, I see Lexie is showing you around our marvellous shelter here. Take whatever you need but not more than that, please. We're getting more clients every week who need clothing and some of the other things on offer. However, you are more than welcome to come back if you need to at any time, okay?"

Meredith mutely nodded. It was all becoming too overwhelming for her. She was grateful for the clothes Lexie helped her choose to keep her warm when the weather turned colder. She really hoped that she was not still sleeping rough once the seasons moved on.

She tucked her new clothes and toiletries into her bag and moved over to sit with Lexie and her friends. Questions were fired at her from all angles. "How did you manage to finish up on the streets? How are you coping? What are your plans? Where are you going next?"

She gave the women a brief and very edited version of the events that had led her to today. She left out Foster's embezzlement and told them she had invested some money badly and been let down by her advisers and that she had lost her home. None of the role she had played in all this was mentioned. Meredith was still unable to accept responsibility for her present circumstances, except that she needed to change her attitude to Sally, or this shelter and others like it were her future – not something she wished to contemplate.

The shelter closed at 4 p.m. and most of the clients had left. Belinda came over and sat down between Meredith and Lexie. She spoke directly to Meredith. "Now, Meredith, I don't want you going back to that park. It's not safe as I'm sure the girls have told you. Lexie has agreed to let you stay with her at a friend's place. You would have to couch-surf, but until you get something better, I suggest you take her up on her offer. She'll look after you until you're ready to move on. I just ask that you contribute something to the household, and if you don't have any money, I can put you in touch with a food bank near here, okay?"

"Thanks so much, Belinda. If it's okay with Lexie, I would like to take her up on the offer but just for two nights because then I can go back to the squat where my friend Sally is staying. She'll let me back in on Friday."

Belinda looked quizzically at Meredith. "What do you mean she'll let you back in? Back in to where? And why do you have to wait until Friday?"

Meredith was reluctant to tell them why she was on the streets for five days. She told them that she and Sally had disagreed on a few things, and Sally had told her to move out and get her head straight. Belinda put her head back and laughed. "Oh, Meredith, that's so funny. If I were you, I would stick with Sally. She sounds like she knows her way around the world. Anyway, in the meantime, do you want to take your chances at the place of Lexie's friend?"

"I certainly do, Belinda. I realise that Sally told the truth when she said I needed an 'attitude adjustment' before I could come back. I have been a bit of a bitch to her, but that's behind me now. It's taken this week to realise that I have a real friend in her, and I think my attitude adjustment is complete."

After two nights on the couch at the place of Lexie's friend, Meredith was more than happy to go back to Sally. Just to make sure she still had a place to return to, Meredith phoned her. "Hi, Sally. It's me, Meredith. Can I come home now, please?"

"Okay, Meredith. You kept your end of the bargain to stay away for five days, so I'll keep my promise too. See you when you get here."

On her way back to Sally, she walked along a busy city street and was surprised to notice that on almost every street corner or in doorways someone was begging. She had been unaware of this in her previous life. One of the women had a sign printed on cardboard that read "I am homeless. I don't drink or do drugs. I can't get work, and there is nothing for rent that I can afford. Please help, if you can. Thank you."

Meredith was taken aback by the honesty of the sign. The woman looked to be about her own age. She was clean and tidy but looked very sad. Meredith had withdrawn some of her Centrelink payment from an ATM and reached into her pocket for a twenty-dollar note. She walked over to the woman and gently placed the twenty dollars in her hand. The grateful look on the woman's face brought tears to Meredith's eyes. *Without Sally, that could be me.*

An hour later, a very different Meredith prised open the covering of their "front door." "Come in," said Sally. "Put your stuff over there, and let's have a chat. You're still on notice, though, Meredith, if you behave to me like you did last week. Is that clear?"

"It sure is, Sally. I'm a changed girl. It's terrifying out there, and I apologise for my attitude to you. It won't happen again."

"Well, we'll see, won't we, Meredith?" Sally opened her arms to give her friend a hug.

Thirty-Seven

Meredith was standing in the queue at her local cafe when she glanced around to see if she knew anyone else who might be trying to get cheap breakfast or coffee that someone else had paid forward. Some mornings, it was the only way she managed to have a decent meal, and she was very grateful for the unknown customer who had provided it. While the queue of takeaway coffee patrons slowly shuffled forwards to order their coffee, she glanced at a man standing nearby, and her heart almost stopped with shock. "Foster," she whispered. But no, Foster was dead and had been for a few years now, but this man looked so much like him that it took her breath away.

She reached the counter and was greeted by her favourite barista, Domenico. "Good morning, Miss M. What can I get for you today?"

Softly, she replied, "Good morning to you too, Domenico. I was wondering if you had any paid-forward meals or coffee today."

"It's your lucky day, Miss M. I have one left for up to $15. What would you like? Take a seat, and I'll bring it to you."

"Thanks so much. I'll sit just over there at table 15."

Meredith ordered her meal and sat at the only vacant table, which happened to be right next to the man she had thought was

Foster. His meal had not been brought out yet, and she was curious if he had any relationship to her deceased husband because he looked so much like him. Although she realised it was highly unlikely, she couldn't stop looking at him. Life can throw a curveball at any time.

When Meredith had her coffee but was still waiting for her meal, she tapped the sleeve of the man sitting next to her. "Excuse me, but could I please ask you a question?"

"Sure. Go ahead. What do you want to know?" he answered pleasantly. "I hope it's not directions to somewhere in Sydney because I'm not from here. By the way, my name's Clint, short for Clinton."

Meredith's heart sank a little. If he wasn't from Sydney, it was unlikely that he was related to Foster, who had lived here all his life, but she went ahead anyway. "Hi, I'm Meredith. Please just hear me out because this is going to sound strange."

He replied, "How about you sit at this table and we can chat? I don't have to be anywhere for a little while."

"Thank you. That's very kind." Meredith picked up her coffee and took a seat opposite the stranger. "Years ago, I married a man who looked very much like you. He died in a car accident, and I can't get over the similarities in height and colouring. Do you know of anyone called Foster Browne?"

The first thing Meredith noticed was that Clint's face went pale. "Do you have a photo of him? I had a twin brother, but that wasn't his name."

For some strange reason, Meredith had always carried a photo of them together cut from a Sunday tabloid with the heading THE NEW POWER COUPLE.

Clint stammered, "I don't believe it. That looks like my twin brother, and he left Western Australia thirty years ago after an argument with our parents about the future of the family business we had. What was his date of birth?"

Meredith told him, and Clint just sat there shaking his head in amazement. When he looked up at Meredith, he had tears in his eyes. "After all this time, you and I meet in a cafe on the other side of Australia. The man you knew as Foster was, I'm sure, my identical twin, Simon. When we finish our meal, is there somewhere quiet we could go and talk? This is a lot to take in for both of us."

When their meals were finished, Clint and Meredith walked down the street a little farther and found a hotel where they could talk. "How much time can you spare? Is there somewhere you have to be?" Clint asked Meredith. She didn't want to tell Clint just what her circumstances were, so she replied that she had a free day and no commitments at the moment. Clint started his story, and Meredith listened intently to what he had to say. It was like listening to a tale about someone she had never known.

He told her that Simon had no interest in the family business and wanted to go to London when he was 21 years old to "find himself." Their parents were upset that he wouldn't consider staying in Australia and, over the years, only had minimal contact with him, usually when he ran out of money and asked for a loan. Simon was more of the opinion that it wasn't a loan but a gift, and none of the money was ever paid back. Their parents didn't mind too much but were hurt by his attitude.

The boys had been well educated, and Clint had moved into the business when his father had decided on semi-retirement about ten years ago. Sadly, he had never made it to full retirement as he had a massive heart attack and couldn't be saved. His mother was devastated, and as they had been married for half a century, she just faded away with a broken heart. She didn't have the emotional strength to want to continue after her beloved husband died, and she quietly passed away one night.

That was about a year ago, and when her will was read, Clint was surprised to discover that a sum of money had been left for him to try to find Simon. It had been his mother's dearest wish that the two brothers get back together, whatever the circumstances. Clint was upset by the news that his brother had also passed away. The family had never known he was back in Australia, had changed his name, or had been married. The social pages of the Sydney newspapers were not read in a town on the west coast, so it was highly unlikely that they would ever have seen a photo of him. Clint asked Meredith, "Do you know why Foster changed his name?"

"No, I didn't even know that he'd done that. I have always known him as Foster, and it feels strange to hear you call him Simon. I wonder now why he did that after what happened."

"What do you mean?" asked Clint.

"I think we might need a drink, Clint, because this is going to be a long story, and some parts of it are not going to be pleasant for you to hear."

Clint came back with two glasses of wine and placed one in front of Meredith. "Okay, Meredith, I'm ready for the news, whatever it is."

The whole history of her meeting Foster, their glamorous lifestyle together, their wedding, his fall from grace because of the embezzlement, and his eventual death were related to Clint. She also told him that, when he could no longer work out how to fix the problems he had created by stealing other people's money, he had died in a car accident because he was drunk. Meredith conveniently left out the part she had to play in their downfall with her overspending and disregard of their financial situation. She didn't mention that she was living in a women's transition home while she waited for more permanent accommodation and had recently moved from an illegal squat. She told him she was sharing with a friend to help out with expenses as she hadn't been able to find a job. Meredith had spent her whole life tweaking a story to show her in as good a light as possible while skimming over the real circumstances of her life, and today's chat with Clint was no exception.

He didn't interrupt while Meredith spoke about her life with Foster and was in admiration of this woman who had lost everything but seemed to have found a new level to her life. Her clothes were certainly not top quality and a few years old by the look of them, but she was clean and tidy. When she had finished her story, Clint leaned back in his chair and said to Meredith, "Wow, that's quite a story, Meredith, and you must be one of the strongest women I have ever met. You've managed to redesign your life against all the odds. You have a lot of skills, and anyone with a business would surely employ you. What happened that you couldn't find work?" he gently asked her.

"I was too embarrassed by what Foster had done to seek work in the events management industry. Too many people were gleeful about my downfall and changed circumstances. I tried for a long time to get employment in other areas but eventually gave up. I was considered too old to be retrained in another industry, so I sold off what was left of my possessions, and that kept me going for a year or two, but my money ran out. I went on Centrelink benefits, and there I stayed. So that's about it." She finished and took a sip of her wine.

Clint was silent on the other side of the table but was watching her with a thoughtful look on his face. "Meredith, I have an idea, but I want to run it past a few people before I say anything further. Could I have your mobile number and give you a call tomorrow? On second thought, it might be better if we meet here at about eleven thirty, and we can have lunch. Does that suit you?"

"It's very mysterious, but yes, I'll be here at eleven thirty, and lunch would be lovely. Thanks, Clint. This has been an amazing day to say the least."

At eleven thirty the next morning, Meredith arrived at the hotel, waiting only a few minutes before Clint arrived, somewhat breathless from hurrying to be on time. He leaned over and gave Meredith a kiss on the cheek. "You look great, Meredith. What have you done since yesterday? Your hair is different."

"Well, I had time for my friend to put colour in my hair and another friend cut it for me. Do you like it?"

"Yes, it's lovely. Have got some news I want to share with you. Yesterday I said there were some people I needed to speak to, and I have come up with a plan, but you are not obligated in any way to agree, okay? How about a drink and then we can go into the restaurant and have lunch?"

"Sounds lovely. I'm intrigued by whatever you have been up to, Clint."

When they were seated, he said, "So here's the offer. You know I'm from Western Australia, but what you don't know is that my parents were in the hotel business all their married life. They owned one of the best hotels in Fremantle, and it is now in my hands. They left money in their wills to refurbish the hotel into a venue for elegant weddings, conferences, and whatever other events we could attract with accommodation as a further benefit. It's almost finished, but I haven't employed any staff yet. Would you move to Western Australia and run it for me?"

Meredith just sat there with a stunned look on her face. "You want me to run the events at your hotel? Did I hear that correctly?"

"Yes, that's right. Is there anything stopping you from doing that? Or does the idea not appeal anymore?"

"Oh, it appeals very much. Where would I stay? When would I have to go?"

"Well, how long would it take you to be ready to leave? I don't want to rush you but sooner rather than later. You can use one of the family rooms in the hotel until you get settled and rent somewhere close by." Clint paused before he said, "I don't want to offend you, Meredith, but hearing your story leads me to believe that you have had it tough the last few years. Would you let me give you a credit card for, say, $2,000 so you can buy some clothes before you leave Sydney?"

For the second time that day, Meredith was without the power of speech. "Thanks so much, Clint. I would like to arrive looking a little like my old self, and I know just the places to go to get more mileage out of the dollar. However, there is one favour I would like to ask of you."

"Go ahead, Meredith. What do you need?"

"I have a friend, Sally, who has had a tougher life than me. She's a really good person, and I would like to ask if you could find a place for her too. She has a background in office work and is straightforward and honest. Is there any chance she could come too?" Meredith held her breath.

"With your experience in organising events, I'm confident that, if you think Sally will be an asset to the business, then I'm prepared to take your word for it. Any chance you can bring her to meet me so I can take down the details for both of you and organise flights?"

"I'll be seeing her after lunch, and I'm sure she'll be thrilled. Will meet you here same time tomorrow? I think a week would give me time to say goodbye to some people who have been very kind because, without them, I wouldn't have survived." She knew that Suzy and Brady were going to be fine together in their business venture, Larissa was happy in her new job, and apart from some of the girls at Patti's Place, she was a free spirit. This news would make Sally's day.

Meredith just smiled and thought about which charity shop would be able to provide her and Sally with suitable outfits. When Meredith returned to their "home," she had a big smile on her face and a bottle of Moët held aloft in her right hand. "You won't believe what happened today, Sally."

"It had better be good if you've spent our money on Moët," replied Sally.

If my book touches your heart, please consider
giving to those less fortunate. Every little bit helps.
Thank you.
Janelle

https://shiningstarsfoundation.org.au

It takes many people in a community to make a difference to others, and this is where Shining Stars Foundation really shines in Macarthur, Sydney. It is a not-for-profit organisation started two years ago by three wonderful women who have a mission to help those less fortunate (https://shiningstarsfoundation.org.au/about/).

Many of these people - men and women, young and old, single, widowed, or divorced - are homeless through no fault of their own. Domestic violence, families torn apart by loss of employment and the downward financial spiral, people unable to meet the ever-increasing private rental market, and mental health issues are just the tip of the iceberg.

Every week in all weathers, these women and their helpers provide friendship, food, clothing, and gifts for disadvantaged children at Christmas, distributing over 550 in 2017. Hampers are given out during the year, but this is totally dependent on contributions from the public to keep their pantry stocked. Throughout the week, meals are prepared and enjoyed by many at a local community centre, and volunteers from Aspect Macarthur (an autism unit in the area) come to help and serve the food. This gives the boys a chance to gain skills and build confidence. Again, it is one hand helping another.

The homeless people you see on park benches or huddled in doorways are just a very small percentage of those without a place to call home. Many people, especially women and some with children, sleep in cars or a converted garage in someone's backyard. Others sleep in the stands of sports grounds or within an unpatrolled, abandoned building; some are couch-surfing, going from one place to another – wherever they can find shelter.

This charity also provides free duffel bags to those who are sleeping rough. These bags contain clothing items, toiletries, and food and cost Shining Stars Foundation $90 each. There is a constant and increasing demand for these bags throughout the year.

Shining Stars Foundation has recently started a campaign, How U Going. This is a mental health awareness program to encourage people to ask others that important question, How are you going? People who are struggling with life need to feel that there is someone out there who cares about them. It might be as simple as asking if someone would like a cup of coffee or a sandwich.

For most people, the life they know can be living the dream until something changes that, and it can be as little as four pay cheques to become homeless. Just think how you would manage if, for the next fortnight or month, your income stopped. Maybe your savings will last for a short time, but when the mortgage or rent isn't paid, there isn't enough for car fuel, and groceries have to be bought in much smaller amounts, how do you think you would cope?

Just before you go, there are many ways you can help those less fortunate, often through no fault of their own. Please consider buying just one extra item every time you go to the supermarket. It can be as inexpensive as a packet of pasta, long-life milk, tinned fruit, two-minute noodles, baked beans, tinned spaghetti, jams, spreads, rice, sugar, or fruit juice. These items will be gratefully received by your nearest charity who struggle every week to feed the people in the community who have very little.

The difficulties facing those organisations trying to care for the homeless and disadvantaged are never-ending.

Here are some real case histories of people who have been helped by Shining Stars Foundation in their local area.

The situations are real, but the names have been changed.

Cameron: Male, about 30 years old

He was working but then lost his job, so he could no longer pay his rent and was out on the streets of Sydney. He was living nights in an alley, frightened and alone. He was arrested one day for an outstanding warrant and sent to prison. His life after prison was desperate. He had a prison record and only a small amount of money from Centrelink, which was insufficient for him to find accommodation anywhere, even if anybody would consider him as a tenant. Recently, he was able to get work and had some money to stay in a hostel in Sydney. He is still trying to sort out his life.

Daniel: Male, about 40 years old

Daniel's relationship had broken down; he'd lost his job and couldn't pay the rent. He found a spot behind one of the stands in the showground of the area he had lived for most of his life. He was given a mattress and some warm clothes, checked on a few times a week, and supplied with hot food. One day he was gone, leaving behind rotting food and three envelopes. Two of the envelopes had his children's names on them, and the third contained a note from his mother and father asking him to come home for the winter. He has not been seen in the area since, and nobody knows what became of him.

This is an excerpt from a Daily Telegraph article on 23 June 2018 titled "Housing Crisis to Cripple the State" by Matthew Benns.

> Tuesday's state Budget unveiled 1,200 new houses for older women as part of its $1.1 billion Social and Affordable Housing Fund. But University of NSW professor of housing research Hal Pawson said spending needed to be tripled for the numbers of homeless just to stand still. "If it was possible to add 21,000 to the NSW social and

affordable rental housing stock over the next decade the current waiting list of 60,000 people would likely remain the same," Prof Pawson said.

Printed in the United States
By Bookmasters